MATCHES IN THE DARK

13 Tales of Gay Men

ANTHONY MCDONALD

Anchor Mill Publishing

Matches in the Dark

www.anthonymcdonald.co.uk

One Funeral And... ©Anthony McDonald, Best Gay Romance 2011, Cleis Press, 2011

Mercutio's Romeo ©Anthony McDonald, Boy Crazy, Cleis Press, 2009

After Stoolball ©Tony Pike, Boy Crazy, Cleis Press, 2009

The Curtain Store ©Anthony McDonald, Best Gay Romance 2012, Cleis Press 2012

Into The Cold ©Anthony McDonald, Death Comes Easy, Gay Men's Press, 2003

When in Rome ©Anthony McDonald, Erotica Exotica, Bold Strokes Books, 2011

The Name of the Wine ©Anthony McDonald, Bend Sinister, Gay Men's Press, 2003

Tiffer ©Anthony McDonald, What Love Is, Arcadia, 2011

Anchor Mill Publishing
404 Anchor Mill
Paisley PA1 1JR
SCOTLAND
anchormillpublishing@gmail.com

Anthony McDonald

I. M.
Tony Linford
1933 - 2012

Matches in the Dark

Anthony McDonald

CONTENTS

Author's Note

These stories do not need to be read in any particular order ... even supposing they need to be read at all. Some have previously been published, some not. I have placed the lighter, more romantic, stories towards the beginning of the selection while the more serious pieces can be found towards the end ... with an exception or two in both cases, to prevent the sequence from being too predictable. There is a range of tones: from the frankly lustful in *Luc, The Fabulous Bakers' Boy* and *When in Rome...* to the wistful melancholy of *Rackham Farmhouse* and *The Name of the Wine*. In the case of the already published stories, the names of the anthologies in which they first appeared give the reader a clue as to what to expect.

I would like to thank my manuscript musketeers, Charles, Drew, Douglas, Josh, Roger and Sarah, for their opinions and suggestions – even when contradictory – on the previously unpublished stories, and Nigel for ongoing support and red wine throughout.

Anthony McDonald

ONE FUNERAL AND...

I was just three when I first went to Endes. It's one of the earliest memories I can reliably date, because of the five-hour train journey from London to Scotland and the fact that it snowed hard all the way up: new experiences both, and guaranteed to make an impression on a small child. Uncle Max met us at Dumfries station – at the wheel of his vintage Rolls-Royce, which was another thing a three-year-old wasn't going to forget in a hurry. Nineteen years later, I can still bring to my mind the smell of its leather seats, as clear and sharp as if they were with me now, though the car is long gone.

The rest of that visit is less clear, details overlaid by memories of another one four years later. But I remember my wonder at the sheer size of the house, a major culture shock after our own modest home in North London. And the breakfasts. Jenny softly banging the brass gong to summon everyone; then Uncle Max at one end of the long, highly polished table and Auntie Annie – who was my mother's first cousin and the only reason for our being invited to Endes at all – at the other. Uncle Max ate differently from the rest of us: grapefruit halves, then Ryvita crispbread instead of toast. He was on a *die-it*, whatever that might be. For the rest of us it was the Full Monty: bacon and eggs with mushrooms and tomato, or grilled Finnan haddock, even for me, and I'm ashamed to admit I remember the food that Jenny served us more clearly than I remember the other people who sat around the table with us: that is, the three children of Uncle Max and Auntie Annie – my second cousins. Isabel and Marie were a few years older than me and to my eyes seemed nearly grown-up. Both had flaming red hair. Their little brother Felix made less of an impression, though he was the same age as I was. His hair was almost black, not fiery red, and he was – the adults all said – *shy*. I remember that instead of giving you a clear view of his eyes when you looked at him, he showed you a pair of long dark lashes. No doubt we played together in the wintry garden and the big old house, but I don't remember that.

We did play together four years later, even if a bit reluctantly. This second visit to Endes took place in early summer, and even my seven-year-old self was conscious of the beauty of the Scottish lowlands then, washed alternately, almost minute by minute, by warm sun and short sparkling showers: a countryside of emerald and diamond. The girls were now fourteen and twelve, far beyond the games of their little brother and myself, so the two of us were thrown together for the week by default. I can't say we clicked. I thought the seven-year-old Felix was stuck-up, snooty, conceited, pompous and cold: all those adjectives (even if they were not all in my vocabulary at the time) that we use to pigeon-hole those people by whom we are subconsciously, and usually unnecessarily, intimidated. I know now that Felix felt exactly the same, back then, about me.

He didn't speak with any suggestion of a Scottish accent, rather he had the posh and assured tones of a boy who has been put down for Eton and knows it. (He didn't go to Eton, in fact; he went to Fettes, which is approximately a Scottish equivalent – the school, incidentally, that had been attended a generation earlier by one Tony Blair.) I'd thought *we* were fairly posh, and me especially, even though there was no way I'd be going to Eton. But Felix's degree of posh unnerved me, put me on the back foot, and so, when our week in Scotland came to an end and I left feeling I would miss so many things – the countryside, the walks with the gamekeepers and the dogs, the breakfasts, the arrival in the kitchen of whole fresh salmon from the River Nith – the company of Felix was not included in the list.

A couple of years later Auntie Annie died, of cancer, at the wastefully early age of thirty-eight. I remember that my parents travelled up to for the funeral, though I didn't; I was away at boarding school. And after that there were no more visits to Endes. My parents and Uncle Max exchanged cards at Christmas, but that was all. When I was about fifteen he remarried. His new wife – somewhat improbably in the wilds of Galloway – was a woman from Argentina, called – hardly less improbably – Lolli.

In the middle of last summer the phone rang. It was my parents' phone, but I was living with them at the time and, because I happened to be in that afternoon and they out, I answered it. It could have been – would most usually have been – the other way round, so it was just chance. Chance! What a maligned word, *chance*. How we undervalue it. Since that day, that moment, I have given a super-healthy respect to Chance.

The voice on the phone was unfamiliar, but once the name was given I knew exactly who it was. I hadn't met many other people called Felix. He was phoning to say – and would I pass the message on to my parents – that his father, Uncle Max, had died. Quite suddenly, unexpectedly, but without pain or fuss. I made the usual polite noises. Condolences. If there was anything any of us could do... Please let us know when the funeral was to be, and we'd make every effort to be there if we could. On an impulse, though perhaps it was just a reflex born of habit, I gave him the number of my mobile phone.

'I don't think they'll expect us to go all that way, you know,' my mother said, when I'd passed the message on. 'Of course I'll phone young Felix and speak to him myself, but I don't think anyone really expects... This woman ... Lolli ... the second wife of a cousin's husband, and we've never met. And the children... Well OK, they're your second cousins, but even so...'

'Well, I think I ought to go,' I said and heard myself sounding a bit over-the-top as I said it. 'As a representative of the family, you know. On behalf of all of us. Show some support for Felix.' My mother looked at me oddly, as well she might. Felix had done very well for the last fourteen years without my support, or even any contact between us, and I'd managed very nicely without him too. My mother had never heard me mention his name, and I'd scarcely given him a thought.

But I wasn't quite as mad as I must have sounded. I was living at home, aged twenty-one, having graduated from university in the middle of the biggest recession even my parents could remember, with no job to go to and no prospect of one. I was doing some part-time work for the Royal Mail, on special deliveries. Real fun? I'll leave you to guess. It wasn't surprising that I'd want to grab at the chance to get out from under my parents' feet with a trip to Scotland. Even so, my parents might still have talked me out of it quite easily. (Simply not offering to pay my train fare might have been enough.) But then, less than half an hour later, I received quite a long text from Felix.

He actually spelled in full the words *could use some support*. No, he didn't expect a full state visit from my family. But if by any chance... Chance.

And as soon as I liked.

I told my parents what Felix had said. I would take the sleeper that evening... The sleeper? Cost a bloody bomb...! Well, all right then, the overnight train. Sit up all night. Neck-ache in the morning. Arrive red-eyed... My father gave in. Let me use his credit card to book a sleeper berth online.

*

Felix met me at Dumfries. Not in a Rolls-Royce but in a respectably mud-spattered Range Rover. It was six in the morning, so it was good of him. It gave me a shock to see him get out of the car and, with a question in his voice, call my name. 'Jonty?' The shock was that he had grown beautiful. He hadn't been at age three or age seven, from what I could remember, but then I'd hardly have been on the lookout for male good looks in those days. Or I don't think I was. But now my immediate thought, the cheap, base one, which you've guessed already, was ... *Is he gay?* Not, I wonder how he's coping, what he's feeling, losing his second and final parent at twenty-one. None of that. Simply: *Is he gay?* How quickly the thought springs to mind when we meet a new person that we fancy. How much longer before we ask ourselves that question when it's someone that we don't.

For all the northern fairness of his skin he had a look more common in South America than among Scots. It was as if he'd inherited them, against all the laws of nature, from his Argentine step-mother, Lolli, rather than from his real mother, my Auntie Annie. His eyes were large, dark liquid brown, his eyelashes dark and long. His eyebrows were beautifully shaped, very dark too, as was his hair, which was curly, thick – but longer than most gay guys our age would choose. He was about an inch less than me in height (I'm five foot ten) and very slim. Though that didn't make him particularly small, he had a delicacy of build – being small-boned and finely made – that made him look both attractively petite and, paradoxically, slightly better muscled than he was. In the same way, though his shoulders were not especially broad they appeared so in contrast to his slender waist and narrow hips. How he might look from behind I'd have to wait to see. His voice was beautiful too, and he spoke, these days, with a very light Scots accent.

So, was he gay? I hadn't even thought to think the question till I saw him. Now it preoccupied me, though there was nothing in his manner to suggest he was – we greeted each other with open smiles and a cousinly but perfunctory hug, then got into the car – but there was nothing in my manner to show that I was either, as I'd discovered long before now. Even my parents had been disinclined to believe it when I first told them, though in the end they were – thank heaven – very nice about it.

As we drove along, the warmth generated by our encounter and greeting dissipated somewhat. I think this was because the reality of our situation was beginning to strike home. I'd travelled four hundred miles on a whim, a whim which was joint property of Felix and myself, to spend time with a cousin I hardly knew, at a particularly delicate and difficult moment in his life and that of his immediate family. Now that I was actually here – and with the funeral itself still five days away – I was suddenly awkward, unsure about what I was here for, what I was supposed to do.

Before going to sleep in my bunk the previous night *(For you dream you are crossing the Channel and tossing about in a steamer from Harwich, which is something between a large bathing-machine and a very small second-class carriage)* I had found myself trying to picture Endes in the throes of full mourning, but laziness and incipient sleep had given me only the scene in Four Weddings and a Funeral where Andie MacDowell marries a dour but wealthy older man in a Scottish baronial castle, and a kilt-wearing Simon Callow dies of a heart attack after dancing the Highland Fling. I'd been just awake enough to tell myself there wouldn't be dancing. I wasn't going to even one wedding but to a funeral, full stop.

The same uncertainty about what was to be done with me now he'd dragged me all this way must have struck

Felix at the same moment as it did me. Trying to make small talk as we drove through the Galloway countryside (emerald and diamond again in the bright morning) I could feel us slipping back, becoming again the stiff, self-conscious and prickly selves we'd shown each other that last time, when we were seven. I didn't know what I wanted in the way of a rapport between us now, but I knew I didn't want that. I took the bull by the horns. 'What do you actually want me to do, now I'm here?'

It sounded really awful. Like I couldn't have been ruder if I'd tried. I added, in a rush to make amends, 'I mean, I'm here to help out in any way I can. Just tell me what you want. I'm at your service.'

Felix had looked startled at my first question – which was fair enough – and had taken his eyes off the road for a second to look straight at me, but then, as he heard my attempt to explain myself, there came a quick smile before he returned his gaze to the road ahead and he said, 'You know, I hadn't really thought. I think I just wanted you to be here. If that doesn't sound too stupid – to say to someone I hardly know.' A hint of awkwardness clouded his voice.

'We've known each other nearly twenty years,' I said, wanting to ease his sudden discomfort. He would know my answer for the silly, fatuous one it was, but would recognise, I hoped, the friendly spirit behind it. The look of his last quick smile was still etched behind my eyes. He had full lips and a cute, pert nose. His smile had made his brown eyes sparkle and transformed him for a moment into a slightly larger than average pixie.

He said, 'It was nice the way you spoke when you answered the phone yesterday. I'd had a whole day of phoning cousins. But you sounded different. Sorry. Forgive me. I'm a bit emotional at the moment.'

'It's OK,' I said, wondering why he'd thought he had to apologise. It wasn't as if he was tearing up or anything. There'd been no crack or tremor in his voice. But of course it was OK if he felt emotional. He'd lost his father just forty-eight hours earlier, an experience I'd not yet had, and didn't know how I'd deal with when I did.

Then suddenly, there it was. That moment of vulnerability, the crack in the armour of his invincible beauty, had done it for me. We hadn't yet asked what we did for a living, if we were still students, neither yet knew even if the other was married, for God's sake. But it was at that moment, as he turned into the long driveway, beneath the tall trees where herons precariously nested – as I suddenly remembered – that I fell for him. I had fallen for him – to mangle metaphors most horribly, but somehow no other one will do – hook, line and sinker.

Endes looked exactly the same. The gong, though silent this breakfast time, was still in the morning room; Jenny, now elderly and plump, was still in the kitchen, to welcome me with a matronly hug. Dogs greeted me as before, though inevitably not the same dogs. Formality was gone though, especially this week that stretched awkwardly between death and funeral rite. Breakfast was not a sit-down affair today, but a casual do-it-yourself in the kitchen, like breakfast in any other busy house. Felix, though he had a hundred and one things on his mind, made sure I got fed, that I was introduced to everyone who came and went – and especially to his step-mother and his two red-haired sisters and their husbands – and he showed me to my room. 'It's the one you had last time,' he said. It surprised me that he remembered that. I hadn't remembered. Perhaps all junior ranking guests were put in that room and had always been.

Doubts about my usefulness, questions about what I was going to do, quickly melted away. Felix had to drive into Kircudbright to see the funeral directors and chase up the death certificate, over which there'd been some admin confusion or delay. Lolli was due to go to a meeting with a solicitor in Dalbeattie, which was in the opposite direction. She shouldn't have to go alone. Would I...? Of course. Could I drive her car? Did I actually...? Yes, of course I could drive. Of course I would. If Lolli would direct me as we went along.

To my surprise I remembered the way into Dalbeattie from all those years before and didn't need to be told. My passenger, dressed in smart but sober grey and white was (I was not surprised by this) surprisingly young. Uncle Max had been seventy but his widow looked to be on the right side of thirty-five. Felix's sisters, I'd noticed, treated her as an honorary elder sister herself.

'So, your wealthy elderly husband's dead, you're a good-looking South American, footloose in Scotland. What's your next move?' There are some people who would actually say that. I'm not one of those people. I'm with the rest of the world – who'd just think it. And, despite the fact that we were on our way to see a lawyer, and presumably that very question was going to be discussed behind doors that would be closed to me, she didn't volunteer any information on the subject. Instead, she talked about Felix.

He was midway through his studies at medical school in Glasgow, where he shared a flat with other medics. In my brief conversations with him so far this morning I hadn't got as far as finding that out. When you go to family gatherings and meet distant cousins in their parents' homes you often make the lazy assumption that that's where they live. Of course they rarely do. Just because I was living with my parents at age twenty-one didn't mean that Felix also was. The other thing that

Lolli told me was that Felix had a girlfriend called Rhona, daughter of another prominent local family, whom he was expected to marry.

I met Rhona a couple of hours later. She came to lunch. She sat very prettily next to Felix at the table, and was charming when she talked to me. Soon after lunch she left. I was alone with Felix for a brief spell after that. He showed me round the house, not all of which I'd seen as a child. If I say there were eight bedrooms upstairs, and attic rooms above that, that gives some idea of how big a place Endes was. 'Rhona's very nice,' was all I managed to say about his girlfriend. 'Oh yes, she is,' he answered, and smiled. We were in the snooker room at the time and, as he spoke, Felix picked up a cue and neatly pocketed a stray ball, as if to show beyond argument that that particular avenue of conversation was closed.

Rhona didn't appear at dinner time, though some elderly neighbours did: a Mrs MacComb and a couple called McClerg. Felix's sister Isabel was there, without her husband. She and Marie were taking it in turns to stay over, night on night off, and be company for Lolli. I thought that very good of them, though obviously it wouldn't go on for ever. Some time after dinner was ended a moment was reached when the guests had gone and Lolli and Isabel had 'retired to their rooms' as some people still say, and Felix and I were suddenly left alone. I was about to say, out of politeness (and shyness also), that I would 'retire' too, but Felix, probably sensing this, jumped in very quickly with, 'Do you want a whisky? We could take it out on the terrace.'

There was nothing I'd have liked better. Well, there was, but with Felix practically engaged to Rhona that didn't seem an alternative realistically to be hoped for. 'Laphroaig do you?' Felix asked. One of those smoky, peaty single malts that taste like burnt toast crumbs – a flavour I don't much care for. I said it would be perfect.

We sat out in the long northern midsummer dusk, and while light lasted in the sky, and the rolling hills and woods went grey, we talked. I told Felix I'd just completed my degree in English but – what did you do with that? He understood: he had friends in Glasgow and Edinburgh in the same position. I told him I was working as a postman. He laughed and said, so were they. I learned about Felix, his studies in Glasgow, his life there... I found we had interests in common, there were opinions and tastes we shared. I dared to think that our personalities were a little bit alike. I told him, rather shyly, that I wanted to be a writer. He said, 'If I knew you a bit better I'd ask to read something you've written.' Everything he said, everything he was, I liked. He was a wonderful new discovery and I couldn't get enough of him. We didn't discuss sex. With someone who's going to be married and who you've only known as an adult for a dozen hours ... well, you don't. Only after several whiskies (I take back what I said about Laphroaig: it's brilliant stuff) was I bold enough to say, 'About this place.' I gestured to the house behind us and waved vaguely across the lawns in front of us and the darkening landscape beyond. 'What happens to it now?'

'It's mine,' he said. 'All mine. Every brick and stone. Every wood and field and pond. Every cottage on the estate.' He didn't sound at all happy about it. 'And I'm just trying to become a doctor.'

'But your sisters?' I said. 'And Lolli?'

'Lolli gets a house on the estate to live in rent free for life – if that's what she wants to do.'

'And you get the big house?' I should have worked this out for myself but I hadn't. I was slightly gob-smacked. 'It sounds more like 1910 than 2010,' I said, which was not very diplomatic of me. When whisky talks it rarely counsels prudence. But Felix didn't take it badly. He laughed and said, 'It may be 2010 in London. Even Glasgow...' and left it there. 'My sisters,' he went on, 'each got a packet when they got married. A very generous one. They don't come in for any more.'

'You mean, like a dowry?' I said. It sounded medieval.

'No, Jonty,' Felix answered, the use of my name making me feel like a reprimanded schoolboy. 'The money remains theirs, it wasn't handed over to their husbands. We may not have joined the 21st century but we've got beyond the Middle Ages.'

'Sorry, Felix,' I said. He topped up my glass.

'The thing is,' he said, sounding like this thing was rather a big thing, 'it's all in the expectation of my getting married. Marrying Rhona. Who as well as being stunning looking and intelligent is pretty wealthy in her own right.'

Mind your mouth, I told myself. Don't let the whisky say anything. 'Hmm,' I said, and asked about the agenda for the morning.

It did get dark eventually and we went inside. 'Will Rhona be over tomorrow?' I asked then, as we washed up our glasses in the kitchen rather than leave them in the dishwasher for Jenny to deal with in the morning.

'No,' he said. 'She won't be over again till the funeral. She lives in Edinburgh. Her own flat in the New Town.'

Edinbugh. I was astonished by that. A pretty long drive from Glasgow, an even longer one from here. I'd drunk two large whiskies since I thought we didn't know each other well enough to talk about sex. I said, 'Do you ... I mean ... do you sleep together?'

Felix looked suddenly awkward and for a moment I saw him as a three-year-old again as his eyes hid themselves behind his long lashes. 'No, we don't.'

To spare him I looked up at the kitchen clock. It said one o'clock. 'Hey,' I said. 'I can't believe that's the time.' I'd been awake since four, watching the dawn on the fells and the Scottish border, and Felix must have woken early himself to come and meet me off the train at six. 'I guess it's bedtime.' We said goodnight at the top of the stairs and went our different ways along the landing.

The next day was another round of errands and tasks that kept Felix and me in separate orbits for most of the time. I drove where I was told to, delivering and collecting things and people as required. You don't realise how much there is to do when someone dies, until you find yourself in the thick of it. It was after dinner, nightcap time, before Felix and I were alone together. I'd spent all day looking forward to this moment. Stupid, lovelorn me. And yet when the moment came, there was a look of something in Felix's eyes – soon to be married Felix, didn't sleep with his girlfriend Felix – that made me wonder, though not too hopefully, might he have been looking forward to this moment too?

We took our glasses – and for good measure the bottle also – out through the French windows and onto the lawn. There was some special stuff you had to burn (Felix had used it last night too) to keep the midges away. We said 'Cheers' to each other, clinked glasses, then Felix, sitting beside me on the grass, turned his whole body towards me, looked me full in the face – his own face looking very serious, troubled even – and said, 'I'm gay.'

There followed an echoing silence, like in a cavern. It was as if Felix had heaved a boulder over the edge of something and was waiting for the splash. I realised that he was waiting for me to speak. I said, 'So am I.' It wasn't the moment to tell him I'd been in love with him for forty hours.

He really did, quite literally, sigh with relief. 'I didn't know you were,' he said very quietly. 'I really didn't. You don't show it in any obvious way...'

'Neither do you...'

'...But I kind of hoped it. Since I heard your voice answer your parents' phone the other day. You were so ... friendly. I mean, I know that doesn't mean a person's gay. I mean... Oh shit, I'm sounding stupid.'

Not half as stupid as I wanted to sound, blurting 'I love you' into his face. I had almost physically to restrain myself. 'It doesn't sound stupid,' I told him instead. 'It sounds ... nice.'

Two guys tell each other they're gay. It doesn't mean they want to sleep together, let alone that they're going to. I mean, imagine it in a hetero context. He: 'I'm straight.' She: 'Me too.' See what I mean? Doesn't get you very far. I took a sip of whisky to give my racing thoughts time to catch up. 'What about Rhona?' I asked eventually. 'Does she know?'

He shook his head, his face tense with worry again. 'No. No-one does.'

I could understand him being reticent with his very traditional family. 'But your friends in Glasgow,' I said. 'You must be out to them?'

'Only one or two. Not with most of them.'

'But are you...?' I didn't know how to put this. Did he have sex with anyone? Had he ever?

'Do I have a busy sex life, you mean. No. Except for the obvious. Though I've done enough to know what and who I am. But that's it.'

I decided not to pursue this further. But he did, with me. 'What about you?'

'I had a couple of affairs at uni,' I said. 'Nothing major. And I don't have anyone now.' Actually I'd had more than a couple of affairs at university but I wasn't going to rub his nose in it. And the last part was true at least. I hadn't had sex with anyone for months.

Now it was I who'd pushed something over an edge or precipice, his turn to react. But he took his time about it, gazing away through the dusk towards the distant fields which all belonged to him. Then he looked back at me, his eyes haunted and big, like dark lamps. He said, 'Can I kiss you?'

We went to his room that night. It was further away from the others' than mine was. Stripped naked he was more beautiful than ever, more beautiful than anyone I'd slept with or even seen. To my surprise, and probably to his also, neither of us had much of a hard-on. We were too awed, I think, by the situation, by whatever – we didn't dare to name it aloud – had happened to us. We simply stood facing each other, next to his bed, taking in each other's naked, glowing form. I reached out a hand and ran it down the middle of his chest to just above his navel, where a tiny central line of hair licked up from below like a slender black flame. He began, silently, to cry.

He had every right to, I thought. The stress of losing a father, and now this. But by what right did I then follow his example, and into the silence spill a load of tears myself? I took him in my arms and he took me in his.

No other kind of load was spilled by either of us that night. We cuddled ourselves to sleep. But first light found us both with robust hard dicks, and we each came, with almost comical superabundance, in the other's hand, overflowing our bellies and soaking the sheet, before I reluctantly tiptoed from his room and back to mine.

For the next two days we led a double life. We spent our nights together, in the full flood of new love, and we spent our days pretending that we didn't, pretending that we weren't. In the evenings we couldn't wait for the others to go to bed. Our whisky intake was reduced (good for our livers) to a single glass, and that was downed in record breaking time, so impatient were we for bed, for the other's body, the other's dick. For the whole, wonderful, wondrous other person. Felix for his Jonty. Jonty for his Felix.

After a couple of days – we were in the garden at the time – Felix said, 'Stay on a few more days after the funeral. Please. Phone your parents. Tell the Post Office you need a few more days off.'

'The Royal Mail,' I said. 'They're not the same thing any more.'

'Whatever,' Felix said. 'I don't want this to end. It can't.'

That was how I felt too. But I said, 'It can't go on for ever. You know it can't. I can't live under your roof indefinitely and nobody twig. Think about Rhona. Unless you intend to tell her, and have the whole thing out.'

'I *want* you here indefinitely,' he said crossly. I'd never known him other than mild tempered in the four days since our idyll began, though he was cross with himself more than with me. Then he stamped away across the lawn.

I didn't attempt to follow him. 'I want that too,' I said. 'I want that more than anything.' But I said the words to myself and no sound came out.

I didn't think we'd have to wait till the funeral before we saw Rhona again and I was right. She came for lunch that day and stayed most of the afternoon. She was friendly towards me as before, and we talked easily over the lunch table, but I let Felix be alone with her in the afternoon, finding jobs for myself to do, taking the dogs for a run... After she'd gone, Felix said to me, 'I've told her you'll be in the front row with us in the church tomorrow. You and me with Lolli and Rhona on one side, my sisters and their husbands on the other.'

I thought this an odd way to proceed. It fell right between what I'd thought of as the only two alternatives – to go on clandestinely as we were until our affair petered out, or for Felix to make a clean breast of it and let his house fall about his ears. For I was quite sure that if he did come out to Rhona and to his family, then his sisters and Lolli would be able to challenge his father's will and kick him out of Endes for good. Then what would happen to him and me? Share a small room at my parents'? Both of us work part time delivering letters? Or would I go to the Glasgow flat and be unemployed and in the way there? I couldn't see our fragile, new-hatched love surviving either of those eventualities. I couldn't see anything that didn't look like a dead end, a brick wall. I guessed the same went for him. 'How did she react to that?' I asked.

'She was fine with it,' was all he said.

We didn't discuss Rhona or any of this further that day. Neither of us was able to. We waited till night came and then took refuge in each other, in sex. We were good for that, at least. Felix had had his first fucks with me, on the giving and receiving end just half an hour apart, on our third night. He was a gentle lover, and a wonderful one. When he first entered me he made sure we were face to face. He wanted to see the blue light of my eyes, he said. He said they were like the sky. Often we were happy enough to pleasure each other by hand, to enjoy the sight of our milk white spurts and our bellies a-flood. His cock was not enormous and neither were his balls. But they were the most beautiful I'd ever seen, his cock elegantly hooded, which mine – he laughingly compared it to a shillelagh – is not. He also called me beautiful, which stunned me. Other people had done, once or twice before, when they'd had a certain amount of drink inside them, but none of those had Felix's looks: that perfect body, that face. I wouldn't have imagined for a moment that I might appear beautiful in Felix's eyes, but apparently I did. That night before we buried his late dad we hugged each other closely, with little hope for the future beyond the next few days.

The service went like clockwork. Felix was a meticulous planner, his sisters too, and I'd helped. The little church in Dalbeattie was packed, and bright with sun; the showers held off. When the coffin was carried in, a swallow followed through the open door and flew quickly round the church before returning to the outdoors. I heard Lolli whisper to Felix that it was his father's soul, freed now to fly through the sunshine. Caterers came to Endes to prepare food and drink. A huge number of people came back from the church to eat and drink it. And though you're not supposed to notice this, the quality of the provisions was seriously good. Felix looked outrageously handsome, formally attired and in a kilt. He looked terrifically sexy in it, those handsome legs of his, which I knew so well the feel of, on public show; those well formed, perfect calves. I wondered, watching him, what everyone always wonders about kilt wearing Scotsmen, and couldn't wait for the opportunity – which I knew wouldn't come before nightcap time – to find out. (I did find out at nightcap time, out on the lawn. I ran my hand up the soft inside of his warm thighs and found no barrier between my fingers and his businesslike cock and balls. He was already very wet up there in anticipation, and hardening at my approach, and my exploring hand was shortly replaced in that warm darkness by my head. But I'm running on a bit.)

Rhona came looking for me among the crowds that drank to Max's memory that afternoon. She was dressed in brilliant black. I was nervous of her now, but could hardly run away. 'It was nice to have you with us in the church,' she said. 'I mean at Felix's side.' I must have gaped at her, because she smiled and said, 'Sorry. I know that sounded really silly. Those things are. But today it mattered. You see, I know it mattered, because I know what it means.'

'You know what it means?' I blustered. 'What does it mean?'

She put a hand on my arm, very gently. 'You know what it means.' She stopped a moment. 'Sorry. These things are difficult. What is expected of us. Who we are. They don't always fit. Jonty, you don't need to look at me like that.' I didn't know how I was looking at her. I tried to smile. It felt a bit flinty. 'Felix is a very sensitive boy. You know that, of course, because so are you.' She paused a half second. Then, 'I know that Felix is gay. We've been friends since childhood, and I know him very well. I guessed some time ago.'

'You're all set to marry him,' I protested.

'Don't be hard on me for that,' she said. 'I thought we could make a go of it, Felix and I. We could be Platonic, even, if he preferred it that way. We're very, very fond of each other, you see. It might have worked. For many people, even these days, it still does. But then I met you. I thought, four days ago, or five, whenever it was, seeing you with Felix... It was nothing the two of you did, or said to each other. But I kind of knew. I told myself I'd imagined it. Then yesterday... Well, yesterday the truth was just too clear. I know you scarcely exchanged a glance all lunchtime, being considerate, I suppose, to me. But when you did... Well, the static filled the air. I was glad he told me about wanting you at the front of the church with us ... I mean, with him. It'll be easier for him now when he's ready to tell me the rest.'

My thoughts were a maelstrom. 'You're going to marry him,' I said. What I meant by that, exactly, I don't know.

'No,' she said. 'Not now. It's you he loves. He doesn't need to say it. It's just so. You love him too.' I was too stunned to speak. She said, 'I'll leave you in peace now,' and walked away.

We hadn't used the word love to each other, Felix and I. Not up to that time. God knew, we'd both wanted to, but we were scared of it. To say 'I love you' is a very daring thing. But that changed that evening, as everything changed that evening, out on the lawn, once I'd freed my head from the embraces of his kilt.

We continued our lovemaking in his bed. Getting away with a blow-job on the lawn when we were both fairly fully clothed was one thing but, though no-one had ever come out, or peered through a window at us, during our nightly garden whisky talks, we thought that stripping naked out there might be a bit foolhardy. And there were always the midges to be reckoned with. Safely tucked up, we both came more times that night than we'd done in the nights before, Felix spurting deep inside me, me emptying myself into him. Felix joined to Jonty, Jonty joined to him. The words 'I love you' came from Felix, came from Jonty, and came and came again.

Nearly a year has passed. The countryside is wearing its diamond and emerald spring look again.

I went back to my parents a week after the funeral – but only to get my things. I never delivered another package for the Royal Mail. But if I ever thought that managing a big estate was easy work, well, I don't think that now. It's incredibly tough, and you have to get up ... well it doesn't bear thinking about how early. But if

Felix is here for the night he has to get up early too. He goes off to Glasgow, by car to Dumfries, and then by train. (It takes for ever.) And if he's not here for the night, then I'm with him in his rather narrow bed at the Glasgow student flat. I'm not going to go on and write more paragraphs about how beautiful he is, how good sex is with him, or about his gorgeous cock, and the sweetness of his character and disposition. You can re-read the descriptions of him I wrote earlier if you want to, and change the tense to the present as you go along.

We see quite a bit of Rhona – and her new man, Callum, who's a hunk. They're good friends of ours. As for Lolli, she didn't take advantage of the rent-free house in the grounds in the end. She's also found a boyfriend – if you can call anyone of fifty that. They're in London most of the time. But when they come to Scotland they stay with us at Endes. We've eight bedrooms, after all.

On the rare occasions when I'm not with Felix, and I'm not working hard around the estate, negotiating with tenants, replacing fence posts or whatever, then I write. And Felix, when he comes back – however tired he may be after a long shift on the wards, will read what I have written and, if I'm lucky, approve.

MERCUTIO'S ROMEO

David was a newcomer once again, adrift in a strange town for the third time in five months. Manchester. He was nervous of course, but not, this time, because he was starting his career as a chorus boy in pantomime but because he wasn't. It was only his third job since leaving drama school and – he still hardly dared to believe it – he was Romeo. Romeo, with all the expectations that that entailed, with all the weight of the great performances of the past upon his twenty-three-year-old shoulders.

He knew the routine by now. Sunday evening: find the digs, find something to eat, try the local pub. Monday morning: meet the new faces, wonder if he'd be up to the job – console himself with the hope that perhaps some of his youthful fellow actors were secretly wondering the same thing.

'I haven't fenced since drama school,' he confessed.

'Neither have I,' said Tybalt with a rueful smile.

'Nor me,' said Mercutio.

'I'm glad we've all got that off our chests at least,' said the fight arranger, handing out rapiers as though they were pencils in a drawing class. 'Very slowly to begin with. One, two three and lunge…'

'You're going to be a bit good,' said a voice at coffee break. David turned round. It was Mercutio. The actor's name was Howard, a handsome raven-haired young man, older than David by a year or so, and taller by an inch.

'Thank you.' David was pleased, and surprised. Although he tried to tell himself the compliment was no more than his due, the fact that it should have been offered at such an early stage was flattering. He felt relaxed enough to say to Howard, 'You're pretty good yourself,' and was rewarded by a bright-eyed smile in return: a smile that showed off a pretty array of pearly teeth.

David did not usually think the word pretty in connection with men. Perhaps it would have been truer to say that he tried not to. He thought his girlfriend was pretty, and other women too, from time to time. But even that was seldom at the forefront of his mind. He had a girlfriend, as many young men do, because he had one. Because he'd always had one. He had sex with her when he was with her – whichever one it happened to be at this stage of his life – and gave her, or them, not a lot of thought when he was away. But to be fair, he didn't waste a lot of time looking at or thinking about other women either. He didn't play away from home. For the fact was, David was one of those ultra-committed, ultra-focused actors whose work and career absorbed him almost to the exclusion of everything else. It was not even that he was ambitious, at least not in the usual sense of desiring status, fame and money. What he loved, what he lived for, was the things itself: the acting, the roles, the theatre; it was the whole of his world. Yet Mercutio's – Howard's – teeth were quite something, David had to admit. And those eyes of his too.

The break ended. The rehearsal continued, with David counting, 'One, two, three, lunge,' under his breath, and showing his teeth a bit competitively when called upon to smile at Juliet.

'What a lovely actor you are to work with,' said Sian, who was Juliet, at lunchtime. 'Your smile is something other. We're going to have a great time. You're so giving.'

She was very attractive herself, David thought, registering simultaneously the twin novelties of being complimented so boldly, and his own new sensitivity to the attractiveness of others. Did it have something to do with the role he was playing? He had found Mercutio's smile attractive as well as enviable, if he were honest. And Sian, well, she had the loveliest deep-set hazel eyes above her high cheek-bones. As for himself, he had never thought that he was especially good looking. Average height, average build, average facial features. And, as far as his limited knowledge went, an average sized cock as well. He'd never made a point of looking at other men's, though he saw them from time to time – in showers or at urinals; in theatre dressing rooms. He'd rarely seen another man's full erection.

But when he was on stage everything became different. If his character was handsome, then so was he, and he could make the whole audience, and himself, believe it. The same held true if he was playing someone ugly of course, but this month, while he was Romeo, that thought could be laid aside. Things were starting well, he thought. He'd managed to charm – and had decided to like – two new people in one morning. As he donned the mantle of Romeo it was as though life was changing up a gear. A sepia-tinted phase of it was giving way to a Technicolor one.

Other people were nervous on first nights. Not David. He could be terrified on the first day of rehearsal, shy with new fellow actors, but soon his performance would take on a momentum of its own. The presence of an audience might change it a little, would usually improve it, but it would not disturb him or make him anxious. Audiences didn't suddenly materialise on first nights anyway. The first dress-run would find the wardrobe mistress sitting in, the second would furnish design staff and carpenters too. The technical rehearsal would leave David in a private world, able to polish what he had not had time to do before: a little gesture tweaked, a new way to give meaning to a phrase… Nobody would be paying attention to him. Everyone would be busy with lighting, cueing, snagging, focused intently on props and buttons, leaving him to pursue his own inner goal: the perfect performance of his given role. Eventually…

'Half an hour please.'

'Oh God, I'm right out of powder. Anybody got some?'

'Got any carmine?'

'What play are you in, darling?'

'Quarter of an hour please.'

'I'm shit-scared. Look at David there. Cool as a whatsit.'

'Anybody else get a card from Viv?'

'Beginners please…' David and Uncle Tom Cobley and all to the stage please.

It went like a dream. All that had been good in the three weeks of rehearsals came together in that evening's two hours' traffic. David came off after his final curtain call feeling ten feet tall. The supporters' club had drinks laid on afterwards. David and Sian were fêted, toasted, separately and together. A magical new stage partnership had been born, people said.

'Party back at Simon's,' word went round. 'Get away when you can.'

'I don't have a bottle,' David said.

'Come anyway.'

David went. An hour or two later Sian was sitting on his knee and making him recount his life story. There was much to be said for playing Romeo, he thought, aware of his own excitement.

'I'll get you some more wine,' Sian said, and disappointingly got up. There was a knock at the door, welcoming voices. 'Tom, we didn't know you were back. How did it go?'

Sian introduced Tom to David. He could hear in her voice the pleasant uncertainty of one spoilt for choice. Then she took Tom away to the kitchen to get him a drink. David remained in his armchair.

'Some you win, some you lose,' said someone who came and perched on one of the arms. It was Howard, Mercutio.

'Your Queen Mab speech was magic,' David said. He really meant it, but the words came out without enthusiasm.

'Aren't you the kind one? Do you know what you were?'

'What?'

'Fucking ruddy brilliant from beginning to end.'

'You're pissed,' said David a bit more kindly.

'So are you.'

'I am?'

'I think so,' said Howard. 'I can tell by that smile of yours. I didn't notice it when I first met you, but it's grown day by day. Now it's bigger than you are. Must be the wine smiling, I thought. Seems to have worked a treat with Sian anyway.'

'I don't know about that.'

'Why not?'

'I'm not sure,' David began, uncertain what he was going to say, uncertain whether it would make any sense, but vaguely sensing that it wouldn't much matter, 'what this smile is doing for me. Or what I'm supposed to be doing with it.'

'With Sian, you mean?'

'Anyone. Anything.'

'Probably the wrong thing,' Howard suggested, nodding his head at his own shrewdness. 'Most people do.'

'Probably,' said David, without knowing what he was agreeing with.

'Perhaps you should be looking in a different direction.'

This woke David up somewhat. 'If you mean what I think you do, the answer is no.'

'What do you think I mean?' asked Howard teasingly.

David only laughed in reply so Howard tried, 'Your glass. You haven't got one.'

'Sian took it out to the kitchen, I think.'

'To fill it up and give it to that Tom fellow. How diabolical. Perfidious. I'll get you a new one.'

'I've had more than enough already,' said David, but Howard had already set off towards the kitchen. David watched him go. He certainly was a good looking man, as well as a good actor. David had admired his panache and his smile and had made a point, as Romeo, of copying them. Now Howard had paid David the compliment of admiring the reflection.

'David, you should be circulating,' someone said.

'I daren't,' he answered. 'I'm afraid the room might, too.'

Howard returned with two glasses of something. It no longer mattered what. There was a new warmth in his eyes that David found appealing. He wanted to say, *you remind me of someone*, but he couldn't remember who, so he left it. Big Norma passed by. Big Norma who had played earth-motherly roles up and down the country for years – she was the Nurse in this production – said, 'I didn't know about you two.' For Howard had somehow half slipped off the arm of David's chair and looked to be nearly in David's lap.

'Just good friends,' said Howard lightly and rested his spinning head on David's shoulder.

'Exactly so,' said David, and completed the tableau by leaning his own head against Howard's.

'Well, well, well,' said Norma, and gave them an old-fashioned look as she walked away.

'She'll have forgotten by the morning,' said Howard from somewhere near David's right ear.

*

'I'm rat-arsed,' Howard volunteered as they spilled out into the street.

'I'll walk you home,' said David. He didn't think he'd been quite so drunk in his life. But Norma's throwaway remark had somehow crystallised the evening for them, and had set it on a tentative course that was previously not even remotely possible, at least for David. They had refilled their glasses twice more afterwards. Now the night air laid about them like a boxer. 'Where are your digs?'

'Furnace Road,' said Howard.

'Jesus, that's miles. Never mind, we'll get you there somehow.' They staggered arm in arm towards a railway viaduct. A late express thundered across it, a dazzling necklace of light, blinding and out of focus as a vision. 'Look at that,' said David.

'Brilliant,' said Howard, as if David had conjured the effect for his own special benefit. The train disappeared like a firework hissing into the blackness and left them in star-less silence, together, alone.

'Look,' said David, 'It's another mile to Furnace Road, and I live just up here on the left.' What had he just said? His mind dredged up the fact that there was only one bed at his disposal. There was the floor, of course... They'd sort it all out when they got there.

David was on a level of consciousness that was new to him. He unlocked the front door of the darkened house and propelled his companion upstairs. In his room he put on the light. Howard immediately dived onto the bed as people in his state do, but he dived rather tidily to one side, leaving a space next to him, and into that space David, with only the briefest pause for thought, slid his own body. 'Come on,' he said, playing the put-upon host, 'let's get you ready for bed.' And he began to unbutton Howard's shirt for him.

'Hey David,' murmured Howard, 'have you come home tonight?'

'Maybe,' said David.

'Maybe for the first time,' said Howard, though mainly to himself.

Howard looked even better naked than he did when clothed. He was a half-size bigger than David in every respect: height, muscle development – and cock. Though David was pleased to notice that the discrepancy of size in this department was not so great as to be threatening. They were both fully hard by now. Both circumcised. And David noticed Howard's cock was wet. But, checking with a finger, he discovered that the same went for his own.

'You can fuck me if you want to, baby.'

David's astonishment at hearing himself addressed as baby by a handsome naked man not two years older than himself only increased his excitement at the novelty of it all. Though he'd never had sex with a man he wasn't ignorant of the options that this kind of sex could involve. He'd spent three years at drama school after all and was now a member of a profession some half of whose male practitioners were gay. He was too choked up to answer Howard in words. He gulped and nodded his head. And even if he'd still had any doubts about what his next move should be, Howard's own next move would have made all plain. He rolled onto his back, drew up and spread his knees, and with an encouraging smile helped David to roll round on top.

David thought it might be difficult to work his way in but it wasn't. Howard was relaxed by drinking – and pretty well practised too, it has to be said. Within moments David was thrusting deep into his insides and not long after that he came exuberantly. It felt as though a series of waves were breaking over him as he lay face down on the shore of a friendly sea.

He had tried to massage Howard's cock. It was staring him in the face after all. But Howard took his hand away. 'Better idea,' he said. 'Later.'

It wasn't much later. After a short interlude of stroking and kissing, Howard reached out from the bed to retrieve a packet of condoms from the pocket of his jeans which were on the floor. With a bit of difficulty he put one on.

'I didn't…' David began, feeling an irrational guilt.

'You said it was your first time,' Howard said smoothly. 'And I believed you. I think I knew anyway though, without being told.' Now he rolled a newly compliant David onto his back and made love to him in a perfect role-reversed action replay of what had gone before. With what remained of his reasoning capability David had thought that this would hurt. And yet, despite the hefty size of Howard's hard-on, both in its length and thickness, David's discomfort was minor and short-lived. He guessed that he was as physically relaxed as Howard had been – thanks in part to the quantity he had drunk. Another thought flashed through his mind: it was as though he'd been born for this moment, as though he'd been looking forward to it all his life. And when, some minutes later, David felt Howard swell and climax deep inside him, he found the hair-trigger of his own cock's workings released again and, with only minimal prompting from Howard's friendly hand, his belly milkily a-flood.

But morning changes everything. Especially when you were drunk the night before. Howard left at first light. David stayed, nursing a headache and more. He had woken to find himself a different person from the one who had woken yesterday. Romeo, he thought bitterly. He was appalled by what he had done. He even smelt different. He got up and had a hot bath. It made no difference. He'd let himself be conned, he thought. The way forward made him feel sick. There was no way back.

All day he planned, scripted and mentally stage-managed his next conversation with Howard. It ought to be in broad daylight, in a public place, the street, a pub. There should be lots of people about, there should be noise. They would see each other, shout 'Hi' and laugh, then go their separate ways, their laughter an unambiguous symbol that last night had been a random, not to be repeated, event: a drunken aberration. They would be able to show that they were still friends, that their friendship was all the better for their one shared moment of eccentric behaviour. One day far in the future they might be able to bring it up in conversation over a drink and say philosophically, 'Remember that night? What was all that about, then?' All this David and Howard would convey in their laughing greeting when they met next in the sunshine, in the busy world.

That their next meeting could not be like that should have been obvious. They had to meet that evening at work instead. They did not share a dressing-room and, though David hoped right up to the last minute they might run into each other in the corridor before curtain-up, they eventually met for the first time on stage, in full Elizabethan costume and make up, with rapiers and daggers complete. They wore handsome matching smiles but there was lead in David's eyes and heart.

After the show David got changed. He stopped being an actor, hung his Romeo and his triumph on a hook and wiped his role from his face with removing cream. In jeans and trainers he joined the queue in the fish and chip shop like any other young man, indistinguishable from the rest. You might have driven past him on your way home from the theatre, still talking about his splendid performance, seen him queuing there and, never noticing, driven on.

David walked home, eating as he went, and bumped into Howard, quite literally, as he was rounding a corner. 'Sorry,' he said first, then seeing who it was, 'Hallo,' flatly. He thought, fate.

'I thought it might be you,' said Howard with as little enthusiasm.

They stood together in a shop doorway, sharing David's chips. 'I don't know what to say,' said David.

'Doesn't matter,' Howard said.

'I meant about last night. I behaved a bit out of character. I don't usually do … you know … the things we did.'

'You don't usually give in to spontaneous natural desires, you mean?'

'I don't mean that. Fuck you, Howard. What I meant to say was, I shouldn't have behaved the way I did. If I gave you misleading signals, then I'm really, really sorry. Please accept that.'

'Misleading signals? A hearty fuck, jubilantly given, and another one just as enthusiastically received… If those were just signals I'd like to know what constitutes a declaration of … of whatever.'

'You twist my words,' David objected. 'I'm not gay.'

'OK. No problem. You're not gay. You slept with a man last night. Live with that. You'll be in good company. All over the world a million men are doing just that – living with that apparent contradiction, and that's just since last night.' David smiled in spite of himself. 'Well, I can live with that too,' Howard went on. 'And I still think you're gorgeous.'

David hadn't known Howard thought that. He hadn't mentioned it before. It made David feel slightly better. 'Those chips weren't enough,' he said. 'Guess we'd better go back and get some more.'

Outside the chip shop, a fresh bundle of supper in their hands, David said, 'May as well go back to my place to eat them, I suppose. Since it's just round the corner. What were you doing round here anyway?'

'Coming to call on you.'

'Why?'

'Not sure. To try to put things right between us, I suppose. That is, if I could. Maybe just to talk, to say hallo... OK, here's a wine shop. I'll call in and get a bottle to keep us company.'

'In case we run out of things to say?' David meant to sound sardonic but it didn't quite work.

They didn't run out of things to say. They talked until the small hours and until the bottle of wine was a distant memory. David said, with what he wanted to be a weary sigh, 'I suppose you may as well stay over if you want to. We don't have any surprises for each other any more.' Standing face to face beside the bed they began to undress each other, and neither was in the least surprised to find the other displaying a full and frank erection when at last their most intimate reaches were revealed.

That night they made love to each other more gently, more tenderly, yet somehow more intensely as they each fucked each other – just as on the previous night – and then got fucked, turn by turn.

They stayed in bed till nearly noon, then spent most of the next day together. In the evening when they met on stage again their eyes shone bright and clear once more, and it was those of Juliet that Romeo's gaze could not meet.

In the days and weeks that followed, the theatre company came first to realise and then to accept that they had become a couple. Even Sian knew a fait accompli when she saw one. And little by little David began to understand that for the first time in his life he was falling in love. He knew Howard deeply now: physically, through their bedtime sexual explorations, and personally, emotionally, through their conversations, through just being together. And everything that David knew about Howard was now wonderful. He would have died for him. Nothing that had gone before, with any of his girlfriends, had measured up to this. And yet he would have to part from Howard – he had no illusions about this – when the run of Romeo was ended. Howard had a boyfriend in London, and Howard would go back to him. He always did.

David had a girlfriend in London, but he would not be going back to her. Their phone conversations were growing more distant by the week. Both of them knew, without David having to explain anything, without her having to ask painful questions, that when they met again they would be meeting only in order to part. It would not be an easy meeting, David knew. However much they might try not to hurt each other, both would get hurt; that was the nature of things; but it would happen anyway.

First love. At twenty-three! The love against which all which followed would be measured. David had discovered from being in love with Howard that this meant infinitely more to him than playing Romeo, more than his acting career, more than whatever golden panoply of talent he might possess. His life was changed utterly and nothing would ever be the same again.

David walked into the theatre bar. The last performance of Romeo and Juliet was finished. The room was full of hold-alls, flight bags and backpacks. Howard's was among them, David's not. He alone had had his contract renewed. He would be playing Konstantin in Chekhov's The Seagull. There was the chance of a London transfer…

Anthony McDonald

Howard had bagged a couple of well-paid commercials, with a little help from his agent, and would soon be smiling encouragement at the consumer from a corner of the consumer's own living-room. Right now he was sitting across the bar room from David, his luggage between his knees. David called across. 'Pint of best?' He'd reached the front of the bar queue.

'Small whisky only. Lots of M6 to cope with.'

David went and sat with him. 'I don't want you to go. I shall miss you.'

There were people all around them. David didn't care whether they heard or not. It was a common enough Saturday night scene.

'Miss you,' said Howard. He touched the back of David's hand for a moment.

'I think I've been in love with you,' said David, understating his case somewhat.

'I think I can say the same.' Howard's voice was soft, almost breaking. 'But what is love without loss? Nobody wins with love. If you are born to love you are born to lose.'

David looked at Howard's glass of whisky. 'Sure you're OK to drive?'

'To love is to lose. Love is loss. That's all.'

David finished his drink and got up. 'Have a safe journey,' he said, then smiled wryly. 'I must love you and lose you now. See you again some day. Actors' paths always cross and re-cross. Hope so anyway.'

Howard stood up and they embraced and kissed for quite some time. None of the people around them batted an eyelid. Then David rumpled Howard's hair, turned and left the room.

He would miss the gentle touch of Howard in the night, miss the rumbustious thrusting of his cock inside him, miss spearing Howard's sphincter with his own, miss his sweet warm breath when they woke sometimes in the small hours just to kiss. He didn't know where he would find such a love again, nor how nor when. But he'd learned at least in which direction he should be looking. And how to recognize it when it next appeared.

Anthony McDonald

LUC, THE FABULOUS BAKERS' BOY

There was a uniform at my school in Scotland. Stepping out of it, so to speak, when I exchanged schoolboy status for that of student at the Sorbonne was one of the many steps into adult life that my move to Paris at the age of nineteen involved.

I wasn't attached to my school uniform. I left it and its implications behind with relief and no backward glance as I entered my new world. No uniform for university students, *dieu merci.*

There were uniforms aplenty in Paris though. Ticket inspectors on suburban trains wore them. Dandy little waiters like wraith-thin penguins wore them too. And from time to time I'd spot, propping up a bar, a muscular member of the Foreign Legion in his full outfit: scarlet tasselled epaulettes on open necked white shirt, blue rifle belt like a cummerbund, gunmetal grey trousers tucked into black laced boots... That sight did turn me on a bit, I must admit, despite my delight at no longer having to wear a uniform myself. And every time I found myself at close quarters to one of these tough fighting men during the day I'd fantasise about him that night in bed, while doing what most men do when they find themselves in that private place alone.

But not all uniforms are imposed by authority from above. As an outsider, a newcomer to France, I was noticing that. Some uniforms were adopted as a matter of free choice, to show that you belonged. One, even more visible in the streets as autumn began to bite, was the near universal male street garb of black wool coat, knee length, with flaming scarlet scarf around the neck. Unchanged in a hundred years, since the Moulin Rouge posters of Toulouse Lautrec, it screamed at incomers, *le*

43

Paris, c'est moi. It did look rather nice, actually, though it was hardly something to masturbate about.

I realised then that even we students at the Sorbonne wore a uniform, though we were mainly unaware that that was what it was. Blue denim jeans, moccasins or trainers on our feet, white socks between, and dark rollneck sweaters an addition as autumn advanced. As much as my schoolfellows and I had done until just months before, we looked as alike as peas in a pod.

But among all these uniforms, whether imposed or adopted willingly, instinctively, there was one which attracted me in a rather special way. It had no equivalent on my side of the English Channel. It was the early morning uniform of the mitrons. *Mitrons* were bakers' boys in times gone by. They probably weren't called that now. And they weren't strictly speaking boys any more – just as people no longer sent children up chimneys to sweep out the soot. They were lads of eighteen or nineteen like myself.

My path would cross theirs when I had an early lecture at the Sorbonne and had to get up at what I considered an ungodly hour, to make my way along the Boulevard des Batignolles to the Place de Clichy metro stop, where I would catch the train south to the Left Bank. At this hour the youths that the bakeries employed were let loose, following a night of toil in steaming kitchens, to criss-cross the lamp-lit boulevard with great baskets of heaven-smelling baguettes, delivering them to the cafés that lined the street, as they began to open for the day.

Their uniforms – these mitrons' or bakers' boys' – were adopted not only out of necessity, I suspected, but also partly out of choice. The necessity sprang from the fact that they worked long shifts in hot kitchens overnight. But also, I thought, this was the way that, perhaps unconsciously, they liked to look. White trainers, jet black ankle socks, bare legs that gleamed white in the street-lamps' yellow stare, then the shortest, tightest pairs of shorts that they could possibly pull up over their sculpted thighs and fasten at their slender waists. Above those waists they wore white T-shirts over which, as winter approached, they began to throw dark roll-necks, just as we did at the Sorbonne.

You need to have good legs to get away with white shorts and trainers and black ankle socks. But without exception these guys did. I was careful to notice that. And cute butts. Cute faces too.

I didn't speak to any of them as they carried their busy wicker baskets along and across the wide tree-lined road. Not at first, anyway. But I saw the same ones, morning by morning, as I hurried to my metro train, and in my imagination found myself giving them all names. Among many others there was 'Jean-Marc', tallest and lankiest of the set: black haired, with big and sombre eyes and elegant straight nose. What his real name might be I had no idea, but he was Jean-Marc to me. Another lad I called Patrick – pronounced in my head the French way, the accent firmly on syllable number two. He was a sturdy, muscular guy with curly chestnut hair and a snub nose. Both these *mecs* featured prominently in my nocturnal fantasies as, every night, I stroked myself to sleep.

After a while another mec took turns with them, though at first I'd noticed him less than the other two. He was smaller, lighter framed, cute faced and blond. If the other two were, like me, nineteen or so, then the little blond chap was perhaps a year our junior: a wide eyed eighteen. In my mind, and in my fantasies about him, I called him Pierre.

It wasn't until January, one morning when I had an early start on what must have been the coldest, darkest morning of the year, that I actually got a chance to speak to one of those shorts clad bakers' boys. The time of day and other circumstances being what they were, it could have been any one of them, but it happened to be 'Pierre'. I bumped into him on the corner of the Boulevard des Batignolles and the Rue de Turin. Bumped into him in the most literal way.

I was walking past the bakery that stands on the corner when its door opened, almost in my face, and out he popped, a pre-dawn vision of white limbs and shorts, a huge openwork basket of long loaves in each hand. We had no time to avoid each other. I barged into his left shoulder and his left-hand load of bread. The impact swung him round to face me but made him lose his balance and his grip upon the ground. He staggered backwards, toppled and began to fall.

These things happen in less than an instant. I saw his big startled eyes – a startling blue – and saw that he was too loth to lose his precious cargoes to let them go, and so stop himself from falling by grabbing hold of the door or wall. I put out a hand to try to save him, but it was a useless gesture, doomed to fail. With all those loaves like rifle butts in front of him, I had no chance to grab an arm or shoulder, let alone catch him around his back. Instead I made things three times worse, pushed at his chest as he fell back and, meeting no resistance, lost my own balance and fell on top of him face down, my chest on top of his as he landed on his back.

The baguettes were catapulted far and wide across the *trottoir* and the road. It was as if they'd been scattered by the explosion of a small grenade. Pedestrians stopped and picked them up from the trottoir, but in the carriageway the traffic had no choice except to squash them flat.

How quickly all this happened, yet how slow it seemed. I'd put my hands in front of me instinctively to break my fall and also – I like to hope – to save 'Pierre' from the totality of my weight as I pinned him to the ground. My left hand did some good here, making firm contact with the paving slab. But my right hand landed on his bare left thigh, slid forward, skidded up the leg hole of his brief, brief shorts – and I grasped his cock.

Grasped? Made contact with it anyway, but immediately my fingers seemed to wrap themselves around it as if in obedience to some freak law of motion that modern physics had yet to explain. It felt soft and squidgy, like a smallish uncooked sausage. Yet as I held it for a second – oh all right, two – I felt the core of rubbery toughness at its centre, the chewy toughness of a whelk.

We gazed into each other's eyes in more than astonishment, though it was only later that I found the proper word – which was *wonder* – and as we did so I felt that little whelky core take charge of the whole thing that I held in my hand so unexpectedly, and felt the whole organ, the lad's *bite* as he would have called it in French, start to toughen up and grow.

I said, *'Pardon, excusez-moi, je suis désolé,'* which is approximately all the words for apology that exist in French strung all together in the same sentence. It was only after I'd said them that I remembered to release Pierre's promising penis from my fingers' clasp and tactically withdraw my hand from the warm-thighed softness of the inside of his shorts. Then we helped each other to our feet.

It was three days before we met again. He was walking down the boulevard in the pre-dawn as usual, under the yellow lamps and the expectant blue black sky, and because he was going on ahead of me, in the same direction as me, and because we'd already sort of met, I boldly caught him up and spoke. 'I'm sorry about the other day,' I said, although I'd repeated the words again and again in the few minutes that followed our first encounter. 'I mean, if you got into trouble or anything … if you had to pay for the baguettes … I mean I'd like to explain to whoever that the fault was mine entirely … and pay for the bread...'

'Pierre' stopped and turned to face me. What lovely eyes he had... That cute little nose... 'I'm not in trouble, don't worry. And nobody has to pay for the baguettes. These things happen. Everyone understands that. It was my fault anyway. I shouldn't have barged out onto the trottoir like that, without looking. Crowds of people going to work... I thought I was late, that was all.' He stopped, then almost giggled. Then he said more quietly, 'Lucky it was you.'

As we stood facing each other in the busy street, just as we'd done after dusting each other down and asking if the other was OK three days ago, he in his tight uniform shorts, I in my regulation jeans, a memory occurred to both of us. I'm quite sure it occurred to him and not just me because he started to smile at me in the same funny, knowing way in which I was beginning, I'm quite sure, to smile at him.

What we were remembering was that, as we had stood there that time, our eyes had strayed to the other's crotch and to our own. We'd each observed two straining curves that pushed out the fabric of our respective leg wear – his short shorts and my long jeans. Curves that pushed out, bent down, and then were pushed back upon themselves, like the brake pipes of uncoupled trains although, to be honest, on a very much smaller scale. We had shared a similar, private smile back then but work had beckoned for both of us and, after asking once again if the other was unhurt, we'd gone on our separate ways.

'I'm Luc,' Pierre said now, and gave me his hand.

'Jamie,' I said, and gave him mine... Not Pierre, I thought, but Luc. Luc. Just as nice as Pierre, I thought next. I didn't tell him any of this. Not then.

'We could meet some time,' Luc was saying, casually, unbelievably, smiling, much as he might have done in one of my bedtime fantasies. The fact that I'd wished, longed even, for just such a suggestion was no protection against the dizzying surge of emotions I experienced on actually hearing those words.

'Oh yes,' I said, hearing myself sound, and feeling myself blush, like a lovesick schoolgirl.

'Tu es gentil,' Luc said. You're nice.

'Toi aussi,' I said. You too.

'Where? When?' Luc went on. I realised there was no misunderstanding of where we were at. We weren't diplomatic thirty-somethings engaged in verbal fencing but two *mecs* in our late teens who were discovering that the other had what we each wanted – and discovering that we wanted it in quite an urgent way. 'You're a student at the Sorbonne,' Luc said.

'How did you know that?'

Luc grinned. 'You wear the uniform.' He looked me up and down. Roll-neck, moccasins and jeans. 'But I work nights.'

'Sunday?' I stammered the word.

Luc frowned. 'I'm at my parents. Porte de Clignancourt.' Not one of Paris's classier districts. Not that I cared. His face brightened. 'Tell you what. I'll come back early. Before my shift starts. I've a room above the bakery I use during the week. A cupboard really. Say four o'clock. There'll be no-one there. Come to the side door. I'll let you in.' By now the baguettes in Luc's baskets were jiggling up and down as their bearer's excitement transmitted itself along his arms. Those loaves seemed to be impatient to get on their way, to be torn into chunks and dunked in morning coffee bowls. So we walked on a few yards together, to where Luc's next delivery split his path away from mine. When that at last happened I stood for a moment where I was. I watched his pert white shorts moving away from me, admiring his ivory thighs and pearl-smooth calves – and then he turned and gave me a cheeky wave, having had no doubt, obviously, that I'd still be watching him, before he disappeared into the café that was his next port of call.

Ever since my encounter with Luc's *bite* – the first cock except for my own that I'd had in my hand for months, the first fistful of other boy's prick I'd squeezed since I'd left school – I'd brought the sensations of the moment back to mind every time I laid a hand on myself. And that had been pretty frequently in those following days. But on Saturday night I managed not to masturbate – it took a major effort of will – and the same went for Sunday morning – which required an even bigger effort of self denial. I was saving myself, saving my sperm, for four o'clock. Saving my spunk for Luc, who had been Pierre.

I pressed the buzzer on the dot of four, as Luc had instructed me to do. He opened it as promptly as if he'd been standing behind it waiting. Perhaps he had. It was something I never asked him in all the time that followed, and never would. Now I found myself in a tiny lobby from which bare wood stairs led upwards: narrow, twisty and steep. I imagined we'd be going straight up those stairs but Luc grabbed me by the hand and led me through the only interior doorway in the lobby. That door was open. It led directly into the tile-floored oven room. Tall stainless steel racks and great ovens like silvery wardrobes filled it, cold, silent, waiting.

Luc was already wearing his trademark shorts, T-shirt and trainers. An angel in white, save for the black ankle socks. There was no reason why he should be dressed like this some hours before his shift started. I had to conclude that he already understood I liked him to look that way.

We fell immediately into each other's arms and kissed among the racks and stoves. No tentative beginning for us, we plunged straight in, lips grasping lips and tongues exploring mouths. We looked into each other's excited eyes and realised for the first time that we were exactly the same height. Exploring hands told us we were the same in build as well. Probably we'd have evenly balanced a pair of scales.

I felt Luc's two hands suddenly come in under my pullover and T-shirt at the front. They swarmed up my chest and grasped a nipple each, startling me. No-one had done that to me before, nor had I to anyone. Like someone tuning a radio Luc gently rubbed and twiddled those tiny knobs of mine, things I'd never thought of as adornments, still less as erogenous zones. I felt them stiffen and enlarge, become rubbery in Luc's hands and, like miniature stand-ins for my cock, take an interest – for the first time in my life – in what was going on.

I did the same to Luc. Ran my hands up under his T-shirt, feeling his smooth warm chest, then grasping his unseen nipples, already big and rubbery and proud. Then, almost instinctively, we raised our forearms, lifting the front of each other's clothes as if we wanted to lift them off over each other's head without letting go of the little rubbery teats we held. Impossible, of course. But we did get our first view each of the other's flat stomach, the round whorl of belly button and youthfully hairless chest. The only concession Luc's torso made to hairiness of any kind was a chain of tiny blond hairs that seemed to spill out of his navel, then run down, straight as a plumb line, to disappear behind the tight waistband of his now domed-up shorts. I knew that Luc would be seeing a similar sight on me, though my own slender arrow of hair was mouse colour and funnelled down not into shorts but jeans.

Luc had to let go of my nipples then. He lifted my pullover and T-shirt over my head as one and let them fall, one still inside the other, to the floor behind me. I made short work of his T-shirt in the same way. Now naked from the waist up, lit through the window by the slanting sun of a winter afternoon, Luc looked lovely, his skin not so ivory toned as the night's street-lamps made it, but light honey coloured, except where his nipples and their areolae introduced the tint of light pink plums.

We knew what we wanted next, and that we needed it right here, now. No time to waste climbing stairs. I unhooked the top clasp of those famous, clingy little shorts, undid the zip and pulled them down. Simultaneously Luc did likewise with my jeans. I'd deliberately set out without underwear and now it was clear that Luc's idea had been the same. Our cocks sprang out and up like jack-in-the-boxes, while my jeans and his shorts went down like flags and concertina-ed round our feet. We didn't waste a second in stepping out of them but each took the other's cock in hand and, standing face to face, went to work on it at once.

'You're circumcised,' Luc said to me. (He was not.)

'Is that a problem?' I asked. The words came breathily, and in jerks.

'No, of course.' Just as jerkily. Hoarse. 'I think it's cute.'

I thought his foreskinned one was cute. Not unlike mine in scale – which meant that while it was far from being the biggest on the planet, it was quite substantial in proportion to his overall smallish size. Sturdy rather than long. The head of it a pinker version of my own pale mauve. Haloed in his case by a slender circlet of fur that was soft and fine and silky white as thistledown.

With my free hand I felt his balls. Small walnut size, so tightly clenched up in their downy retaining pouch that they'd half retracted up inside him. I felt his spare fingers exploring mine.

We quickly came. Our darting liquid pearls be-dewed the floor then, less energetically, dribbled into the puddles of our shorts and jeans. We looked at each other approvingly for a few seconds more, then pulled our leg-wear up, without bothering to mop up or to fasten them properly, and Luc took me by the hand without speaking and led me up the stairs.

Arriving in his tiny bedroom we both found we needed to pee. We stood together by the small washbasin and did it there, playfully crossing our silver water swords above the plughole like two kids. Jeans and shorts were round our ankles again by now, but once we'd finished at the basin we took them off properly, removing socks and shoes. We lay on Luc's narrow bed together, our hands and legs exploring every part of each other that we hadn't yet touched – as well as all those parts we already knew. When Luc suggested, *'Soixante-neuf?'* I thought for a startled second that he meant a card game. But then he squirmed round and lay on top of me, his knees bent up at the pillow end, his thighs across my shoulders, and his head and genitals... Well, you know where.

I had never had another guy's cock in my mouth before, nor put mine into the mouth of anyone else. I'd only done with other lads what Luc and I had just accomplished in the bake-house downstairs. I discovered an absolute star-burst of new sensations. The soft and luscious warmth of Luc's lips enfolding wetly my most delicate, most tactile sexual part. The pulsing thickness of Luc's organ (not over-long, for which I was grateful) inside my lips and cheeks, sharing the soft space with my tongue. The mirror image sensation of doing as you were being done to. And other things besides. The unanticipated loveliness of Luc's blond mop of hair tickling me ever so gently between the soft inside curvings of my thighs as his head moved gently but decisively up and down. His hands sought out my calves from time to time, lightly stroking them, setting up tingles of static among their nearly invisible sprinklings of fine hair. I did the same for Luc from my different, on-my-back, position, reaching up and around him to caress the giant cleft peach that was his bottom, his soft-skinned thighs, and his calves which, because his knees were bent up against the bed head, hung above me like a pair of ripe exotic fruit. His chest against my tummy, his thighs against my chest... I could go on and on.

That afternoon we did. We came almost together, as we'd done earlier downstairs. This time each felt the other's cock swell in his mouth, then drank in surprised and gasping gulps the up-welling salty springs. We rested after that, cuddling in our twin nakedness, and then we played soixante-neuf again. It was the first time in my life, I think, that I'd come massively three times in an hour.

Eventually we dressed and went out onto the boulevard for a beer in the Bar L'Europe. And then we started talking properly to each other for the first time, getting to know each other a little and, as we did so, liking more and more what we found. In the warm lighting of the bar – a light which was picked up, warmed and cast around by the glowing copper of the counter and other fittings – his legs were no cold white, but the colour of stirred together vanilla and strawberry ice-cream. He was in his shorts again, of course, as an unmentioned courtesy to me. (Naturally he was the only shorts-wearing customer this January evening, and he attracted a few glances of surprise.) I couldn't help noticing, though, that looked at in this light those shorts were not as pristine as they appeared in the lamp-lit street every morning before dawn. There was a grubbiness about the front of them that was not owed entirely to our recent activities, and I found myself imagining him masturbating inside them occasionally – perhaps through a hole in a pocket – during the longeurs of his bakery night shift. I must confess I found the idea an attractive one and I thought I might enjoy toying with it when I got into bed that night and toyed again with my own dick. And then I realised suddenly that neither of us had remembered to wipe up the oven-room floor...

Luc moved into my rented room, a block away from his bakery, a week later. My room was, like his, an old servant's room, a *'chambre de bonne'* under one of the steep grey mansard roofs that characterise the Paris skyline. My room was small, I'd always thought, but nothing like as small as Luc's, and that was what made the move make sense.

I was introduced to Luc's handsome bakery stable-mates, the people I'd christened Jean-Luc and Patrick and other names in my fantasies in the months before. Of course they had other names, they were all nice lads, and none of them was gay. It didn't matter: I didn't need them to be now.

Bravely we joined my Sorbonne friends for drinks a few times and none of them – all credit to them – turned a hair. Luc worked at night, I studied by day, but somehow we found time to be together, either at home (then generally in bed) or out and at large in the wonderful city.

One day, after we'd been living together for about two weeks, I came home early one afternoon to find Luc lying on his tummy on our bed, naked except for those tight white shorts – his uniform. In that position his calves and thighs made you want to bite into them. As for his peachy bottom, its contours emphasised by those hugging shorts... Well, I knew suddenly what I wanted to do, and knew at the same time that I was going to do it, though I never had before.

Luc didn't move as I stripped naked, but he watched me, his head turned sideways, half buried in the pillow. It was difficult to see if his mouth was smiling, but there was a mischievous light in his blue eyes that I was beginning to know quite well. 'What are you going to do?' he asked deadpan.

'You'll see,' I said, watching him clock the fact that my *bite* was already hard and pointing.

I'd never fucked anybody in my life up till now, nor had anyone fucked me. I knew that went for Luc too; we'd exchanged those intimate details one frank and alcohol lubricated evening early on. But we hadn't been in a hurry to experiment in that particular way; I suppose we had a sort of unspoken agreement to wait until the moment seemed right. Now though, with him lying there in his shorts like that, and with me all stiffened up and ready to go, it seemed that the moment had come.

I lay, tummy down, on top of his back on the bed. He didn't speak or move, but gave a throaty little chuckle, and a faint tremor ran through his body. I could have pulled his shorts down but I didn't. Neither did I reach for a condom: this all happened a long time ago, a whole year before Aids first came to Paris and gay Parisian men started having to protect themselves just like their counterparts everywhere. I lifted the hem of the right leg of his shorts with my fingers. Though the term leg seems an exaggeration. The inside seam measurement can hardly have been more than about three inches, and my pulling at the hem with my fingers didn't move it very far. I spat on my other hand and rubbed my dick with it. Some primal instinct must have told me to do that. Then, using the hand that held his shorts leg a bit like a shoehorn, I pushed my highly excited penis up inside his shorts. By some miracle it found his anus almost immediately and, by another one, slipped in first time, as if it had been made to measure for Luc's individually fashioned *cul*.

I asked Luc if he was OK and, when he grunted yes, let my prick slide in gently all the way. Like sword swallowing, I thought, marvelling at what was happening and at how good it felt. When I found myself inside Luc up to the hilt I paused a moment, then rolled myself and Luc sideways, till we lay morticed and tenoned together on our sides. With some difficulty, because Luc's shorts were now tighter than ever, due to the additional presence in them of my cock, I wormed a hand up inside the other leg hole at the front. Happily, there were no knickers inside to impede me, just the tightness of those shorts. But soon I had fondled my way up over his tight small ball-sac and was grasping his twelve o'clock positioned *bite*. Simultaneously I started to thrust in and out of Luc, up and down the leg hole from behind, and to masturbate him in the tight confines of his shorts at the front. I got the rhythm of the thing quickly. As I thrust in, I slid my hand along his cock towards me, away from his cock-head, back into the downy halo of his pubes. As I pulled my cock back, my caressing fist slid up towards Luc's foreskin-hooded tip. I hadn't thought to lubricate his penis by spitting on my hand before I pushed it up his shorts. But it turned out that I hadn't needed to. His cock was doing that very nicely by itself...

It never took us long to come when we were together, Luc and I. We were very young, we were more turned on by each other than by anyone we'd previously met and anyway, neither of us was as experienced as all that. So it was no surprise when Luc's body went into spasm, he became a bucking bronco, and I felt his hot sperm pour out of him into my clasping palm and fingers and then flood his shorts. A second later I was taken by surprise by the sensation of my cock swelling inside Luc and starting to pump. I didn't have the wit to keep on thrusting. I just lay there in wonder, in the fully inserted position, feeling myself pump out slowly, draining invisibly into Luc, until I trickled to a stop.

We lay where we were for some time after that, me still inside Luc, too overcome with everything to speak. But eventually my cock grew small again and slipped out of Luc and out of his shorts of its own accord. Luc turned round on the bed to face me. 'Look at that,' he said, pointing to a truly vast irregular wet patch on the front of his shorts. 'You've made me do the map of France.' And then, pretty soon after that, he had to head out rather urgently to the *toilettes*.

We lived together for two more years after that. Then, because life is life, and we were young, because we found in time that our aspirations, like our backgrounds, were very different, we found other people and other things to do. But we parted on good terms and for several years afterwards had sex every time we met. But to go back... After that first shorts-clad fuck we got into the habit of having anal intercourse in the more conventional manner: naked, either in, on or beside the bed, or (occasionally) against a wall. And though I'd been the first of us to fuck the other, Luc had made pretty sure that once we next got into bed together he would have the second go. He rolled me onto my back, hauled my legs over his shoulders, and pushed his dick into me as easily as I had done with him – though he had the advantage of not having to contend with tight shorts: we were both naked this time.

I might have thought that there was no possibility of Luc returning my compliment of fucking him while he was 'in uniform'. After all, shorts are short by nature, no matter how tight, whereas my 'Sorbonne uniform' jeans

measured 30 inches up the inside leg and Luc's cock –
like my own – was precisely six. But I'd have been
wrong. One day, I was wearing an old and tattered pair
of Wranglers which we both knew were due to be
thrown away, and lying – I must admit, a bit
provocatively – face down on our bed, with no other
clothes on, not even anything beneath the jeans except
myself. Luc came up with a pair of nail scissors and
started (very carefully – I was glad of that) to cut the
stitches of the back seam. It took a while but when he'd
opened up about three inches, and checked with a
probing finger that he'd got the right place, he decided
he'd unstitched enough. He took all his clothes off and,
lying on top of my back, pushed his familiar,
comforting, and comfortably wet *bite* into me through
the hole he'd made in the denim. The novelty caused his
cannon to fire almost at once but he gamely went on and
made sure I climaxed too, reaching his hand down inside
my waistband to grasp my own eager penis from the top.

Those jeans did have to be replaced, of course, just as
his shorts had been after that first time I'd thrust myself
up the legs of them at front and back, which caused
them, we discovered afterwards, to split. (I bought him a
new pair from Prisunic before he went to work that
night. Cheekily I bought them a half-size tighter than the
old and abused pair.) But we didn't throw the old ones
away – neither my bottom-holed jeans nor Luc's spunk-
stained shorts. Over the next two years we occasionally
hauled them out and fucked each other while wearing
them, just like those sex-mad first times. They went into
the wash a few times during those two years, I'm pleased
to recall … although not as often as all that.

AFTER THE MATCH

Stool-ball is played – by teams comprised of both or either sex – among the villages of rural Sussex, England. It's like a rudimentary form of cricket, only the bat is rather wider and quite flat, while the wicket... Oh, all right, you're not reading this to learn about stool-ball. You might not even be all that interested in the finer points of cricket. Anyway, this isn't about the match, but about what happened afterwards, what began on the furthest edge of the outfield, in the lengthening shadows of the lime trees in the dimming dusk, back in the magic hot summer of 1983.

John had regularly worked on Marlpits Farm during his summer holidays from school. This year was no different, except that summer holidays had been renamed summer vacations: he had left school and gone to university at Cambridge. He drove tractors, mucked in with the strawberry pickers – who were local women mostly – in July, then in August followed the tractor-hauled potato spinner along the furrows, back-breakingly picking up the tubers it unearthed. He had to get up at an unearthly hour every morning while he was doing this and, because of all the hard work in the fresh air during the daytimes, crashed into the deepest of sleeps the instant his head touched his pillow every night. This played havoc with his most intimate nightly routine, but over the last few summers he had learnt to deal with this. He adapted to circumstances for the duration, and found alternative opportunities for getting off whenever his trips on the tractor took him to outlying, unwatched-over parts of the farm. There he would dismount from his massive blue-painted steed, lower his jeans to half-mast and pull on his ever-ready, obligingly dick until it let fly across the stubble, or into the brambles, or up against the rear wheel of the tractor, depending on which way he happened to be facing at the time.

Like any nineteen-year-old he was proud of his prick. And he was pleased with its power to deliver, reliably and often. Pleased too with its impressive projectile power. The only downside to all this was the fact that, except on a very few fumbling occasions when he was much younger, the pleasure had been all his: it had not in recent memory been shared by anyone else.

He couldn't reasonably have expected that to happen during his summer farming stints. Those of his fellow workers who weren't women – most of whom were disqualified by age as well as by sex – were either young married men from the nearby villages or younger boys, some of whom were very appealing, but all of whom had girlfriends. A fact which they took the earliest opportunity to drop into the conversation. This was to make absolutely sure that John, an alien being who attended first a school and then a university many miles away, should not form any misleading impression that might lead to the embarrassment of both parties at some future date.

As for university, he had gone up to Cambridge the previous autumn in the condition of virgin, though a busy little wanker, and returned at the end of his first year in exactly the same state.

Now nineteen, John knew plenty about sex from a theoretical standpoint, in spite of his lack of experience. But he knew nothing about love – precisely *because* he had never experienced it, and because theoretical standpoints on this subject are worthless. He wasn't to know that this year, in the rough soil of a holiday job on a fruit and vegetable farm, both sex and love would germinate and flower for him in the space of a few days.

For this year Stuart appeared. Not for the strawberry picking, but at the beginning of the week that followed it. Nobody had told John to expect him. John had been assigned for the week to the lettuce plots. Most of the work here would consist of mind-numbing, back-breaking hoeing between the rows of growing seedlings, bent double hour after hour. It was not one of John's favourite jobs, especially as it was usually just him on his own. And this Monday began wet. Arriving in the barn he immediately picked up an oilskin cape and sou'wester from the row of hooks, put them on, grabbed a hoe and went into the workshop to sharpen it.

But there, standing by the workbench, his hoe already clamped into the vice and already at work on it with a Carborundum stone, was someone who might have been himself from what could be seen of him – though that wasn't much. A young figure of medium height, also clad from head to Wellington boots in protective waterproofs.

'I guess I'd better join the queue,' John said in a friendly manner to the back of the other's head. That caused the head to turn round and a pleasant voice to say,

'Oh hi. You must be John. I'm Stuart. Just starting today.' He offered a hand, which John shook.

'They didn't tell me about you,' John said. 'Not that that matters,' he added hastily. 'Hoeing lettuces all on your own is the pits. It'll be good to have company.'

And it was, after a fashion. Hoeing in the rain was a dispiriting business, a clog of mud and seedlings adhering to the hoe and to your boots and building up till you could hardly see what you were doing among the growing green shoots. But then to look up and see someone else a hundred feet away, as extravagantly dressed as you were, so that you looked like two trawler-men in an Atlantic gale, was quirkily comforting, even if you only exchanged a sardonic wave by way of communication.

They had their coffee break (which Susssex farmers call lunch) and their packed lunches (referred to as dinner) sitting in the barn, looking out at the rain. John learned that Stuart was also a university student. He went to Bristol, about as far away from Sussex as Cambridge was, but in the opposite direction. His family had moved into the village next to John's just a few months ago. They both liked cricket.

There wasn't much to be seen of Stuart, bundled up in oilskins. But what there was looked nice: a face that was not in fact dissimilar to John's. They both had fair complexions and light brown, unruly hair. Both had bright blue eyes, rather on the large side and framed with long thick lashes, which always seemed to have the spark of a smile in them that was ready to ignite at the slightest excuse. Where they were different was in Stuart's finer bones, his straighter, sharper nose – John's was snubbier – his more prominent cheekbones, and lips which, though no less sensual than John's rather kissier pair, were a little thinner, and more elegantly sculpted.

It was enough to keep Stuart in the forefront of John's mind when he went to bed that night. For once he didn't go straight to sleep but masturbated energetically while he thought about him– ironically he had been prevented from doing so during the day by Stuart's very presence.

By the next day summer had returned, and John and Stuart found each other dressed in shorts and plimsolls and very little else except their shirts when they arrived by bicycle at work. At first John found himself slightly awkward in Stuart's company, as was often the case when he'd had a wet dream, or a wank, over someone the night before and had to deal with them in real life in the morning. But pretty soon that feeling was overtaken by a more present lust. Stuart, dressed in very little, struck

John's eyes as utterly gorgeous. His big blue check shirt magnificently brought out the colour of his lovely eyes. He had a beautiful pair of legs, lightly muscled and lightly tanned, adorned with a sprinkling of light-catching golden hairs; his calf muscles hung off the backs of them like a pair of elongated fruits awaiting a caress, while his crotch was impressively ornamented with an almost indecently large something that formed a dome in his shorts. Was he wearing a cricketing box, for God's sake? During their lunch and dinner breaks John had to make an effort to keep the conversation going between them, in order not to be seen to be too obviously running his eyes over Stuart's body and gazing raptly into the other boy's eyes. But it did cross his mind once or twice that ... no, it couldn't possibly be true … that maybe Stuart was having a similar difficulty himself. Stop that, John told himself. Don't flatter yourself. You're not that beautiful.

But John was.

The stool-ball match took place the next weekend. Marlpits Farm fielded a team, half male half female, against Stocks Mill Farm on the other side of the village. Of course, in the best of British traditions, it didn't matter who won; the important thing was the booze and the grub afterwards. Which, this Saturday evening, on trestle tables under the trees, was an impressive array. Pies, quiches, salads, hot roasted chickens on spits, Italian sparkling wine, cider in jugs and a 'pin' or small wooden cask of Harvey's Sussex ale.

How it was, or exactly when this point was reached, John never really remembered, but at some point there was Stuart waving an opened but still full bottle of white wine in front of John and taunting him with it. 'Take it off me,' he was saying. 'Come get it.' And John was making playful but ineffectual dives towards it. But after a few moments John's dives grew more determined and

Stuart was forced to shift his ground. 'OK,' he said, laughing, 'Rugby then,' and turned and ran, the bottle tucked under his elbow in imitation of the oval ball.

John followed. At first Stuart went at a teasing jog-trot, zigzagging as he went, with John hopping after, both laughing. Then the pace quickened and they had no breath to spare for laughter. John could feel the wind rush in his face. He was never more than a yard behind Stuart, his fingers just inches out of reach of the wine bottle, or Stuart, whichever it was he was trying to take. But the faster he ran the faster Stuart managed to go, till John thought he had never made such a speed in his life, not even when he'd won the hundred metre sprint on his last sports day at school.

They had left the pitch and the party far behind now, and were in thick rough grass, running down hill, approaching the tree-hung boundary of the field. From out of sight the cries and half-drunk laughter of their team-mates and work-mates were fading to an indistinct wave of sound. And then John caught Stuart. Almost by chance. Not tackling him low, correctly, but in a sort of foul, catching the waistband of his shorts on both sides at once with a hook from his two thumbs.

Stuart fell. There was a tearing sound of cloth, the pop of an exploding button or two, and as Stuart's shorts first revealed a bottom like a peach, and then came ripping down his thighs, there came another sound: that of Stuart's suddenly released cock springing upwards onto his bare belly like the spring of a mousetrap.

Stuart let out a whoop of laughter. 'You've ripped my sodding shorts, fuck you!' Landing on the ground, face down, he immediately rolled round to face his attacker, bottle still firmly held under one arm. 'Look what you've done!'

John looked. From Stuart's startlingly unclothed crotch his penis jutted forward from out of his pubic bush as uncompromisingly as a wall-bracket. It was the same size as John's was, though it tapered gently towards its hooded tip, which John's circumcised number did not... 'My God,' said John, 'but I hope you're not blaming me for that as well.'

'Come on now,' Stuart taunted. 'Don't tell me you haven't got a hard-on too.' And he reached forward to the spot where he guessed it ought to be, made a grab, and proved at once that he'd been right. 'Go on, let's see!'

John was laughing too now, in sheer delight. He could hardly believe this was happening. 'You'll have to let go of it if I'm to get my fly open,' he protested. But Stuart paid no heed. He served John with the same treatment he'd had himself, yanked at his shorts with both hands till they in turn ripped at the seams, pulling them roughly down over the boy's hips and releasing John's own pent-up penis in its turn. 'Jiminy, you're hung,' he said. 'Like a wolf. Hung like a bear.' He made a grab for it again, and this time caught it, naked and pulsating in his hand.

'Oh my God,' John said – almost a gasp. 'I'm going to come.'

'And so am I,' said Stuart, just realising this at that moment. He thrust his whole body forward against John, toppling John back till they lay belly to belly on the ground, their two cocks mashed together between them, and there, without further prompting by hand or anything else, they pumped out their hot white floods, which melted together between them into a single slick of sperm that glued them tight, for a moment, as if that might be the way of things for all time to come.

But it was only for a few moments of course. Muffled voices at a distance called their names from beyond the brow of the field, and *where are you?* Reluctantly they pulled apart. Breathlessly, looking down at them both,

Stuart said, 'We can't go back like this. Torn shorts. Matted with spunk and grass…'

John was close to panic as he said, 'But how can I – can either of us go home, show up at our parents' looking like…?'

'It's OK,' Stuart said, his voice unsteady but trying to be calm. 'My parents are away tonight. You stay over with me – if you want to, that is. Phone your parents from my place and tell them you'll be back tomorrow.'

John was mightily relieved by all this, but he said, 'What about our bikes? They're right over by the gate. No, wait. We can get out through the bottom of the field, go round by the lane, and pick them up from the outside. No need to go back past the others at all.' Then he remembered to thank Stuart for his merciful invitation.

It was getting to be dusk, and they floundered rather, crossing the uneven tussocky regions beyond the field's edge, sometimes falling into each other and having to grab hold of the other to avoid falling. Somehow that helped to bond them and to keep them relaxed in each other's company, rather than falling into the dark and doubtful states of feeling that sometimes follow a first in a lifetime experience of sex with another boy. They reached their bikes, lying flat just outside the field's front gate, only just in time. The party was breaking up and beginning to wander in their direction. They mounted quietly and slipped away, without lights, down the twilit lane.

It was only ten minutes to where Stuart lived. He let them in with a latchkey. Smart house, John thought, as Stuart gave him a tour of it, a bit diffidently and trying not to seem to be showing it off. By some miracle he still had the bottle of wine with him. They drank it, sitting outside the French windows in the summer not-quite-dark. They had put their two pairs of shorts in the washing machine. They planned to let them dry overnight and re-stitch the burst seams, which were actually only slightly torn, in the morning. They sat for a long time on the lawn, in their T-shirts to protect them from the light summer-evening breeze, but otherwise naked: barefoot, bare-legged, bare-cocked, bare-balled. Sipping their wine and enjoying the novelty view of each other that their position and sartorial state afforded.

In Stuart's bedroom they removed their fig-leaf T-shirts. 'I've never done this before,' admitted John huskily. 'Gone to bed with anyone.'

'Nor me,' said Stuart. 'You're sure you…?'

'Of course.'

They reached for each other and stood embracing for a long time, teaching each other how to kiss. Then they climbed into bed, or at least onto it – for it was a very warm night – exploring with their fingers the shapes and contours of their slightly different but by now fully extended cocks. They tried to fuck each other, but didn't yet know how, not realising that for tonight at least they were still too tense. Their efforts ended in ticklish, giggling failure, dicks buckling and sticky between thighs. Then Stuart said, 'You've heard of something called sixty-nine?' John had not, but once Stuart had rearranged himself so that he lay on top of John, his head between John's legs, it was more than clear what the expression meant, and what was going to happen next.

It was the most magical experience of John's life. The feel of Stuart's cock inside his mouth, the touch of his drum-tight ball-sac beneath his finger tips, and the crazy Doppler effect – that the same things were being done to him at the other end. John's head drove back and forth as he felt Stuart's doing the same. With a free hand he reached out and stroked Stuart's warm thighs and calves. Minutes later they came in each other's mouths in bouncy, salty springs. First John, then Stuart, excited by his sudden mouthful, a few seconds behind. And in all those good things happening to John at once the best of all was thinking about *who*. It was Stuart. That was who. Stuart and no-one else.

When they awoke it was still Stuart, and for Stuart, still John. 'No regrets?' Stuart asked from the pillow.

'None at all,' said John. He was slightly surprised. 'And you?'

Stuart answered with a chuckle and a grin. Then he said, 'Well, since we don't regret that, why don't I say something we might really have regrets about. But here goes anyway. I've never had sex with anyone before you. And I fell for you the moment I saw you, over my shoulder, dressed in oilskins, as I was sharpening my hoe. Fell for you like falling down a hole… Perhaps I'd better stop now.' From the change in his voice it was clear that doubt had undermined his resolve.

'No,' said John. 'Go on.'

'I'm in love with you. There. Sounds stupid, doesn't it?'

'Yes it does,' said John. 'Quite, quite stupid. And wonderful at the same time. And brave. Because it's what I woke up wanting to say to you, and almost had to bite my tongue. I love you too, Stuart, however silly that sounds after just one short night. I love you too.'

They didn't share a bed again for some time. But their coffee breaks and lunch breaks on the farm were transformed now, as they sat in the lee of a hedgerow in the sunshine, with their Thermos flasks and sandwiches and open shorts. They learned how to fuck each other, as they relaxed into the sureness of each other's love, jeans rucked around their ankles, as they lay in the long grass. And when there wasn't time to do that, would compete to see which of them could project his sperm the further out across the lettuce field with the help of the other's hand.

Those turned out to be the easy things. They were more cautious when it came to revisiting the declarations they'd made in bed, the night after the stool-ball match, under the influence of wine and heady first sex. But each knew that they would revisit that conversation – that they would have to, even as they put off doing so until the last possible moment. That last moment came as they were about to part. It was the end of the apple harvest and the little workforce was breaking up, being laid off, at the end of a Friday afternoon. In a few days the start of term at Bristol and Cambridge would pull John and Stuart a further two hundred miles apart, but for the moment things were ending with a four o'clock drink in the barn. Along with the beer and cider, weird bottles were produced, that contained things like elderflower or parsnip wine. John and Stuart left at the same time, but would only have half a minute to say goodbye outside, before riding off in opposite directions, if they didn't want to attract attention to themselves through the watching windows of the barn, where the remaining women were running out of people and events to gossip about.

They did their goodbyes as they stood tiptoe astride their bicycles. Both wanted to lean in towards the other, to kiss or hug. But it was out of the question. They said, 'Well, have a good term,' and, 'See you next vac...' Then Stuart came out with it.

'We said, I love you,' he said, in an unemphatic tone. The words were potent enough. 'Were we allowed to say that after we'd only known each other a week?'

Stuart's directness overwhelmed John. He thought he was going to cry. He got a grip of his voice, though, and managed to say, to his own very great surprise, 'I think we had to say it. Otherwise it might never have got said.'

'Did we mean it, though?' Stuart asked.

'Yes,' said John. 'We did.' He was suddenly sure of that, and saw in Stuart's eyes that this avowal had given his friend the confidence to believe it too. The thought came to both of them – they could each read it in the other's face – that perhaps this was how love always began. Because love was something that could only prove itself over time you had to begin, you could only begin, with a hunch about it's being real. It was like putting money on a horse you felt sure would be a winner. If you didn't place your bet, put your money on, then you could not collect. John decided to re-confirm his stake. 'I love you, Stuart,' he said matter-of-factly across the handlebars. 'I always will.'

'I love you too, John,' Stuart said, growling the words out to prevent his voice from cracking. 'And I always will.'

Then they rode off swiftly, away from each other, each thinking as the road separated them, that his heart would break.

They wrote letters to each other that first term after they'd met – there was no email in 1983, there were no mobile phones. They met again, once the Christmas vacation was on, by arrangement, in a pub in a nearby village where neither of them was known. They slept over at their respective parents' houses. Separate rooms of course. Waiting till the house was quiet. Tiptoeing soundlessly to the other's room. Tiptoeing back again before December's late dawn...

Diffidently they exchanged details of occasional sex adventures they'd had at university, told the bitter-sweet but titillating tales of experiences with other young men. 'It was only sex,' they'd say, and then hold each other tighter between the sheets they shared, as they tried to make sense of that awkward teenage muddle of loving one person while having sex with all the rest.

But as term followed term and vac succeeded vac, those other encounters, those other guys, grew fewer and farther between. They began to hear themselves saying to those occasional others as they rolled condoms on, 'I shouldn't really be doing this. I've got a steady boyfriend back at home...' And then university was over, those casual contacts disappeared like smoke on the wind, and John and Stuart were back in Sussex. Working together for the summer at Marlpits Farm again. They didn't present themselves to the world – to their parents, to their workmates on the farm – as a couple but by now the world had sort of guessed. And when the time came for them to go and get 'proper' jobs it was no surprise to anyone that they both found work in the same city and chose to share a flat.

What had begun as a simple lustful teen adventure developed into something else. Was that an unusual thing, or commonplace? Neither of them knew, or really cared. After twenty-five years of city life the pair of them returned to Sussex, where they set up in business together as market gardeners and plant nurserymen just a few miles from where they'd played in the Stool-ball game that changed their lives. They talk about the occasion sometimes. Neither of them can remember which team won the game – Stocks Mill or Marlpits Farm. In retrospect that seems the least important thing of all. For nearly thirty years after that consequential match, it is another match, the pairing of John and Stuart, that endures. They haven't forgotten that on the morning after that first mad sexy romp on the outfield, they incautiously said, 'I love you,' to each other. With no real justification or evidence. It was just a hunch they had.

Anthony McDonald

THE CURTAIN STORE

It wasn't love at first sight. But it was attraction at first sight. And it was mutual, though I didn't know it then. We were both sixteen.

I'd landed a Christmas holiday job at our local theatre, thanks to my grown-up sister who worked there. I was going to operate one of the follow spots during the run of the pantomime: Aladdin this year. I met the chief electrician a few days in advance, and he took me up the seemingly endless staircase to the back of the gallery. Two big spotlights were installed there, with a seat for each operator, on either side of the central aisle, behind the back row of seats. I say seats but right up here in the gods they were actually benches. (Downstairs, the stalls and dress circle were all gilt and red plush.) I was shown how to swivel my light, and move the barrel up and down. Like an anti-aircraft gun, I thought. I was shown how to use the dimmer, following instructions received through headphones from the lighting box behind the stalls. My sister obligingly walked to and fro across the front of the stage, far below us and brilliantly lit, so that I had the chance to practise making the beam follow her, instead of waiting till I made an idiot of myself at the tech.

All casuals, as we were called, were summoned to the green room, where we met each other for the first time, an hour before the technical rehearsal started. Green room sounds grand, but it was nothing of the sort. It was a wide, windowless, linoleum-floored passageway between the dressing rooms and the stage. It was furnished with threadbare sofas from which the stuffing was escaping, a sink, a kettle and a fridge.

The stage manager divided the backstage crew into two teams – stage left and stage right – and handed them black clothes to wear. The ASMs took charge of them and off they went. Which left the two of us.

I'd noticed Charlie at once, of course. Couldn't not. Eyes met across a crowded green room... I know, but it really was like that. We were easily the youngest there. I guessed he was about sixteen, like me, and he, like me, was small for his age. Small but not scrawny. Now the room was nearly empty I could see more of him. There was space for me to notice that his very tight jeans were roundly filled with muscular trim thighs and calves, prominent buttocks and, at the front, a jaunty little dome that seemed to announce: look what I've got. I knew already that I was attracted to boys, not girls, and this worried me quite a lot. But all I'd ever done, and all I thought I'd ever do, was look.

'Know what you're doing and where to go?' the stage manager asked us. We said yes. He showed us where we could stow our coats and pullovers. No blacks for us: just the jeans and T-shirts we already had on. We pulled off our redundant pullovers. It was cold in the streets outside but at the top of the house it would be hot, especially behind those lamps. 'I'm Tim,' I said. 'Charlie,' my new acquaintance answered, and stuck out his hand. We climbed the stairs together. Not one in front and one behind but side by side.

There is a special kind of darkness in a theatre when the house lights are down and the stage lights are up. It's dark yet not dark at the same time. Emergency lighting brands the word EXIT on your retina in underwater green. This is how the night-time must appear to cats.

There was enough light for me to see in my peripheral vision the side view of my fellow follow spot. During the next days I memorised every contour of that view, across the aisle, just out of reach. (We could have held hands across the aisle, I suppose, but obviously we did not.) I can bring it all to mind today: the springy taut, bow curve of his thigh; his short, straight nose and biggish lips; the proud young muscles of his forearm and biceps. Little by little, then, I learned those details of beauty, as technical rehearsal was followed by full-dress, then day after day the people poured in, in their hundreds, till even the gallery was full. The noise, the kids, the heat.

Because we were the youngest two, we gravitated together in the green room during breaks. We went to different schools. Otherwise we'd have known each other already. But because we were both easy-going characters, inclined to like rather than compete with new people we met, we got along together very well. You could almost say we became friends. But all the time we stood or sat together, drinking oily tea and talking about school or last night's TV, I was imagining myself tearing off his tight jeans and... My imagination failed to come up with exactly what would happen next. I only knew that, whatever it was, I wanted it. I felt like King Lear, in the play I was then studying. *I will do such things, what they are, yet I know not, but they shall be the terrors of the earth.* Although Lear was talking about something else.

When you're sixteen you are very aware of who you fancy, but often quite slow on the uptake when it comes to noticing who fancies you. At least that was my case. So it didn't cross my mind that all my lustful thoughts about Charlie might be mirror images of Charlie's thoughts about myself.

Until that Saturday.

The stage manager asked the two of us if we'd like to earn a little extra cash. One of the rooms beneath the stage, the curtain store, was in a mess, he told us. A fire hazard. If there was an inspection the fire chiefs would have a fit. It was arranged that Charlie and I would go in the following Saturday morning and tidy it up.

There were a number of interconnecting rooms in the bowels of the theatre below the stage. The band had to make their way through them on their way to the orchestra pit. One room contained small items of furniture, another, which we explored at the start of our visit that morning, was full of an intriguing assortment of props. We saw some broadswords and gingerly took them into our hands for a few seconds, feeling their balance and weight. The last room, the curtain store, answered to the SM's description of it: a mess. Tabs and drapes of all sizes, colours and thicknesses, from plush red velvet numbers to plain black masking had been thrown down in there by people in a hurry, month after month, instead of being folded and stacked on shelves. Most of the floor was occupied by a sort of compost heap of curtain, about four feet deep.

Two people folding theatre curtains go about it much like two people folding tablecloths or sheets; it just takes longer, and requires a lot more muscular effort, which becomes more noticeable with the passing of time. Again and again Charlie and I walked towards each other with a fold of fabric scooped up from the floor, passed it into the clasp of the other's outstretched hands, and backed away to pick up the next section of curtain and create a new fold. It was like performing some absurd variation on an ancient courtly dance. Every time we came together, hands touching hands, we felt the warmth of each other's breath, looked searchingly into each other's eyes. And whatever that thing was that I wanted to do with Charlie, I wanted it more with every series of forward steps, with every pleat. I felt that something in me was being wound up to a dangerously high pitch, like a violin string, and that if this went on much longer, like a violin string it would snap. Maybe the whole instrument would smash too.

But Charlie snapped first. He suddenly dropped the heavy velvet tab we were working on, grabbed a smaller one and shot out through the door with it. I gazed after him, rooted where I was and perplexed. But in a second he was back. The curtain was draped around him dashingly, like a Roman cape, and he carried two of the broadswords we'd handled earlier in the other room. He held one out to me.

Obviously I needed my own curtain cape. I plucked one up at random and luckily it was not impossibly big. I threw it around me with an optimistic swish, hoping it might achieve the same swashbuckling appearance as Charlie's did, and then we began to fence.

Actually, to say we fenced would be seriously to over-describe what now took place. A broadsword is a mighty heavy thing and neither of us was very big. Also, I didn't know how to fence. Neither did he. So all we did was to stand and face each other, rather slowly clashing the sides of our weapons together, forming iron crosses each time in the air between us. I think we were both aware that had we tried anything bolder or more dramatic we would probably have taken off each other's head. Even so, the noise was pretty good.

Then Charlie dropped his sword and ran – ran three feet? More like jumped –towards me, forcing me to drop my weapon too. Excitedly Charlie threw his cloak around my shoulders so that it enveloped us both, and I felt his body press against mine. Oh God, I thought, he'll discover that I'm hard, and how embarrassing that's going to be. But I didn't spend long thinking that.

Charlie had got one hand inside the cloak and was fumbling with something. I wasn't quite ready to believe it was his zip. But then I felt him tug mine down and had to believe it. Our two cocks seemed to emerge of their own accord, both hard, both hot, mine pressed up against his, unseen in the curtained dark.

We abandoned our hiding place, letting our cloaks fall to the floor. And discovered that the sight of our two cocks was not enough. We wanted balls too, and pubes, and tops of thighs. It was less than a second before our jeans were halfway down our legs.

The sight of Charlie's partial nakedness, all that part of him between pulled-up T-shirt and pulled-down pants was the most wonderful thing ever. It etched itself upon my inner eye and is with me to this day. His cock, short, thick and circumcised, stood straight up against his belly, flattening his scanty pubes. You couldn't have got a cigarette paper behind it. Mind you, the same went for mine.

We threw each other, toppling, onto the still deep pile of curtains on the floor. Each took the other's cock in hand and pumped it at ferocious speed. We lasted less than thirty seconds, I think. Then our milk came gushing out of us. We let it find its way down through the curtain pile.

We found it impossible to chat normally and look each other in the eye during our green-room breaks that Saturday matinee and evening. The shock and dislocation of self that occurred as a result of my first sexual experience with another were even greater than they'd been on the occasion of my first private orgasm, in bed, two years before. I felt that Charlie and I had somehow broken something – like breaking a family heirloom, or something of that kind. During the Sunday that followed I was glad not to have him around. I didn't want to face the confusion that had been caused between the two of us. Caused by him. Caused by me.

But, guess what? By Monday evening my cock was ready for Charlie again, even if my bruised soul was not. When we met in the green room at seven o'clock we exchanged a shy grin, which somehow accepted and explained that, though we weren't yet quite ready to speak, given time we would be.

We did speak. Later that evening. And a few days later we found a moment, and an excuse, to visit the curtain store together once again. It wasn't easy to arrange such a tryst without being noticed. We only managed it six more times before the panto ended its run. And then we parted. We said we'd phone each other, but we never did. Life moves on quickly when you're sixteen. We went to different schools, had different friends. Things happened to us. We did other things. We grew up.

The theatre bug had bitten hard and deep. When I was at university I got involved with the theatre in the town, working backstage part time, on and off. Around the time I graduated a vacancy for an ASM arose there. I applied and – no big surprise – got the job. Degree in economics? Forget that.

Over the next few years I moved up the ladder fast. If you were willing to up sticks and move to another part of England or Scotland hundreds of miles away – something that many people were not prepared to do – you could do that. ASM means assistant stage manager. Most theatres employ three or four. DSM means deputy stage manager, and there is only one. I was DSM in Glasgow at the age of twenty-two, stage manager at Plymouth at twenty-three, then production manager – a senior post with big budgets to control and ten full-time staff to manage – at twenty-four. Aged twenty-five I was the general manager – top dog except for the director of productions – at a theatre in Wales.

You learn fast in that job. You discover that the manager is, in the last resort, the changer of roller towels, fixer of decrepit ball-cock valves in the toilets and un-blocker of drains. He must stand up to the bullying of directors on the board, and hold his own against experienced senior staff, some of whom have been in post since before he was born. I found myself the licensee of two bars, one in the circle, one in the stalls, and would have to attend court every year or two, dressed in a suit, to plead my case for those licences to be renewed. I was also, de facto, a member of the Regional Theatres Council, which meant attending a meeting in London once a year, again in a suit. The same suit. The only suit.

There was a certain grim delight, I found, in meeting on an equal footing those venerable souls who had interviewed me for jobs during the past four years. Especially those who'd happened to turn me down. At the first meeting of the council that I attended I was by far the youngest present. I already knew, or thought I knew, that I was the youngest general manager of any regional theatre in the UK. But then I saw him, also in a suit, across the... (Yes, yes, I know.) Across the crowded room. I remembered at once not only who he was, but that he was two months younger than me. But never was a record holder more delighted to relinquish his title.

There was barely time to say hallo before the business of the meeting began. At least, with that hallo I'd established that he remembered me. We sat together. From the corner of my eye I could see the taut bow curve of his thigh in the close fitting trousers of his suit. That familiar short, straight nose. The full lips of his handsome mouth. His head of shining black curls. He'd grown a little taller in the years since I'd known him, and so had I, but in both our cases not very much.

But if someone fancied you at the age of sixteen there is no guarantee that nine years on they still will. So much happens in those particular years, so much of your life is crammed into them. You've changed. You've learned to earn a crust for a start, and you've taken some knocks in the process. You've been in love a couple of times, and had your young heart broken once or twice.

And, quite importantly, I had to remind myself that not every teenager who's played with another boy's cock grows up to be gay. If that were the case we wouldn't be worried about overpopulating the planet. Rather the reverse.

It was an afternoon meeting. Neither of us actually rose to speak during the course of it. It was a first time for both of us, and the cockiness with which we'd arrived and greeted our older peers had quickly evaporated. We were over-awed by the seniority and expert knowledge of the other delegates, intimidated by the very thing that made us special there: our shared, exceptional, youth.

When the meeting was closed and people stood and general chatter broke out, Charlie turned to me and said, with a diffidence in his voice I hadn't heard before, 'Do you have time to go for a drink?'

I smiled, reassuringly I hoped (though it's a clever man who knows his own smiles) and said, 'Yes.' Did I have time? The rest of my life. But I didn't say that.

The meeting had been at Covent Garden. We walked to Rose Street and into the old Lamb and Flag. We bought pints of Young's bitter and sat among the age-black furniture and beams. We talked about how we'd got to the positions in the theatre that we now held. There were two standard routes to the job of general manager. I'd come up by one of them, Charlie by the other. His way had lain on the other side of the safety curtain: front of house. Box office assistant, box office manager, front of house manager, PR and advertising manager, and now here he was, doing the same job that I did, but in Cambridge, two hundred miles away from me. Like me he'd achieved his rapid rise by going for jobs again and again, in no matter what God forsaken part of the country they might be. Like me his track had criss-crossed the kingdom. It was surprising that it hadn't, until now, crossed mine.

We had so much to talk about. We could have talked for hours. Actually we did. On our third pint I looked at my watch for the first time and saw it was nearly eight. Then Charlie said, 'I suppose you're married and all.'

I didn't reply at once. I'd wanted, yet not wanted, to ask the same question. His answer of yes would have sent the evening on a downward curve. Not at once, but gently. We would have parted friends in an hour's time and promised to stay in touch. Only we wouldn't have done. We might meet again at the next annual meeting of the Regional Theatres Council. If we still had our jobs then. Charlie was looking at me. There was something a bit despondent in his eyes. Time to answer. I said, 'No. What about you?'

'No. Nor me,' he said, and looked away.

Charlie, the bolder of the two of us, had done his best. Now I had to help. 'Actually,' I said, 'I'm not very likely to be. I've turned out gay.'

He said very softly, 'Me too.' I didn't try to meet his eye. I don't think he tried to meet mine.

There were stages to this, I realised. The conversation would proceed tantalisingly, as if we were unwrapping a gift parcel that might, only might, have something inside, or disassembling a Russian doll, or unlocking some door or treasure chest with an elaborate succession of catches and bolts. There was only one order in which to proceed; the sequence could not be short-cut. And when the process was complete, the treasure chest might yet prove empty, and there be nothing behind the door.

'Boyfriend back in Wales?' he tentatively asked.

I shook my head. 'No time.' I'd actually had no sex with anyone since starting my newest job, pressure of work and time being elements of this situation, though not the only ones, but I wasn't going to volunteer all this just yet.

'Ditto ditto,' he said. Then he looked at me. Those blue eyes of his looked troubled now. Surprising myself, I laughed. Not rudely, not loudly, but I laughed. And he reacted by doing the same. His eyes looked less troubled now. Curious perhaps. 'Do you remember the curtain store?' he asked.

I was surprised into a sort of splutter. 'How could I ever forget?'

There was another pause, while we looked at each other. We still didn't have absolute proof that we fancied each other. Hindsight is one thing, dealing with the situation on the spot is quite another. Charlie spoke. 'I suppose you have to get back to Wales tonight.'

'Work in the morning,' I said. 'Same as you.' I could feel, rather than see, Charlie's disappointment. I wriggled. 'I mean, I should go back.' I paused for a split second. 'We could catch a show, I suppose.'

'Yeah,' said Charlie. 'But isn't that a bit too much like work? I mean, for you and me. Doing the jobs we do. Show every night.' He gave me a look. The kind of look that writers call quizzical. 'We could go for a meal. You can talk in a restaurant, you can't at a show.' There was a slight pause during which he looked away. 'We could get a room for the night.' He waited apprehensively for my reply.

That switch from bold to diffident went to my heart. But that wasn't the only thing. The idea of spending a night together set off such a rush of feelings that it was like a firework display inside me. 'Let's do that,' I said quietly.

When you work for a boss you have to phone them and make your excuse if you're going to arrive late. When you are the boss you have to phone a member of your staff and do the same thing. Charlie and I got our phones out there and then and phoned our front of house managers – the most senior people present at our two theatres at that time of evening. When you tell them you're going to be detained in London and won't be at work till tomorrow lunchtime they know exactly what this means. Charlie and I mugged grimaces at each other as we trotted out our lame half-truths.

We didn't have to go far in Covent Garden to find a good restaurant – an Italian one. Then we found the nearest cheap hotel. 'Twin room?' the woman receptionist asked.

'Can you make it a double?' Charlie asked. Two months younger than me but twice as brave. As he'd been in the curtain store all that time ago. The receptionist did blink, but then she politely handed him a key.

We looked solemnly into each other's blue eyes as we undid each other's shirt and took it off. For practical reasons we then dealt with our own shoes and socks. But we returned to each other in order ceremoniously to remove the trousers of each other's suit, pull down each other's underwear, release each other's springing cock. Then we stood back to admire our work.

I thought he looked gorgeous. Not big, but gently muscled, still boyish. A little tongue of dark hair licked up from below, straight up the centre line of his belly where it petered out. There was no hair on his chest; as if to compensate, his nipples were proudly big. Back in the curtain store days we'd only ever seen the middle third of this view of each other that we now appraised in full. We'd known the other's body only from belly button to knees. I already knew I'd love his legs when they were revealed. But, heavens, I found even his knees beautiful. Even his long-toed feet. I told him so.

'You're beautiful all over,' he said, very solemnly and running a finger tremulously down my chest. 'We're not much bigger than we were,' he went on thoughtfully, as his finger encountered the resistance of my own little flame of belly hair, flaring upward from my pubes. Then he grinned. 'Except in the matter of this.' He gently touched the up-reaching tip of my penis, which immediately caused the foreskin to slide back and a dewdrop to appear like magic on its tiny lips. 'How we've both grown.'

It was no longer true that a cigarette paper could not have been slid between our bellies and stiff cocks. Now a cigarette packet would have done. But that's the price you pay for growing bigger, growing heavier. Growing up. With my own forefinger I touched the chunky head of his cut, sturdy cock. It reacted just like mine had done. Spilt a little juice. We giggled. Then, serious again, we moved in to each other till we touched at every possible point. We began to kiss.

It wasn't long before we had to move to the bed. My cock was threatening to spill over, weighty with a load that seemed to be already gathering inside. I guessed it was the same for him. Neither of us had brought condoms: it was a business meeting we'd come to London for, or so we'd thought. And we didn't want, tonight at any rate, to have to interrogate each other with uncomfortable questions, possibly to hear answers we didn't want. I was certain of my own status – negative, but Charlie didn't know that, just as I didn't know his. We lay clasped together, duvet pulled down so we could see each other properly, and did exactly what we'd done on the curtain pile all those years before. Because of that bank of experience from way back we were supremely comfortable and confident with each other's physicality and need. We pulled just far enough apart at the end to have the satisfaction of seeing each other's creamy spurt, just as we'd done when we were little more than kids, then lay pressed together as if we might stay that way for all time.

'I think about you very often,' Charlie said, close to my ear.

'Me too,' I said. It was true. The memory of Charlie was a kind of background rumble through all my waking moments, and had been for all those years.

'Even when you're doing *that*?' he asked, and I felt his hand clasp and squeeze my melting dick, to leave me in no doubt about what *that* meant.

I admitted it. 'Occasionally,' I said.

'Me too,' he said, and chuckled, and fell asleep.

We did *that* again in the small hours, and again just before we got up. But in between those landmark points in time we both half woke when a blade of steel-grey light was prising open the new day. I murmured to Charlie, 'I don't want dawn to come.' He said, 'I never want to leave this bed.' We were wallowing in the warmth of each other. Warm tummies, thighs, chests, shoulders and encircling arms. Warm pricks. Newly vulnerable in our shared warm nakedness, and intermittently wet. He said, 'Don't want to go back to Cambridge.' I said, 'Don't want to go to Wales.' But all those things had to happen, and they did.

My phone burned like an ember in my pocket all that day. Which of us would make contact first? How long before we did? What were we ever going to say? Or text?

It was Charlie, at nearly ten o'clock that night who made the call. Bold, tender Charlie, not for the first time, cracked first. It wasn't a text. He gave me his voice. 'I want to see you, Tim,' he said.

'Me too,' I answered. No other answer was remotely possible. We had unlocked the doors to each other, unlocked the treasure chests, taken apart those Russian dolls, but only so far as to deliver a one-night stand, even if that had been a very lovely one. But there was further to go, more work to be done, more locks to pick.

The following morning I woke up and saw Charlie's face immediately, as if it were really before my eyes. I knew already what that meant. I knew I'd see it morning after morning until we met again. As I made my solitary breakfast I imagined him making his and wondered, pathetically, if he was thinking of me. He phoned an hour later. 'I saw you in my mind when I woke up,' he said. 'Sorry,' he went on. 'Do I sound sad? But I just can't stop thinking about you.' I told him that was just fine and that it was the same with me.

We met in London that weekend. We could have seen a show, gone to a club. Neither of those options appealed to us in the least. We sat talking in a pub, pouring out our lives and thoughts like mountain streams in spate. We drank each other's words, each other's intimate revelations, with the sensual joy of parched travellers.

Mutual lust can be great. Charlie and I had acknowledged that during our overnight stay in London a few days ago. But it has a sell-by date, like a cut flower. Only sometimes does it put out roots, become a living plant and start to grow into something bigger than it was when it began. Talking to Charlie, getting to know him better that evening, I dared to believe, just to begin to believe, that something bigger might grow in us.

We ate at a Thai restaurant. We checked into the same cheap hotel. Deadpan, the receptionist gave us the key to the same room. We'd both brought condoms, and we laughed at that. We made love. I was able to think that expression this time: we made love. The previous week I hadn't dared to think it.

A week later we met in Cambridge. I went to the flat Charlie shared with a young architect – who was straight, but easy around gay men. The following weekend Charlie came to Wales. I too shared a flat. With two young teachers, one of each sex. They too were straight but had no problem with the idea of *us* – as Charlie and I (though still only privately, separately) identified ourselves now. I showed Charlie round my theatre in the dark quiet of Sunday morning. We had a curtain store in the backstage area. We looked at each other and had to smile. Then – tacky was it? Can't be helped – we went in there and did *that*, for old times' sake. (Though we were more careful not to stain the curtains. We were responsible managers now and these particular curtains were a responsibility of mine. I didn't want some ASM unfolding them and saying, Dear God, who did that?) Later I walked with Charlie to the station. This time I was the bold one. 'Are we falling in love, Charlie?' I asked.

'You may be,' he answered, poker-faced. Then he grinned. 'Me, I've already fallen. Pretty bloody hard. Pretty damn deep.' There comes a moment sometimes when two people who thought they'd been in love a couple of times before in the course of their lives realise they haven't. For Charlie and me that moment had been reached.

The long-distance phase of our relationship lasted over a year. The transport costs were dismaying, and at times during the winter the rail network fell apart due to heavy snow, and one or other of us would be stranded for half a weekend at some remote and unheated railway junction. (In Britain the rail companies excuse themselves in this situation by explaining that the wrong type of snow has fallen.) We each spent our twenty-four hour Christmas – the maximum that theatre life allows – with our respective families, who lived only two miles apart, but there was no time for the upheaval and explanations that would have been involved in meeting up. Though we made up for that with a private feast of our own in Cambridge a few days later. Meeting me off a train on one of those snowy weekends, Charlie complained, 'It's like bloody Brokeback Mountain. Talk about high altitude fucks four times a year.' On top of our long working weeks those weekends of tedious travel would have left most people exhausted, but it wasn't like that for two young men in love.

Then the front of house manager at Charlie's theatre gave her notice in. She too was moving up the chain, going on to a bigger job somewhere else. Now it was my turn to be the bold one: I told Charlie I planned to apply for the vacancy created by her going. 'You can't,' he said. 'It'd wreck your CV, spell the end of your career.' He meant to sound shocked, but I heard other things in his voice: a kind of thrill; something like awe. I said, 'So what?'

'No, but really...'

'Too late,' I said. 'My wrecked CV is already in the post. It'll land on your desk tomorrow morning.'

I got the job, of course: the interviewing panel consisted simply of Charlie and his director of productions, an older gay man. It meant a big pay cut, and a lot of explaining to my parents, but there you go. I thought there'd be a lot of explaining to do at the theatre in Wales which I was leaving after little more than a year, but I was wrong. Apologetically I explained the situation to my PA. 'Of course,' she said, and took my hand. 'We all knew. You silly goose. Best thing that could happen.' I tried to give her a peck on the cheek by way of thanks but she wasn't expecting it and I ended up kissing her nose.

I moved to Cambridge and Charlie and I lived and worked together, day in day out, for a year that passed as quickly as a holiday. Then Charlie took a proposal to his board. The post of front of house manager to be abolished, for as long as Charlie and I both worked at Cambridge. We'd combine our two jobs and share them, splitting the salaries equally. This was coming out at work in a very big way: it not only startled the board, it got a column or two, and a picture of the pair of us, in the local rag. But the proposal was passed, and now we take it in turn to wear the evening bow-tie, take it in turn to face the assault course of the morning. It is an assault course, as all jobs are. We handle it OK. Better than OK in fact. Being together gives us a strength we couldn't manage on our own. It's the strength that only one thing can give you: the strength that comes from love.

Cambridge is unique among British theatres – at least, among the ones I know – in that it provides a small apartment within the main building, for the front of house manager's use. That apartment is now ours. On Sundays, in the quiet time, it's almost as if the whole building is our home. A great eccentric mansion, furnished with several hundred chairs, a dozen mirrors in ormolu and gilt, and as many swords and costumes as anyone could wish for. Actually, we don't. We haven't turned into batty theatre queens, and we don't hang around the building when we're free. We get out and go places, do things, just like anybody else.

On the other hand – I write this with a certain amount of embarrassment, and can already imagine smiles – there is a sizeable, often untidy, curtain store behind the stage. And just occasionally, very occasionally, for old times' sake, for the sake of memories which are silly and sentimental but also nice... I think I'll leave it there.

Anthony McDonald

INTO THE COLD

Suddenly it was raspberries. For nearly a fortnight it had been carrots but now, just after two o'clock this Friday afternoon, raspberries. The luscious scent of them filling the packing room promised a glorious release from the tedium of those orange discs. Matthew looked out of the window and smiled. In the yard there was snow and beyond, bare wintry trees were outlined above the rooftops against a grey sky. Raspberries. In a few days everyone would be heartily sick of them and an occasional plaintive voice might be heard extolling the virtues of carrots – one thing was, they didn't stain your hands – but today the raspberries were the heralds of change and bore the illusory promises of things new and exciting.

Slowly the last pallet-load of thirty-six-pound boxes of fluted frozen carrot rings toiled up the sloping corridor, Matthew pulling and all the women pushing. They negotiated the narrow doorway into the top room where Tom and the others were racing to get one more load of mushrooms processed before tea-break, then out across the concrete, through the slush, to the New Freezer which was by now practically full of boxed carrot. There was just one space left. Matthew squirmed the pallet into it, let the wheels down with a bump and pulled them out at a run. The freezer was filled with a dense fog in which tiny ice crystals sparked as the light caught them. Air blew fast and freezing from the fans. It was too cold to linger.

Matthew shut the heavy door behind him, then, as he turned round, there was Ray, standing silently at his side, making him jump. Ray was the boss, the owner of the freeze and packing plant, and he had a disconcerting habit of materialising right next to you when you least expected him. There was another disconcerting thing about him. He was rumoured to be gay. And the disconcerting thing about that was that Matthew, who was just turned seventeen, suspected that he himself might be, too.

'And how's young Maths today?' Ray asked. Friendly enough, but with a familiarity that Matthew didn't exactly welcome. His friends at school had called him Maths. He didn't know where Ray had got the nickname from and he didn't like it when Ray used it. But, since Ray was the boss, Matthew could hardly tell him so.

'Farting fit,' said Matthew. It was a way of getting back at Ray, who might or might not have misheard, and could hardly ask, *what did you say?* 'And it's nearly the weekend.'

Ray smiled, choosing to ignore what he thought he had heard Matthew say first. 'Well, keep up the good work then.' Then he walked briskly off towards the top room, to Matthew's relief. He didn't like the way Ray stood so close to him. He didn't stand that close to the women, or to Tom, and, since Tom was sixty and the women were women, Matthew could see only one reason why he got singled out in this way.

Being gay, Matthew thought, might be OK as long as you looked like Matthew, or like Kevin, the friend he experimented with sexually, cautiously, at the weekends and in the evenings. But it wouldn't be OK if you ended up looking like Ray: going bald, not noticing that your body had got bigger than your clothes, creeping around with that stupid apologetic grin on your face... being forty.

He trundled the pallet-loader, the wheels, towards the Old Freezer, where the raspberries were stacked, Dutch tray upon Dutch tray, in the same punnets into which they had been picked more than six months before. They stuck to his fingers as he loaded a few trays onto his pallet. You couldn't take too many at a time. For one thing, they tended to thaw out rather quickly. For another, if they were piled too high you were liable to upset the whole lot on the way back across the uneven concrete of the yard. Especially if you were Matthew.

By the time Matthew had trundled his wobbling load down to the packing room the women were ready and waiting. The room had been rearranged to meet the requirements of the different product. Equipment had been hosed down and wiped clean. Customers didn't like to find even small pieces of fluted carrot in their twelve-ounce bags of frozen raspberries and you couldn't really blame them. Ellen and Ethel waited at the aluminium-sided table-top, rubber gloves on hands, mallets upraised. Plastic bags were attached to the chutes. Beside the scales stood Mary, holding the jug she would make adjustments with; Diana waited by the sealing machine and, at the far end of the little production line, Peg was making up the cardboard boxes in which she would soon be packing the sealed bags of fruit.

Matthew tipped the first tray of punnets into the table-top and gently squeezed the frozen blocks of fruit out of them. With a little persuasion they usually crumbled neatly apart into individual berries, but occasionally a smart tap with one of the mallets was needed to make them yield. Sometimes the mallet was applied by one person before someone else had quite given up hope of success with bare fingers... Matthew placed a raspberry on his tongue and let it melt there, the taste of June preserved for him till January and served fresh and cold as the snow outside. He tipped another tray and then moved over to the scales to help Mary with the weighing and adjusting, for the bulging bags were piling up. 'Ellen, you're putting too many in.' Mary disgorged an over-full bag. 'They weigh heavier than carrots.'

This was the start of one of the regular free-for-alls which Matthew was getting used to, in which Ellen would criticise Mary for her slowness in weighing, Mary would belittle Diana's skill as a sealer of boxes, Matthew's capabilities as a stacker of pallets would be called into question, until…. 'Ooh, look at that!' said Ethel.

'Ooh-urgh!' said Ellen.

Everybody stopped bickering and came over to the table-top to have a look. *That* was a caterpillar, frozen solid in the act of walking along the edge of one of the raspberry punnets some time last June. There he had remained ever since, his translucent green body hard as jade, lightly frosted as an ice-lolly: a study in arrested motion. Matthew reached over and lifted him carefully off his perch. He wasn't stuck to the punnet at all and he came away quite easily without breaking. Matthew transferred him gently to the windowsill. 'He can stay there,' he said, 'until he wakes up.'

It was teatime soon after that. The frozen trays and part-filled boxes were shunted into the nearest freezer to stop them thawing, and then Matthew made a dash for the rest room before Tom could finish his mushroom-freezing in the top room and make the tea first. But he was too late. Tom had beaten him to it and made the tea already. He was now ensconced on an upturned crate watching it keep warm – the old iron teapot sitting on the red-hot electric ring with steam pouring from the spout, and the lid going up and down with an energy that would have delighted James Watt. Not the kettle, notice, but the teapot. That was how Tom liked his tea – and how Matthew didn't.

When tea was done, and fruitcake eaten, and *The Sun* peered into and discussed, all went back to work. Matthew tipped the first tray of punnets and paused, peering absently at the window and the snowy sky beyond. Then a tiny movement in the foreground caused his gaze to refocus on the windowsill. There he saw the caterpillar, exactly where he had placed it half an hour ago. No longer frosted like an ice-lolly, it had thawed out completely. By rights it should have collapsed completely into a flaccid tube of pulp. Frozen caterpillars usually did. But this one had not collapsed. It was standing there on its own six real and ten false feet. It looked dry, and as pristine as it must have looked that fateful day last summer when it took its last, unlucky, stroll among the raspberries.

Matthew peered more closely at it and as he did so, a ripple ran down its long back. Matthew refused to believe his eyes. But the spasm was repeated. It must have been a similar movement that had caught his attention a moment earlier. Matthew watched, spellbound. For perhaps half a minute nothing more happened, and he tore himself away to tip two more trays of fruit into the table-top. And then the caterpillar raised its head and waved it slowly from side to side, the only expressive gesture that its kind have at their disposal. It seemed to say, quite simply, 'Here I am'.

After a certain amount of limbering up in this way the caterpillar began to walk, very slowly, like someone convalescing after a long illness, along the windowsill. Matthew's mind began to race. A frozen caterpillar restored to life after six months in an ice-box. Was this a scientific discovery? And was the discovery his? He would be famous. He would be…

'Matthew! What are you doing over there? We're running out of fruit.'

'Come here,' he called, excited. 'Look at this.'

They came. They crowded. They gasped. And Tom, who came into the room at just that moment, joined the little group at the windowsill. 'Oh,' he said. 'You don't want that in here.' And before anyone could explain, or thought to stop him, he had picked up Ethel's mallet and squashed the caterpillar flat.

'You must have been gutted,' Kevin said. They were in the pub later that evening. But not just any pub. They were in the only pub in town that had pretensions to being a gay venue. Not that, looking around them, they could see much sign of it. Perhaps it was too early. Still, it was exciting to be here, in a gay pub for the first time, still slightly under age. They were excited too by each other's presence, and by thoughts of what they would do together later when emboldened by a little beer. It showed in the way they talked, looked, occasionally touched each other. Still...

'Yes, I was gutted. There I was, on the brink of ... and all my evidence just destroyed before my eyes.'

'I call it vandalism,' said Kevin. 'Sheer bloody vandalism. When you think of the money you could have...' He took a mouthful of beer.

'Of course all the women turned on Tom. Poor bloke. Didn't know what had hit him.'

'And then?'

'Well it all calmed down in the end, of course, and we got talking of other things.' As now, so did Matthew, who didn't want to hear Kevin reminding him any more times about all the money he might have made. 'You know I told you about my boss, Ray, and that he's supposed to be gay. Well, apparently it's true. So Ellen was saying, anyway. And that there used to be two of them running the place. Ray and this bloke called Andy. Only Andy pissed off and left him.'

'Oh wow,' said Kevin, who was still rather new to the idea that two men might choose to live together in the first place and had not yet got his head round the concept of marital breakdown between two people of the same sex.

Then Matthew, who would normally have nudged Kevin in the ribs, only because this was a gay pub he didn't, pulled his head towards him and whispered in his ear, 'Don't turn round but he's just come in.'

Ray hadn't just come in. He had been watching the two boys for some time, not knowing what they were talking about but realising, from their body language and the sexual energy-field that radiated around them, that the youth he had employed to stack pallets and load lorries had the same sexual orientation as himself. Now he walked up to them with something like confidence and said hallo and he hadn't seen them in here before.

'It's our first time,' said Kevin unselfconsciously. And then, when Matthew had introduced them, blurted out, 'Did you know about the caterpillar?'

No, Ray had heard nothing about it. Matthew was obliged to go through the story all over again, from the beginning.

'And just think of the money he might have made,' Kevin said, when Matthew had finished. But Matthew was aware of a look on Ray's face that suggested a reaction out of all proportion to the story he had just been told. Matthew wasn't sure enough of the meaning of the word *apoplectic* ever to use it in public, but that was the word that came into his mind. He looks apoplectic, he thought. But not with rage. It looked more like … elation, jubilation, exultation. Not that he would have used those words either, at least not with Kevin. But could you be apoplectic with … joy?

'Quite extraordinary,' said Ray. 'Quite … quite wonderful really. If you should find another one, well…'

'I'll make bloody sure no-one squashes it, that's for certain,' said Matthew.

Then Ray bought both the young men a pint and Matthew began to think that he wasn't such an unpleasant, creepy person after all. Perhaps he just wasn't very happy, his boyfriend having left him. They talked, and Matthew found that Ray was quite entertaining once they had got him away from the subjects of frozen broccoli and equipment-leasing. Eventually Ray took his leave of them, sensibly realising that if a little of his company could be welcome, too much of it would not be, and he didn't want the boys to have the awkwardness of wondering if they should buy him a return pint.

By this time Kevin's tongue, at least, was much loosened by drink, and wanting only to be friendly he said by way of parting words, 'I'm sorry Andy left you. It must be lonely being on your own.'

Matthew was horror-struck, silent and as suddenly red-faced as if the faux pas had been his. Ray looked startled too. He stood very still for a moment and silent. Then he said to Kevin, quietly, 'How do you know about Andy?'

'I told him,' said Matthew, almost too loudly. 'I had no business to, I know. Someone at work told me and … I'm sorry. I shouldn't have.'

Surprisingly, Ray smiled. 'Don't be sorry. Everybody likes to gossip sometimes. We can none of us help it. Only I can't let you go on thinking that Andy left me. He didn't. And he will be coming back. Goodnight. Enjoy yourselves.' He raised his eyebrows almost too expressively, Matthew thought. 'And have a good weekend.' He turned and went

Monday mornings were always the same. The freezers, having been shut up all weekend, were perishing cold. It was dangerous to enter them without gloves. If your fingers accidentally brushed against any metal fixture you were stuck there until someone rescued you with warm water or else you tore the skin from your flesh. And this morning of all times Ray collared Matthew the moment he arrived. 'Job for you, Maths,' he said.

'You're helping me this morning. There's stock to rearrange in the Old Freezer. Boxes of apples need pulling to the front, they're going out later today, and some of that carrot can go to the back. It won't be wanted for another month at least.' Normally Ray would have done this on his own. Now he wanted Matthew to do it with him. Was this some kind of promotion, resulting from their social encounter on Friday night? Funny way to show you were pleased with someone, Matthew thought: to give them a morning in the coldest place on earth. Still, Ray was the boss and Matthew had to do as he was asked.

Together they heaved and hauled the huge boxes around with two sets of wheels, their breath coming in white sparkling clouds. At one moment it went through Matthew's mind that Ray planned to seduce him in this most private of hideaways among the boxes, but he dismissed the idea as absurd. The temperature was quite unconducive to sex. The thought of even the preliminaries in such a climate made his blood run cold.

'You must find another caterpillar, Maths,' Ray suddenly said. 'And bring it alive for me.' Now this did sound creepy, baldly stated in this dark ice-cavern of a freezer-store. 'Because then I've got another job for you. A harder one. And secret too. You mustn't fail me, Maths.' Ray said this with a sudden intensity that made Matthew look towards the door. They were almost at the back of the freezer now, having worked through rank upon rank of palleted containers, their exit practically blocked by a solid phalanx of them, ten deep and ceiling high. Then, to Matthew's horror, Ray reached forward, pulled him towards him by the lapels of his thermal coat, and kissed him on the lips. It felt like being kissed by a piece of ice. 'Don't fail me, Maths,' he said again, his voice a whisper. Then he let him go, raised his set of wheels under the container at his side and pulled it out from the back wall. There was something in the shadow behind it, something crumpled and on the floor. It looked like nothing more than a bundle of clothes. But Matthew did not need to lean in closer to look, didn't need Ray to take his hand and drag him – 'Come and see. Nothing's going to hurt you.' – Didn't need Ray to remind him once again that it was secret, and that he, Matthew, must not fail him. He knew already that he was being introduced to Andy.

SAILOR BOYS

We've just written our wills, Harry and I. It's something we should have done long ago. Anyway, it's sorted now. Everything will go to Alfie and Rick. The restaurant, the two pubs. After we're both gone. Though we don't expect to disappear for a long time yet. It seems a good moment to look back. Fifty years. Half a century this year. I can't believe I've just written that.

Sexually I developed late. Had I known more about myself I might have hesitated before joining the Royal Navy when the time for my military service came. I'd scarcely seen a grown boy naked before. Certainly I'd never seen one undress for his hammock just inches from my face. Never seen a hard-on stuffed quickly into bell-bottoms and buttoned there, confined like a trapped animal while we all clattered up iron steps to breakfast in the mess.

At sixteen I'd only just started to masturbate – which seems late by the standards of today. But, inspired by the proximity of my fellows, in my hammock I soon caught up. There was a yearning, and some heartache attached to this. I wanted to reach out and touch those other bodies, the naked and the half-clothed. Yet it was quite impossible. They might have been behind a wall of plate glass. And my wanting to touch them led to an appalled realisation about myself. I wanted other lads. Wanted to touch, to hug, to cuddle, to fondle – I couldn't get my head around other physical things just yet. Only queers did any of those things... I wanted to love. Did queers want that?

We put in at Portsmouth. Had some time to run ashore. Sometimes that was in the evenings – though by midnight we had to be back on board ship. It meant that young sailors who wanted to get tanked up and then get laid with a short-time girl needed to know what they were doing, and needed to be quick. It was on our last night in Portsmouth... Isn't it always the last night, by the way, on which the momentous thing happens? And don't we then regret all the previous nights, which seem in retrospect a waste?

Where had the others gone to? My crew mates. I don't remember. Probably because it became a matter of supreme unimportance a moment after they left. Left me alone in one of the Spice Island pubs. Not alone exactly, because there were other customers. But without company at any rate. Then, over by the bar, sitting at the counter, there he was. His uniform was identical to mine; on the counter in front of him he'd laid the familiar cap. The bar counter turned a corner between us, so that he sat half facing me. He could see me if he wanted to. Apparently he did. Within a second of my catching sight of him he gave me a friendly nod.

The world holds its breath at such moments. The future forks like a lightning bolt. The nod might have been the end of it. That was one possibility. There were two more. I could have walked over, taken my drink with me and joined him at the bar, chatted with him there in full view, and rubbing shoulders with everybody else. If I'd been the bolder one I'd have done just that. We'd have chatted and, again, that would have been that. But I wasn't the bolder one. Thank God. On this occasion at least, he was. I merely nodded back to him from the partitioned-off little alcove in which I sat all by myself. While he got down from his stool, wove his way through a crowd of other drinkers without taking his eyes off me, and was at my table a moment later. 'Join me,' I said. Did I tell you I wasn't bold? At that moment I was.

He looked rather like me, actually. (He still does.) Straight nose, dark blond hair, nice lips. And eyes... Well, I can't lay claim to anything of the sort myself. His were sky blue, dark lashed. They looked like stars, I thought. 'What's your ship?' he asked, as he sat.

'Rother,' I said. The third word I ever said to him.

'Sprite,' he answered, volunteering the name of his own ship. The sound of that word made Rother go flat. We nodded to each other. It didn't need saying that we'd seen each other's ship at moorings across the big dockyard every day that week. Then we talked sailor talk, comparing notes, exchanging anecdotes... I realised after a moment or two that I didn't want to talk about all that. I wanted instead to climb inside the chambers of his heart. In just a few short minutes my own inexperienced little heart and cock had both fallen in love.

We were sitting very close to each other, I realised. The alcove was very small. The table in it screened us, from chests to knees at any rate, from everyone else's sight. In sitting down he'd placed himself, quite by chance I supposed, as close to me as I now wanted to be to him. The feeling that gave me was wonderful. In fact, once we'd relaxed a bit and each was growing confident that the other was enjoying his company and not just being polite, I could feel that relaxation take physical shape: we both minutely moved our legs.

I felt our knees touch. It was like an electric shock. The contact spread, our thighs took part, and it felt as if a warm wave were sliding up my leg, as that first pin-point of connection expanded out. I had never known anything like this before. Never felt anything so good.

'And then the skipper says...' He stopped in mid-story and smiled; his eyes joined in; the stars twinkled. 'You weren't listening,' he said.

'Sorry,' I gasped.

'Wasn't really listening meself, tell the truth. I'm Harry.'

'Will,' I said. We shook hands. This must have looked funny to anyone watching, since we were already so close to each other, leaning in towards each other and now touching at the shoulder as well as the knee and a couple of places in between, that we had only to move our hands a couple of inches each in order to exchange the formal greeting. And our hands, having shaken each other, seemed to have their own agenda now: refused to disengage themselves but stayed clasped for a moment, despite the awkwardness of our positions side by side and slap-bang up close.

Eventually those hands dropped into our laps. Although not quite. Harry was sitting to the left of me; the hand he'd used to shake mine dropped vertically and landed on my left thigh. That couldn't happen so easily with my right hand. I withdrew that. And slipped my heart and all its contents gently onto his right thigh with my left. We sat an age like that. We continued to talk, but absently. It didn't matter now what either of us said. Then slowly our hands began to move, just an inch or so in any direction, like hands on a Ouija board at a séance. Then after about another minute, Harry's hand stopped. 'Wait,' he said. 'I'll get us another drink.'

I watched him go. He was almost exactly my age. Two months older, he'd told me, than my sixteen and a half. He – whose face was so like mine – looked as lovely from the back as from the front. So poised, so confident. I didn't dare imagine I looked like that. He didn't go directly to the bar. He called in at the gents' toilet first. I ached to follow him in there but dared not. I waited till he came out and went to the bar, and then I went to follow his example, prudently, not wanting to have to interrupt our second pint. I placed my cap on the table before I left it, so that no-one else should claim and usurp our charmed spot.

And we went on from there, after we'd sat back down again, resuming from the point at which we'd left off. We were soon stroking each other's thigh quite energetically, and rubbing calf against calf. After a while I dared to look directly at his crotch. I was thrilled, though almost horror-struck, to see the ridge of his erection there. Looking down vertically I beheld myself in the same state. To my relief it seemed that in our relatively modest size we were equally matched.

'Yeah, yeah,' said Harry quietly. He sounded very much in control of things. Of himself. Of me. Then his voice changed totally. He sounded like a panicking kid. 'I've never been here before. Have you, mate?' He wasn't talking about the pub.

'No,' I said, in a broken thread of a voice. His hand was trembling and tentative as it grasped my cock through the fabric of my uniform trousers.

'Oh God,' I said. 'Oh no, please don't.' But I didn't mean that, and he knew it, and he did it anyway. And, coming like a machine gun, unexpectedly, I fired off round after round into my pants.

The feelings that suffused my body, heart and mind were followed, as overhead lightning is followed by its thunderclap, by mortification, shame and the deepest embarrassment I'd known in my life. The words, 'Oh no,' escaped, less than a whisper, on my breath.

But Harry put his lips close to my cheek and whispered, hoarsely, urgently, 'Do me too.'

'What?' I whispered back. 'Now? Like that?'

'Yes,' he said, and I realised then how close he was. 'Go. Now.'

I clutched at the ridge in his trousers: it angled up sharply from his groin. Rubbed at it with my fingers a couple of times. Ineffectually, I thought. But apparently effectively enough. For after just two seconds he gave a gasp and his whole frame shook. With startling suddenness I found his trousers and my fingers hot and wet – as if someone had turned on a hot tap.

I know now what I didn't know then. To expect a moment of mutual recoil after sex with a stranger, if the situation between you isn't … how can I word this? … extremely right. But that recoil never came. We stayed, closely snuggled against each other's flank and hip, saying nothing, just happy to be where we were and not wanting to move to anywhere else. With hindsight I know why this was. We were simply … extremely right. Our only source of anxiety was the dark blots on our bell-bottoms –that, and wondering how we were going to hide them when we eventually stood up.

Exchanging conspirators' smiles we picked up our pint glasses and resumed our interrupted drinks. 'Cheers, mate,' Harry said. And then, because we were young and quick, we started after ten minutes or so to fondle each other again. Fingering shoulders, chests and necks as well as hands and legs. We were bolder with each other this time round, more confident. Too confident in fact. Indiscreet. The barman clocked us and came over. He stood against our table, a tall barrel-shaped man with dark curly hair, bald on top. He overflowed our view, seemed to fill the pub. 'Now lads,' he said. 'You can't do that here. And you know that. Either sit here quietly and keep your hands to yourselves or go somewhere else. Understand?' He turned abruptly and went back to his domain behind the bar. He'd spoken like a firm but kindly schoolmaster. We'd been lucky in that, we thought. It was England, 1963, and he could have – many of his ilk would have – called the police.

'At least he didn't get a proper look over the table top,' I said, thinking about our blotted pants. We both sniggered. But we were too cowed by the barman's intervention to do other than he said. We finished our pints quite quickly, not saying much. Then Harry drained his glass. 'Come on, let's go,' he said.

'Go where?' I asked.

'Dunno,' he said 'Alleyway? Round the back?' I was thrilled, and my cock stirred again at the daring of that thought.

We had to do quite a bit of exploratory walking around the centre of Old Portsmouth before we found an alley that was quiet and dark enough. Having entered it we turned to face each other, touched each other's forearms, then kissed.

Then kissed. So simple, so ordinary a thing that sounds in later life. But the astonishment, the wonder of it, when it's the first time for both of you! The sweet, sour, complicated, taste of it, the needy thrusting of the strong and bony parts of another boy's head, the soft, soft wetness of another boy's warm lips.

I felt Harry's hands at my waist, checking I had an erection again. (I did.) I felt him undo the buttons and spring my trapped cock. And I felt my own hands, again as if they had minds of their own, do exactly the same to him. I gasped at the discovery at that moment that I held another person's penis in my hand. That this tough, wiry-muscled teenager – probably well able, as I was, to take care of himself in a fight – was ready to allow his most delicate and fragile adornment to be clutched by my rough strong fist... That seemed to me, and seems so to this day, an expression of the most profound and humble, and humbling, trust. I held Harry's erection as gently, reverently, carefully, as a gun-dog holds a live bird captive in its mouth.

'Pull them further down,' I said – I meant his bell-bottoms – with a kind of desperation in my voice. I wanted more of him to see, to feel, to smell: his balls, his thighs. I loved the boy-man scent of his nakedness and I wanted more of that. I made the heart-stopping discovery that he wasn't wearing underpants. No wonder he'd earlier made my hand so wet and hot. But Harry had the same desires as I did, evidently, for while we continued to kiss I felt him tugging my own waistband halfway to my knees, then tenderly fingering, exploring, my tight small ball-sac.

Then in a businesslike way we wanked each other off, standing facing each other, feet a little way apart, one hand each around the other's shoulder for physical as well as emotional support. Lacking the experience and the know-how we hadn't the wit to twist sideways when the moment came, but ended up spraying the inside of each other's thighs... Actually, I was glad of that: for a couple of days afterwards I managed not to wash it off.

We buttoned up and walked back to the dockyard. Some of the way we went arm-round-shoulder, in the manner of sailors everywhere, pretending to be drunker than we were. At last we came to the place where our ways parted; we had opposite directions to walk in, skirting the dock's brink, towards our different ships.

'That was your first time, then?' Harry asked me, for the second time, suddenly diffident and needing to check.

'Like I said.'

'Me too,' he reiterated, almost whispering the words.

A wave of emotion poured itself over me, drenching me through and through. I said, 'Stay with me. Come back to my ship.'

'Don't be a child,' Harry rebuked me gently. 'You know we can't do that.'

'Then let's run away together, Harry. Jump ship.'

'Oh bloody hell, mate!' His exasperation showed, though he was trying to be gentle about it. 'Go where? Do what? Desertion's not exactly without risk.' (I don't remember now whether they still shot you for it in

1963.) He laughed a bit bitterly. Then, 'OK,' he said, suddenly the senior one. 'Time to say goodnight.' He ruffled my hair.

'I want you!' I croaked hopelessly, fighting sobs that rose from previously uncharted depths.

'You'll be OK in the morning,' he said, either cheerful or else feigning it. Then he turned and walked away quickly without looking back.

I wasn't OK in the morning, of course.

We met again on Malta. A year had passed. I walked into a bar alone, out from dizzying sunshine into shadow for a second; then, as my eyes adjusted, at a table with a group of other sailors, again in the familiar uniform, there he was. A lot of water had flowed under my bridge in the year since we'd first met. Other fluids too, if you'll forgive a moment's crudeness. I hadn't exactly kept myself for him. I might have fallen heavily for my first ever jack-off mate, but I wasn't as silly or self-denying as that. And I could see – my first glance at him told me this, as if his past year's history had been tattooed all over him – that all the above went for him too. His seventeen-year-old face had acquired a world-used, lived-in look, or so it seemed to me, aged two months younger than he was. Though from where I stand now he'd have looked fresh faced and innocent enough. My heart missed a beat in any case. He was still Harry. Harry again. On Malta, just when I was. He still looked… Even now I grope for a word... Perfection, I thought.

He saw me at once, got up from the table, left his mates without explanation or excuse and came to greet me. 'Will!' he said. I was grateful just that he remembered my name. Then more grateful yet for the smile on his face. 'Will! Oh hey!' He shook his head. 'Seeing you here.' He sounded almost overcome. And the contrast between this and his brusque rough parting from me in Portsmouth a year ago was almost too wonderful, too painfully wonderful, to take. I didn't remind him of that parting, or of the bitter taste it had left. The present moment was too precious, too beautiful and exquisitely fragile. I feared that if I pushed at it too hard it would crack and break.

'How long are you on Malta,' I asked, dreading his answer.

He gave me the answer I dreaded most. 'We sail tonight.'

'Oh fucking hell!' I said. I touched his fingers for a fleeting electric nanosecond the way that, on the Sistine Chapel ceiling, Adam touches God. 'I've never forgotten you, Harry,' I said.

'I haven't forgotten you,' he said. He chewed on the words a bit, as if he'd come across something in a mouthful of pie that he wasn't quite sure about.

'Is there somewhere we can go?' I asked wildly. 'An alleyway? Something?'

His eyes of stars opened expressively wide. 'It's broad daylight out there.' He flicked the stars towards the table he'd just left, scarcely moving his head. 'I'm with me mates.'

There was nothing to be done. I joined him and his mates back at the table and, with a beer or two and lots of laughter and false bonhomie, passed the most miserable hour and a half of my entire life.

Luck strikes occasionally like a spark, but we have to have the tinder in place, ready for when it does. It was I who had the forethought to provide the tinder in this case. As we parted – the time had come for him and his mates to return to HMS Sprite – I said on a sudden impulse, 'Give me your address. Home address.'

He shook his head defeatedly. 'You wouldn't know it. Capel-le-Ferne. Little place outside Dover. Near Folkestone cliff.'

That was the spark – the lightning bolt – of luck. 'I live in Dover,' I said quietly.

We wrote our addresses on a couple of finger-wipes, plucked from the metal dispenser on the table nearest the door. 'When are you next there?' I asked.

'September,' he said. He didn't sound very hopeful as he said it. It was now March.

But September will always come, whether we live to witness it or not. I was young, we were at peace, not war, so there was a good chance I'd make the next September at least. But, precisely because I was young, the six months passed as slowly as months have ever passed for any teenager in love.

My stint of national service was behind me when September finally turned up. I was wondering what to do next. And as I wondered I walked, or took the bus, daily up the long hill that leads south-west out of Dover to Capel-le-Ferne atop the white cliff. Then, from a grassy slope that looked down on a row of terraced cottages, I staked out Harry's parents' house. A dowdy piece of 1950s terrace, it looked like my own parents' home in fact. It took eight days of waiting but then at last I saw him coming out of the shabby front door. He was wearing a one-piece overall, with bib and brace. Plimsolls on his feet. And – presumably because the weather had remained unseasonably warm – apparently nothing else. I ran down the slope to him. So fast that I had to stop myself with flailing arms to avoid knocking him flat. I would have liked to embrace and kiss him, but walls have ears and windows eyes, and they'd already seen quite enough.

'What are you doing here?' he almost shouted, startled. 'We can't be seen to meet!'

I'd had eight days to rehearse this. Calmly I said, 'Red Fox. Eight o'clock.' I'd named a pub, halfway between our two houses, which I'd never been inside. Nobody there would know me. I hoped the same would be true for him.

At eight o'clock I sat there. And at ten past eight. With the passing minutes I felt my rapture turning to despond. By half-past I was a whimper away from breaking down in noisy sobs. He wasn't going to turn up. And then he did. My heart rose to meet him like a flock of bright-feathered birds. And for the second time in minutes I wanted to cry so much that it hurt.

'Sorry,' he said. 'Tea was late. I won't go into it. I told my folk I was meeting mates an'd be back late.'

'I said the same to mine,' I said.

If the last time we'd spent in a bar together, on Malta, had been hell, then this was already a taste of heaven. We talked, we caught up, we opened ourselves up; our hearts became like molluscs without shells. 'Do you...?' our youthful questions all began. And, 'Yeah, so do I,' or 'Me too,' all our answers came. But remembering our experience on Spice Island eighteen months ago we dared not touch. We sat on opposite sides of a table, our legs drumming involuntarily up and down in that engine-running reflex that is the give-away indicator of excitement, anticipation and – in this case certainly – sexual longing. The expression *body language* hadn't been invented back then, I don't think, but the language existed all the same. And it gave us away again, just as it had done in Portsmouth. But rather wonderfully, we found we'd given ourselves away to the right person this time round. To the very person who, that night, could help us most and who – though we couldn't guess it then – would change our lives. But our hearts sank as the landlord strolled over to us and joined us at the table. We feared a repetition of the Portsmouth incident.

'Well, boys,' he said gravely. 'Haven't seen you in here before. You're very welcome. In a minute I'll buy you a welcome drink. But I wanted to say something to you first.' He said this in such a serious yet nice way, that we looked carefully at him. He was a slim, curly-haired man in his late thirties. (We worked that detail out later, when we knew him better. Had we been older we would have realised that he was a very handsome man, but we were young and in love and so didn't notice that.) 'I'm Charlie. I run this place with a friend of mine called Pete. You'll meet him later, I expect.' He was looking very carefully into our eyes for signs that he and we were all on the right track. 'We're partners, if you know what I mean.' We saw what he meant. It came as a blinding flash of revelation: a Saul on the road to Damascus moment. And he could see in our eyes that we'd got there, and that we were indeed all on the right track. 'I just wanted to say to you, we know how difficult it is at first. You may not have anywhere to go, for instance. I can well imagine that.' We didn't answer him, but he read our response in our faces as we looked at him, and he carried on, 'We've got rooms aplenty upstairs, going empty. Beds in them even...' He gave a saucy grin as he said this. 'If ever you need a place to … well, just be together, or stay the night.' He paused. 'Just making the offer, you understand. Just in case. No charge, obviously. And it'd be just between us, of course. Tick the No Publicity box. OK?'

Harry astonished me then. He was wonderful. He said, 'How about tonight?'

Undressing for the first time together we had the deep, lovely but also rather difficult, feeling that we were stripping bare not just our bodies but our souls. We watched each other the whole time this was going on, so that we kept tripping in our clothing as we pulled it all off. I loved the look of him. He loved the look of me. How do I know that? He told me, and has done many times since. Both recently returned from operations in the tropical seas, we sported golden tans; taut well-exercised muscles clothed our slender frames; we showed off pretty swirls of light brown hair in all the places where hair grows on seventeen-year-old boys. We played with our newly naked other halves awhile as we stayed standing up, enjoying – a bit naughtily perhaps – the fact that we looked, and were built, a bit like twins.

But the room was not warm, hadn't been used for some time. We were soon in bed. Exploring with our hands and tongues – with our hearts too – all those parts of each other we hadn't touched before, and laying claim to them, while not forgetting those other bits, the hard and jutting bits, the furry musky bits, we'd claimed eighteen months before. 'Have you ever been fucked?' Harry asked me in a tremulous voice after a little while. 'Fucked another boy?'

'Not yet,' I said, a bit nervously.

'Nor me.' He was nervous too.

'Look, I said. I caressed his cock very softly. 'Do we need to do everything all at once? Shouldn't we take it slowly to begin with? Step by step?'

'Good idea,' he said. He sounded relieved. He kissed me then, again. Placed his hand, again, delicately on my cock. We stroked each other's till we came. And then we repeated that. And in the morning yet again. We had our first go at sixty-nine the second night. And fucked each other for the first time – face to face on both occasions – on the third. We managed not to hurt each other as we each poked experimentally into the other's backside that third night, and smiled cautiously into each other's eyes. That was partly because we trusted each other implicitly and were perfectly relaxed. And partly because, physically, in terms of size as well as other things, we were a perfect fit. I still think that in proceeding in that softly-softly way those first three nights we exhibited wisdom beyond our years.

Pete was as handsome as Charlie was and, like his partner, a lovely friend to have. It was Pete, even more than Charlie, who put us on the road to our first jobs in civilian life. Car ferries, and in those days train ferries too, sailed almost every hour from Dover to ports on the French and Belgian coasts. Each ferry carried a complement of sailors, of course, and we might have thought, off our own bat, of applying for a job of that kind. It was Pete who had the better idea. 'Apply for jobs as stewards,' he told us as the four of us sat in the bar of the Red Fox discussing this one night. 'You know. Bar work, kitchen, restaurant... Fact is, it might make more sense. The man who hires the stewards for...' (he named the biggest operator on the Cross-Channel routes) '... is a mate of mine. He comes in here. You've met him. That can't do any harm...' We spoke to the man Pete knew. We wrote to him. He interviewed us. We got the jobs.

Why do I keep writing *we*? *We* did, *we* thought. Off *our* own *bat* – not bats. How could that be? What right have I to say that it was so? Because it was. We never said, we are a couple, we'll stay together for ever, in those early weeks and months in Dover, or in those years when we worked aboard the ferries – always wangling to be on the same watch, in the same cabin, on the same boat. It just was so, and it never crossed our minds that there was any other way that things could be. We simply accepted it, starting that first night in the cold bedroom at the Red Fox. Because, I guess when I think about it now, the long time that elapsed between our first meeting and our second, and the time that passed between that meeting on Malta and our coming together the third time at Dover, and the way we responded to each other every time… Those things taken together told the unconscious bits of ourselves all that they – we – needed to know. We hadn't been celibate during those times apart, yet now it was somehow understood by both of us – we didn't say it, we didn't formulate it in our heads – that *we,* Harry and I, and that *I-love-Us* thing, were … extremely right.

We worked hard on the ferries for three years. Heads down, buried in our work. Sometimes we were so caught up, so busy, so cream-crackered after hours of relentless toil, that we didn't know if we were headed south or north or if we were due to disembark in ten minutes onto a quayside where we would hear English spoken or French. There were moments of beauty all the same. Not only in our shared cabin at night, cuddling, our two hard bodies tough as dogs, having sex together in whichever way occurred to us that day, enjoying the scratch of each other's body hair, wallowing in each other's musky scent. Occasionally we would find ourselves out on deck at sunset, coming out of Calais, turning north at the limit of the dredged channel along the shore, when Dover cliffs presented a white crescent on the horizon ahead of us and the sun, going down, seemed to raise the other ships in view a metre or two above the calm blue, so that they floated like white castles in the air. We'd taste the cold, salt, sexy sharpness of the breeze; hear the excited mewing of the gulls above the regular whoosh of the bow-wave. We'd want to kiss at those and other moments. Never possible, of course. At least we always knew we'd be making up for that in a few hours' time.

When ashore we'd stay at the Red Fox. We'd tell our parents we were staying over with friends, just as we had done, from the call-box outside the pub, on our very first night. Our room there was our own now, decorated and furnished – albeit simply – by us. Never cold now, not even on a winter's night.

In the summer of '67 the British parliament made it legal for men over twenty-one to have sex together. So whatever Pete and Charlie did in bed at night (we never got too involved there) was suddenly no longer punishable, if discovered and reported, by a prison stay. Over the next few months first Harry then I turned twenty-one. And became legal too. Charlie and Pete took the opportunity soon after that to lure us away from our ferry jobs. They were buying a second pub. We'd helped out in the Red Fox from time to time, for three years. It was our way of saying thank you for a safe haven on shore. Now they asked us if we'd like to manage their new acquisition for them. Joint managers of the new pub. In Dover. Centre of town. At twenty-one, a place of our own. We accepted. For two gay men in '68, an opportunity like that was pretty rare.

Years passed. A restaurant was mooted, near the port. Cuisine was to be French-inspired. Harry and I were asked to set it up. We did so with some trepidation. Yet our experience of on-board catering, and of spending time ashore in France pulled us through. 'You were thinking of this all along!' we challenged Pete. 'When you sent us off to work on the ferries, this was what you had in mind.' Pete protested he'd never had any such idea.

A never-ending honeymoon it sounds. Fifty years from '63 to the present day without a hitch, maybe. Well, of course not quite. Life – or love, they're two words for the same thing really – never is an ongoing honeymoon, and we all know that. Some things did go wrong between Harry and me. Surprise, surprise. When would that have started, then? In 1970, to be exact. Seven years after we first met. (Seven years. Ring any bells, does that?)

A French lad called Olivier came to work for us that year, as second chef in the restaurant. He was three years younger than the two of us. A handsome boy of medium height, he had dark brown curls which – because this was 1970 – he allowed to grow down over his collar. He had nice full lips, chestnut brown eyes that were lustrous and laughed and, as far as we could tell through his clothes, a beautiful physique. Quite early on he developed the habit of turning up (by coincidence?) in the restaurant's gent's toilet from time to time if I happened to be having a pee there, and having a pee himself. He did this quite flamboyantly, happily showing off his cock and, when he caught sight of me giving it a glance, smiling quite brazenly in my face. He had something to smile about: although he was of about the same height and build as Harry and I were, his cock was on a larger scale than either of ours. That was a matter of interest but of no great importance. Similarly, he was circumcised, which Harry and I are not. I found that cute, but again hardly eyebrow-raising. Just one of those things. OK, that's two of those things – but life's like that. Inevitably … you know what's coming next, I think … those moments of glancing across at each other's equipment grew ever so slightly longer as the weeks passed, and so, I have to admit, did our cocks. Eventually things reached a point at which we had difficulty stowing them away each time, since they would both be almost fully erect. Neither of us commented on this, but we'd mug a grin or a grimace at each other as we tried to stuff them back where they belonged. I had no intention of taking this any further, for all Olivier's physical and personal charms. First, I was committed to being faithful to Harry, and hadn't found that difficult up to that time, and secondly, Olivier was our employee, so that was that.

Anthony McDonald

One night that summer I sensed a difference in Harry when we got to bed. He'd come back from a meeting with suppliers in London and had spent the evening being nervy and irritable and tense. In bed he felt different somehow, like a car that has been driven by someone else. And he had a different smell. I spent some time that night mulling all this over as I lay awake. By the next morning I'd come to the conclusion, though I said nothing at all about it, that he actually had been driven by somebody else.

I bided my time. And then there came another day when Harry was out somewhere, doing business on behalf of both of us. I had some time off in the afternoon and so did Olivier. We coincided in the toilet as we finished work. I looked at his handsome, full-grown penis as he rather slowly tucked it away, and said to him baldly, boldly, 'Nice afternoon, don't you think? Wonder if you'd fancy driving up to the Warren for a walk?' Despite all his previous signals in the course the preceding months I knew there was still the chance he'd say no to that, but he did not.

Folkestone Warren was a bit of a paradise for lovers. It probably still is. An undulating criss-cross of chalk paths and grassy clearings among bushes and small dense trees atop the white cliffs. There was a good view of the sea too in places and, when the day was clear, of France. France wasn't visible that afternoon as it happened, but we hadn't gone up there for that. The sun shone hotly, brightly on us at least.

Olivier was more than beautiful once he'd stripped. Tanned and cutely muscled. Almost without body hair, except for one dark arrow of it, pointing down from a little above his navel, and merging eventually with the soft fur collar that encircled his little balls and big wagging dick. Not that I'd expected less. He paid me the compliment of saying I looked good too, and that he

119

liked my cock. That though it was a size smaller, he thought it more beautiful than his. More elegant, he said, more stylish and shaplier. He was simply charmed by the idea of a foreskin, I now think, looking back. He lay down on the grass on his back, smiling up at me, and wordlessly, though with eloquently raised knees and parted thighs, invited me to enter him. And without any difficulty – he must have been used to this – I did.

He did something I never saw anyone do before or since. As I rode him most enjoyably, propped on my hands as if doing push-ups, enjoying the sight of his rigid dick beneath me bouncing a little in time to my thrusts, and almost ready to come inside him, he came suddenly himself, without any help from his or my hand, raining milk-white threads of semen all up his tummy and onto his chest. It looked, since his spurts seemed to coincide exactly with my thrusts, as though my own sperm were pumping through him, the outpourings of my own cock channelled mysteriously out through his. It goes without saying that I came immediately after that. Then I lay forward and we kissed each other happily for half a minute. 'Are you OK?' I asked him tenderly, and he said he was. For a minute or two I believed myself to be in love.

That was a feeling that dissipated on the car journey down the hill. By the time we were back in Dover my heart was as heavy as lead. I hadn't gone off with a random stranger by way of paying Harry out for whatever he'd done in London a few days back. I'd fucked our chef, with whom Harry and I would have to go on working now, day in, day out. Only we didn't. Olivier gave in his notice within a week, then left. Which made me feel ten times worse.

Of course it all came out. It nearly always does. Harry and I experienced a week or two of awfulness and separate beds, during which it seemed the floor had opened up and swallowed us, and taken us to hell. Yes, he'd met someone in London. Yes, I'd fucked the chef. We picked over every squalid detail endlessly, even though it was like rummaging in a box of drawing-pins: there was nothing to be encountered there that didn't hurt. We went to hell, yet we came back. Somehow we forgave each other, and discovered once again as the weeks passed how much we were in love. Love does that. And, because we were both human, not creatures from some angelic mould, similar falls from grace occurred a few more times during those early years. More often, if I'm honest, on my part, not his. We suffered the pain of discovery anew each time, the shaming humiliation of it, no less horribly than before. Yet again, and yet again, love healed us every time, and has kept us together since.

Charlie and Pete died ten years ago, just six months apart. They left the whole business to us, the restaurant, the two pubs, as they'd told us they intended to in advance. We'd started penniless, Harry and I, two poor kids from two poor streets four miles apart. Now we had a thriving business, or three to be precise, to run and to build up. Something that would cushion us, when the time came, in later life. We were determined to manage things carefully, make a go of the business just as Pete and Charlie had done before us, and so far we've done all right.

Five years after Pete and Charlie died – five years ago in other words – two lads came into the Red Fox one evening, then again the next night. I happened to be working behind the bar there on both those nights. I couldn't help noticing them, then taking a particular interest in them, for reasons which will become obvious as I set the details out. They were two blond fellows of about eighteen, I guessed. Both rather shorter than average height, but showing enough muscle through their clothing to suggest they were fit and would be able to take care of themselves, if things came to it, in a fight. They looked rather alike, though not so much alike that they might be actual twins: there was no question in my mind about that. The resemblance was heightened by the identical uniforms they both wore. They were junior ratings – as Harry and I had been long before – in Her Majesty's navy. They were also – their body language gave it away – very much in love. I could see their frustration with their situation: it was expressed through their engine-running, drumming legs.

I went over to them, smiling inside, though with quite a serious expression on my face, I think. 'Listen, you two,' I said to them. 'I'm Will, and I run this place with Harry, my mate. Just thought I'd tell you this and – just in case you ever need a place to stay the night...'

They moved into one of the spare rooms that very evening, Alfie and Rick, and lived with us when on leave from then on. A year ago they quit the navy, and started to work with us, helping to manage the pubs and restaurant, full time.

Today, after Harry and I made our wills in favour of our two young friends, our boys, the four of us had a celebration meal – at a restaurant that wasn't ours, for once. We lingered at table after we'd finished eating, over another bottle of wine. Alfie was a little pink in the face by now, and ready to be mildly indiscreet. He's still only twenty-three. He said, addressing Harry and me, 'Do you remember the moment at which the scales tipped?'

'In what way exactly?' Harry asked, frowning a little across the table.

'I mean,' said Alfie earnestly, 'the moment when it all clicked into place. The moment when the new person in your life, the one you talk about excitedly to your friends, is suddenly off-limits to everyone else. He's become un-talkable-about. D'you understand what I mean? The moment when he's suddenly become a very private space. You talk to him, but not about him any more. It's like you're one person now, not two, and that God, or whatever there may be, has drawn a veil of privacy over the two of you that nobody else can lift.'

'That's rather beautifully put, Alfie,' I said. But I didn't answer his question straight away. Instead I asked him very gently,' When did that happen to you and Rick?'

Alfie didn't hesitate before answering but plunged straight in. 'It was the moment that second evening in the Red Fox, when you came over and talked to us. It happened then, didn't it, Rick?' Rick nodded energetically. Alfie wanted to get back to his original question, though. 'But what about you and Harry? When did you first know you were a couple? Your first night in the Red Fox with Charlie and Pete, all those years ago? Or not till after that?'

'I think it was earlier,' I said, after a second's thought. I glanced across the table. 'Don't you?' Now it was Harry's turn to nod. Encouraged, I went on. 'I think we sort of knew on our first evening on Spice Island, in Portsmouth.' I looked across to Harry again, suddenly feeling diffident and needing his support. Again he nodded, smiling. In that second nod of Harry's I saw suddenly his very first nod to me, a nod from one lonely boy at a bar counter to another one at an alcove table on his own. And at that moment I saw Harry as his sixteen-year-old self again, fresh faced and starry eyed, with dark blond hair. I turned back to Alfie. 'I think God, or whatever may be, had earmarked us for a couple even before we met.' I found I was struggling suddenly with my voice.

RACKHAM FARMHOUSE

I

'There's a job for you if you want it,' his mother said.

'Oh?' He didn't sound enthusiastic. It was the first day of the school holidays. Colin had told his mother he wanted to make some money over the coming weeks but that wasn't the same as saying he wanted to work.

'This afternoon. Miss Marston wants you to cut her hedge.'

Colin thought for a moment while his mother smoothly told him what Miss Marston was planning to pay. The money sounded good. It was an outdoor job, and just for the afternoon. It could have been worse. 'OK,' he said.

Colin knew vaguely who Miss Marston was. She lived up a lane, about a mile from the village centre. He'd been driven past her house a time or two and he'd seen the mighty hedge he was now going to cut. It was so tall and thick that he'd never glimpsed the house that lay behind it. Rackham Farmhouse. Till the land had been sold off a generation ago it had been simply Rackham Farm. He was learning to drive that summer, but could not yet legally take himself to work on four wheels. He set off that afternoon, a pair of shears in his backpack, pedalling his old bike.

He dismounted in front of the towering hedge. It was pierced halfway along by a small gap in which was framed a low wrought-iron gate. A brick path led up to the front door. Overgrown rose beds and hummocky lawns flanked the path and two enormous bent old apple trees overhung it. The grass was a mass of daisies. The house itself was long and low, just two storeys high, with three windows in each. The front door was to the left of centre and directly behind it a huge chimney reared up through the roof. The upstairs was clad in white weatherboard that needed repainting, while the ground floor front had at some time been rendered with cement. It must have looked hideous when newly done but time had mellowed the cement to a warm honey colour and lichen clung to it, grey and gold. Somehow that dreadful makeshift cementing job, that clumsy act of desecration, didn't matter. It was as though the house might have a soul that could not be destroyed no matter what you did to it. The physical wound had healed. Only the scars remained and they were bravely worn, the disfigurement turned almost to advantage.

Colin was a sensitive boy. Although barely old enough to drive he was susceptible to adult emotions when faced with beauty, charm and loveliness. He stayed a moment longer, one hand steadying his bicycle, the other resting on the gate, continuing simply to look. The front door, Colin noticed, with a kind of frisson he'd never experienced before, stood open. Open, inviting, as though that was its natural state. Colin felt that it would always be open, welcoming, even if it rained or snowed. That in this charmed spot there was no barrier between the indoor and the outdoor worlds.

Miss Marston appeared suddenly in front of him, on the other side of the gate. She must have been gardening out of sight behind the hedge. Her sudden materialisation as if from nowhere made Colin start. She was tiny, frail and white-haired, with a hooked nose and high cheekbones. She had amber eyes. They were extremely striking, like those of a very superior kind of cat.

Miss Marston's gaze travelled over Colin's shoulder and lighted on the tips of the shears poking out of the top of his backpack. 'You didn't need to bring your own shears, you know,' she said. 'I sharpened mine with a Carborundum stone last night.'

'Oh,' said Colin. He looked upwards at the hedge that towered massively to either side of him. 'But I didn't bring a ladder. I hope you've got one of those.'

'Hmm,' Miss Marston snorted. But then she smiled, just a twitch, and they both knew they were going to get on.

Teetering on the top of the ladder, leaning sideways from it halfway up, at other times reaching downward, standing on the ground, inching his way along, Colin snipped away at thickets of holly, hawthorn and beech for a perspirational two hours. Then Miss Marston appeared in the open doorway and called across the lawn to him. If he wanted a cup of tea he was to come in.

He walked up the path to the front door and crossed the threshold. He was in a tiny lobby, a row of coats on hooks in front of his nose. One door opened to the left, another to the right. Of Miss Marston there was no sight or sound. He walked into the room on the left. It was damp and faintly, interestingly, musty. It was obviously never used. The fussy-patterned brown and cream wallpaper had dark patches and in places it was coming away from the wall at the joins. Old black beams crowded side by side across the ceiling and from one of them hung a single light-bulb with a frilly shade. The room was full of photographs; they were Edwardian, all sepia and sentiment, and they stood on lace doilies which concealed startlingly lovely antique tables and chests. Net curtains covered the lower half of the small-paned window, like those spectacle lenses that fill just the bottom half of their frames. There was a little Victorian fireplace, cast iron, enamelled black with a design of coloured flowers forming an arching wreath around. Where the floor was visible at the edges of the faded carpet it showed as massive slices of dark oak.

It was not a promising place to look for the tea that had been offered him. He retreated, back through the lobby and into the other room.

This one was as lived in as a living-room could be. Books and newspapers lay on chairs, and on the dining-table sat a colander full of peas waiting to be shelled. Not just the ceiling above but also the walls displayed close-spaced beams. The floor was of brick and it undulated gently beneath thick rugs. The deep windowsill was jostling with pot plants. But the focus of the room was the fireplace. On this side of the massive chimney stack was no Victorian grate. The old chimney recess had survived the centuries. It took up the whole of one wall, and stopped only short enough of the ceiling to leave room for a mighty chimney-piece twelve feet long. Tiny cupboards were recessed in the brickwork at the back of the fireplace – niches where the salt used to be kept dry in olden days. The stone-flagged hearth accommodated two armchairs. The fire back was a cast-iron relief depicting Charles II sitting in an oak tree while beneath, his pursuers galloped by.

Across the room from Colin another door clicked softly open to reveal a dark enclosed staircase, and a woman at the foot of it, in early middle age. She was dressed, startlingly to Colin's eyes, in white muslin from neck to calf. 'I think my aunt is in the kitchen,' the apparition intoned in a strange chant-like voice, then she disappeared through the room's third and final door. She returned a moment later. 'My aunt would like to know if you'd care for scones and damson jam.'

Colin found that he would. They were delicious, and there was fruit cake as well. Her eyes pouncing from plate to plate as she poured the tea, Miss Marston told Colin she'd been born at Rackham Farm. She'd also inherited the niece, who was called Joan and had been deaf from birth. Colin turned towards Joan across the table on hearing this and, not quite sure what the etiquette of the situation was, made her a slight bow. Joan contributed little to the conversation. But, like Colin, she ate a hearty tea.

'I wonder,' Miss Marston said, as she was showing Colin to the door, 'if you'd be free to come again tomorrow and dig the vegetable beds. Last winter was the first one I didn't manage them myself. Rheumatism.' She gave a snort of disappointment in herself, resentment of her age.

Colin worked for Miss Marston two days a week for the remainder of that month. His passing his driving test coincided with Miss Marston's spraining her wrist while trying to start a reluctant mower with the pull-cord, so he now became her occasional chauffeur as well. But then his final year at school began. His parents moved to a new house on the other side of Rye, the nearest town, and Colin never saw Miss Marston again. But he never forgot her, or Joan, or the house in which they lived. The house especially. The years passed and his memories of it became enchanted ones. The enchanted house, it appeared, had in its turn laid an enchantment upon him.

II

'Good heavens!' said Colin.

'What?' asked Jake, a bit tetchily. They were in the dentist's waiting-room. They'd booked consecutive appointments. Jake's was first, so that he was a bit more tense than Colin, who still had another twenty minutes or so in which to relax while idly turning the pages of Country Life.

'Rackham Farm is up for sale. Rackham Farm near Rye. In the village where I grew up.' He thrust the glossy pages under Jake's nose. 'I must have told you about it. About the summer I did the gardens there.'

'Hmm,' said Jake, but then the buzzer sounded and the receptionist called his name.

'We could buy it,' said Colin on the way home in the car. 'Now.' By now he meant now that they'd both made more money in their ten years in business together than they'd expected to make in their whole lives. When, in their twenties and in the first flush of love they'd set up a film company together, they'd expected to pootle along on the fringes of prosperity while basking in the acclaim of the art film world. The opposite had happened. The world of high art had sneered at their pretensions, had spurned, scorned and snubbed them, and still did. On the other hand they had become severely rich.

'Buy a farmhouse in the countryside? You are joking. Bury ourselves in darkest Sussex? 'The world forgetting, by the world forgot'?'

'We'd only be there at weekends, or when we wanted to be,' said Colin. 'I don't mean we'd pull the plug on London for good.'

'You mean, have London pull the plug on us.'

'There's no harm in going to look. I'd like to show it to you anyway.' They drove down the next weekend.

The estate agent walked them up the familiar path. Familiar to Colin anyway. He felt his chest tighten as he re-entered his past. There was no need to knock at the front door. It stood open, as it had done those many years ago. The agent called through it very loudly. 'Miss Marston.'

'Good God,' Colin said aloud. Miss Marston had been in her eighties when he'd been a schoolboy. It couldn't possibly be...

It wasn't. It was Joan.

'Of course, Auntie died,' Joan told Colin as they all walked round. She spoke still in that voice that Colin remembered, uncertain of its pitch, between a boom and a wail, the voice of the deaf. 'She fancied she heard spirits in the bedroom in her last few days, but at least she died at home.'

Colin was conscious that the house remained almost unchanged despite the passing of the years. Which it had done all those years ago, of course. Things from every different period were jumbled up together still. There was no indication that anyone had ever thrown everything out in order to start again. There was a continuity about it, a sense of reaching out into the past along an unbroken line. There was the little damp parlour, still full of its sepia ghosts, the living-room and its great inglenook. The kitchen remained as Colin remembered it, preserved as it had been then, in the amber of time. The old range, the flattish stone sink, the hand pump for raising water from the well.

'It hasn't changed much,' Joan boomed and wailed. 'You'd better see the back of the house, though. You'll say it was just as it always was, but your friend,' she looked at Colin but inclined her head towards Jake, 'will want to see for himself.' From the kitchen she opened a latched door that led into the bakehouse. The old bread oven was still there but, as in old Miss Marston's time, the place was stacked with firewood from floor to ceiling. Then they entered the old dairy, which ran most of the length of the house. It was the biggest room in the place but remained, as it had done when Colin was a boy, almost unused. 'Too big for one,' Joan intoned. 'I'm moving to Ashford. My horn teacher lives there.'

'You're learning the horn?' Colin both said and mouthed this to her, trying to keep the surprise from showing on his lips. 'The French horn?'

'I've been going every week on the train,' she said. 'It takes all day.' Joan slid her hands along the slots in which wooden shutters ran. Shutters that had kept the dairy cool when Rackham was a working farm. An old ladder clamped to a wall led into the loft where, long ago, farm-boys had slept among the hay. The room was bare save for some empty bottles and a work-bench on which were scattered a few tools. Cobwebs were everywhere, while between the bricks that made up the floor sprouted plumes of ribbon fern. Joan touched one with an outstretched toe. 'Dairy faced north, of course.'

'You could do a lot of things with this,' the agent said quietly to Jake, deliberately facing away from Joan.

'Auntie had some old dresses belonging to her mother,' Joan said later, when they'd climbed the stairs. 'I took them to the Victoria and Albert to be valued. The museum offered to buy them there and then. I'd taken on a job at the village school. As cook.' Colin's eyebrows shot up in spite of himself. In Auntie's time Joan hadn't known how to boil an egg. 'But thanks to those dresses – well, I'm a woman of independent means, foot-loose and fancy-free. Now, have you all time for scones and damson jam with tea?'

Long before they'd finished the drive back to London Jake admitted to Colin that he'd fallen as hopelessly in love with Rackham as Colin had done more than twenty years before. They put in their offer as soon as they reached home. An hour later the estate agent phoned. He was dreadfully sorry. Within half an hour of their leaving Rackham a neighbour of Joan's, a farmer, had turned up on her doorstep and privately put in a higher one. Joan, flustered, had accepted it. And that, as much to Jake's disappointment as it was to Colin's, was that.

III

An awful silence falls upon you after you break up. The absence of your other half, surrounding you like a noiseless fog, follows you everywhere you go. Just as a plane travels the sky pursued by its own footprint of noise, so Colin was now condemned to travel, to work, to interact with others, pursued by the silent footprint of Jake's absence: the biggest silence in the world. Colin found himself thinking, once or twice, this is what it must feel like to be Joan. No wonder she'd wanted to wake the world up with the uproar of horn blasts she could never properly hear.

Colin was surprised one evening, about four months after Jake had gone, to find a message on his phone from an estate agent. He didn't catch the name of the person's firm. He'd had no dealings with any estate agent for more than five years now. Not since the one in Rye, and the disappointment over Rackham Farm. He checked the number. The code was Rye. Colin returned the call.

Someone in that Rye office had been a diligent keeper of records during the intervening years. Rackham Farmhouse was on the market again, Colin learned. Might Colin be interested a second time around?

Colin felt dizzy. He remembered how distraught Jake had been that last time, to lose the house to a higher bid. Jake had gone down to Sussex unwillingly almost, to humour Colin at best, but had returned in love, not just with the house but with a new idea about his and Colin's future life. The fact that that new life hadn't materialised, Colin felt, had contributed something to their relationship's failure to progress in the last few years. It was as if it had run instead into an unpromising siding, to hit the buffers five years down the line. Jake lived in a poky flat in Stockwell now. With a much younger man – whom he didn't really love. Colin was quite certain of that last fact.

He wasn't naïve enough to imagine that if he bought Rackham Farmhouse – something he could now manage without needing to split the outlay with Jake – he would automatically be able to win his ex-partner back. Yet who knew what might be the consequences of an invitation to Jake to spend a weekend or two down there – with the young man from Stockwell in tow if needs must.

Broken relationships did sometimes mend again, if the situation became right. Couples parted, then got back together. And you didn't have to be either mercenary or shallow – Jake was neither of those – to weigh your chances of future happiness on the scales. On one side of the balance was a tried and tested relationship that went back twenty years, to which would now be added a house and way of life in the countryside on which he'd set his heart once, only to have it cruelly snatched away. On the other, a fragile new relationship with a youngster who would one day fly the coop as all youngsters did, and a stuffy Stockwell flat. Weighing those two against each other, Jake would surely pause for thought at least.

Colin arranged to meet the estate agent the following morning. But having done so he found himself pacing his empty Chelsea flat, and realised he couldn't stay the evening there. He got back on his phone and booked himself into the Mermaid Hotel, then drove the sixty miles to Rye.

It was still light when he arrived, and too early for dinner. He was so close now. He couldn't just walk the streets of Rye, or prop up the bar of the hotel. He drove to Rackham Farmhouse; it was only ten minutes away; he needed to set his eyes on it again. It was as if seeing it in front of him would bring him closer to owning it: it was like putting down an intangible deposit. While securing the purchase of it this time round – he tried hard not to let himself think this, but the idea kept sneaking into his mind anyway as if through a side door – would be like putting a deposit down on his ultimate prize, the recovery of his lost love.

He parked his car a hundred yards short of the house; his appointment was for tomorrow, not tonight; and besides, a kind of panic had got hold of him; he could feel his temples beginning to throb. He went the last part of the way on foot, that stretch of the familiar lane that was hemmed in with tall hedgerows and trees growing from high banks. Above his head birds sang unseen in the heights of the trees. But then the banks came down and the view opened out. Rackham Farmhouse appeared. Trees had been cut down around it, the front hedge had gone, and there was a clear view of the building from the lane.

It had been altered beyond belief. It was approached by a gravelled sweep from the side. French windows gaped from what had been the parlour's side wall, while plate glass ran the length of the old dairy at the back. The old shuttered windows had gone. At the front the old cement rendering had been ripped away and replaced with yellow cladding-stone. A metal-framed porch half hid the front door, though Colin could see enough of it to realise that it too was new: a mock-Tudor affair in illiterate semi-Gothic style. And the door was closed.

Colin turned away and walked back towards his car. It was almost dark, and the birds which had been singing as he walked along two minutes earlier were now finishing their songs one by one, as if candles were being snuffed out. His temple throbbed violently for a second. The immense silence of the countryside descended upon him like a shroud. The infinite silence of his absent Jake. His imagination supplied a sound just then. It came as a melancholy booming wail, like the ever so far-off sound of a French horn.

WHEN IN ROME...

Dominic awoke in terror, alone in the darkness of the small hours. Darkness but not silence. He had been woken by the smash-smash sound of an axe raining violent blows on a piece of furniture – he guessed the chest of drawers – less than two metres from where he lay. He fumbled for a light switch. He seemed to remember a bedside table lamp with a switch some way along the cable. The smash, smash of the axe continued. It must surely wake the whole *pensione*, Dominic thought: his panicked brain clutching at straws just as his panicked fingers made contact with the lamp cable and felt their way along it like someone fumbling with rosary beads. *Ave Maria, gratia plena…*

His fingers found the switch. He pressed … and there was light. And sudden silence. Dominic looked around him uncomprehendingly. There was the plain little room: the rug on the tiled floor, the old-fashioned wash basin in the corner, the bare table and the wooden chair, the hanging cupboard … and the chest of drawers, intact, as he had last seen it a few hours ago, just before turning the light out and going to sleep. The door was shut, the windows closed. Dominic's heart was pounding, his forehead clammy with sweat. Slowly he got out of bed. Checked the door – firmly locked. The window – latched. With trepidation he opened the hanging cupboard. No-one hung there. He ran his hand over the surfaces of the chest of drawers. He had expected to see it halfway towards the condition of firewood. But there were no axe-marks, no more scratches than were consistent with normal wear and tear. He stood still, naked, in the middle of the floor, for a full minute. At last his pounding heart began to slow. He found that he badly needed to piss. He still felt too frightened to leave the room to make use of the communal facility along the dark corridor. Instead he took two strides towards the wash-basin, pulled back his foreskin and emptied his bladder down the plughole, chasing the torrent down with a hygienic dispensation of cold water from the tap. Viewed in the mirror above the taps, his cock appeared larger and heavier than it did when seen directly from above, and he felt reassured and curiously comforted by the idea that that was how it must appear to others, and in particular to John, who would be joining him in a little over twenty-four hours. In fact, he thought, the whole of his mirrored top half – the smooth lean chest, the flat stomach, the faintly visible but not ostentatious muscles of his arms – looked pretty good, and that thought gave him succour as he climbed back into bed, still quite frightened, alone on his first night in Rome. He was nearly twenty-one. Nevertheless, he kept the light on while he drifted, none too quickly and with some apprehension, back to sleep.

And it was only the fact that the light was still on when he awoke again into bright autumn sunshine that convinced him that the whole nocturnal disturbance had not been a dream. Even so, he began to think that, though his waking terror had been real enough, the violent sounds that had occasioned it were mere products of his imagination. He dressed and prepared to go out in search of breakfast in the sun. On his way downstairs, and rounding a bend in the corridor on the floor below his, he passed a young man in the act of locking the door of his own bedroom. He was someone of his own age and very nice looking, not to say beautiful, with dark hair and eyes, but he stood out mainly because of the clothes he was wearing: he was draped from collar-bone to ankles in a black, button-fronted *soutane* or cassock – the street garb of a Catholic priest. Dominic said *buon giorno* and the priest, if that was what he was, said *buon giorno* back. Something about the way he said it made Dominic guess that the young man was no more Italian than he was, but he didn't give himself the chance to find out, continuing instead around the angles of the corridor and down the last flight of stairs. Then he hung his key on the hook on the board behind the un-tenanted reception desk and stepped out into the bright sunshine.

Pity about the cassock, Dominic thought. The young man had looked both sexy and nice. Much too young to be a priest… Unless they caught them in their teens here, like the *castrati* of times past. A silly line of thought, Dominic told himself. He wasn't here to ogle the young men of Rome; John would be here tomorrow. And even if that were not the case and you were looking for fun in the Eternal City, to start your search among the priestly classes would have been exceptionally perverse.

He found a café, sat at a pavement table, ordered a cappuccino and a brioche and sipped and munched contentedly in the warm sun. He took his phone from his pocket and dialled John's number. Only John must have switched his mobile off, since the machine invited him to leave a message. He was alive and well, he said. Would talk later. 'Love you,' he finished. Had John answered, Dominic might have told him about his night-time terrors or he might not have done, but it was not a piece of news he was going to leave by way of a phone message.

By the end of the morning Dominic had explored a substantial part of the old city. He was surprised by its compactness. He had seen the Piazza Barberini, the Spanish Steps and the Mausoleo de Augusto, had stood beside the Tiber and looked across the water towards Castel S. Angelo and the Vatican. He did not cross the river. In-depth exploration of the city's treasures would wait till John joined him the next morning, after arriving by overnight train from Brindisi. This afternoon he would be on a ferry, coming to him from Greece.

How bright the sun was here – and by contrast, how deep and black the shadows. Together, sun and shadow turned the whole cityscape into a pattern of jet and bright ochre. Indeed the window and door recesses of the sunlit buildings around him seemed so fathomlessly black that Dominic found himself thinking of the sockets and orifices of skulls.

More cheerfully, his other principal impression of the city was the sheer physical beauty of its young males. They swaggered through the streets and piazzas with a breezy sexual self-confidence that seemed to say, *I'm up for it, just say the word.* Dominic had to remind himself that nearly all of them would be straight and would not welcome any kind of come-on from him – and also that he wasn't supposed to be 'up for it' himself. John was coming tomorrow. All the same, he thought he might check out one or two spots in the Trastevere district that night and see if Rome's gay youth came up to the standards set by their heterosexual counterparts.

By way of exception to the general rule of male peacockry were the priests, walking black shadows themselves, who streamed in both directions across the bridges between the old city and the Vatican, heads downcast as if to avoid sight of the temptations all around them. But even here it was as if beauty could not be completely quelled; it triumphed here and there and shone out, beacon-like, from a good number of youthful faces, and Dominic remembered the young man he had said good morning to in his *pensione*.

After a mid-day pizza and a beer had rounded off his morning's exploration, Dominic returned to his room. He felt surprisingly tired and thought that perhaps a siesta was in order. First though, he went to his window, opened the shutters and casements to the autumn warmth and leaned out. It was a room without much of a view. The *pensione* was built round four sides of a courtyard and his window gave onto that. There was no sign of life here. Until a movement inside a window opposite caught his attention and he focused his gaze on that. The window was on the floor below his, and through it he could see the bottom half of a bed and, stretched on top of it, a pair of jeans-clad legs and bare feet that looked as if they belonged to a boy or young man. It was the legs that were doing the moving. Dominic couldn't see the whole of them: his view was cut off about halfway up the thighs by the top of the window. But they were twitching about in such an extravagant way that Dominic could only conclude that their owner was either having some sort of a fit or else… The feet suddenly lifted off the bed and were drawn rapidly back, up and apart, almost following the knees out of sight. A few seconds later and they were back in their original position, but this time they lay relaxed and still. Dominic was aware that inside his own jeans his cock was thickening. There was not much doubt left about what he had just witnessed – or rather, tantalisingly – not quite witnessed. He watched from his window for a half minute more, but there was no further movement of any kind. The show was clearly over. He turned away from the window, towards his own bed. An idea of what he might do next was stirring, not so much in his mind as in his pants.

He stopped, rooted to the floor with shock and fear. His bedside light was on. It hadn't been when he had entered the room a few minutes ago. But it was worse than that. No longer did the lamp sit demurely on his bedside locker, but it was on the floor, on the far side of the room towards the door. The flex – how extraordinarily, unnecessarily long the flex was – stretched all the way from the wall socket, past the end of his bed … and … and this was the worst thing … the flex was being pulled, straight and taut.

For the second time in twelve hours Dominic found himself terrified into immobility in the middle of this *pensione* bedroom. And, if anything, this time was even worse. For the implication of this second manifestation had quickly flashed upon his mind. The bedside light had been his ally last night. Switching it on had caused the shattering noise of the axe to stop, had returned the room to normality. But the light was no longer at his command. *It had gone over to the other side.*

After what felt like an eternity Dominic approached the shining light. After all, he had to do something. Step by step he crept towards it. Equally cautiously he bent down, reached out a hand … and was thrown back across the room like someone who has attempted to do a repair on an electric cooker without first switching it off. Whatever had dragged the lamp across the floor was not about to let go.

Back at the window again, Dominic glanced quickly out of it and down at the window he had been watching just a minute ago. The bed was now unoccupied; the legs had gone. There was no other sign of the room's inhabitant. Not brave enough to attempt to switch the light off – the switch on the cable was rather too near the lamp itself for comfort – Dominic had a new idea. He made his way gingerly towards the wall socket and, with the quickest movement he was capable of, unplugged it. The plug jerked away from him, the bulb went dark, the lamp appeared almost to jump a foot or so towards the door, then fell over with an anticlimactic bump.

Dominic had never felt less like a siesta, with or without an auto-erotic prelude, in his life.

Gingerly skirting the now inert lamp on the floor, Dominic left the room and locked it behind him. Was it possible, he asked at reception, to change rooms? No, he was told, the *pensione* was full. It was a Saturday, after all. Why did he want to change? Dominic's Italian was not up to this challenge, nor, he supposed would the receptionist be able to make much of his answer supposing he decided to give an account of events in English. 'It's OK,' he said. 'It doesn't matter.'

He went out into the street. He tried to phone John again but couldn't make contact at all. He'd never before tried phoning someone on board a ferry in the middle of the Ionian Sea; perhaps it wasn't as easy as all that. He looked for another nearby *pensione* – even though he had arranged to meet John at the one where he'd spent last night. He found two and enquired at them both. They too were full. Did he not know it was Saturday night?

He sat at a pavement café and ordered a coffee and a Grappa in the hope that a plan of action would occur to him while he drank them. Still the sun blazed on the ochre walls, still the shadows ran black through the alleys, still the windows and doorways had for Dominic the sinister aspect of the portals to the inner recesses of human skulls.

And then the obvious struck him. If his room was spooked or haunted in some way – the word *poltergeist* had already come into his mind some time ago – then the solution lay close at hand. There was a young priest in his *pensione*; they had said good morning right outside his room. He'd go to him and ask him to carry out an exorcism or whatever might be required. The young priest would know what to do. When in Rome…

As Dominic made his way up the stairs he realised that the priest's room must be on the same corridor, on the same side of it even, as the room in which he'd seen… The thought made him smile. Then, supposing it was the very room? In spite of his very real state of anxiety, by the time he was knocking at the young man's door there was a grin on his face which he could not remove.

Until, that is, the door opened and he was confronted by the attractive face he'd seen that morning but without the black *soutane*. Instead, the young man was naked to the waist, barefoot, and dressed only in the faded blue jeans that Dominic had seen from the window. He looked just great. Polite Italian formulae deserted Dominic. 'I think I need your help,' he said in English.

'Come in,' said the other.

Ten minutes later they were drinking an incautious quantity of Grappa out of tooth-pastey glasses. The young man was not yet a priest – if he ever would be – but a student for the priesthood at the Luca College. A few of the student rooms had not been ready at the start of term and he and a dozen others had been farmed out to various *pensiones* for the first week or so. His name was Alex. He explained all this in faultless English, though he was in fact from Luxembourg and had an Italian mother. That explained the raven hair and deep brown eyes, thought Dominic. Alex listened attentively while Dominic told his story and was silent and thoughtful for a moment after he'd finished it. Then he said, 'I'm not sure if I can help you as much as you would like me to, or deserve. As I said, I'm not a priest. But even if I were, the responsibilities of exorcism are not undertaken lightly. Usually, each diocese – that's the area under the jurisdiction of a local bishop – has one priest appointed as official exorcist and specially trained, though obviously it's not their sole responsibility. And they don't shout from the rooftop about that aspect of their work either. I've no idea who the official exorcist for Rome might be. And if any other priest wants to carry out the rite they need special permission from the bishop.'

'Don't you know a priest that you could get hold of quickly and then ask the bishop yourselves?' asked Dominic.

Alex paused and smiled. 'I think even you know who the Bishop of Rome is.'

Dominic thought for a moment. Then, 'Yes, I see what you mean. It wouldn't be all that easy to get hold of the Pope.'

'So, as you see, I can't be much help from a sacramental point of view,' finished Alex. 'But I could try to be a friend. Would you like us to go and take a look at your room together?'

Dominic was touched by the fact that, in his concern for his new friend's welfare, Alex didn't stop to put on shirt or shoes but walked up the stairs with him, bare-chested as he was. He wasn't a big fellow but lithe and slim and Dominic, having spent some time enjoying the sight of Alex's naked top half, couldn't help wondering about the rest. He unlocked his door and the two of them walked in together. All was as he had left it, including the bedside lamp which was still in its capsized state on the floor at their feet. 'Shall I?' offered Alex, and bent down, picked the lamp up and placed it in its usual place on the bedside locker.

'Thank you for that,' said Dominic. 'But do you mind if we don't plug it in just yet?'

They strayed towards the window together and looked out.

'You can see your bed from here,' said Dominic. Perhaps it was the Grappa making him flirtatious.

'Oh yes,' said the other. 'So you can.'

'In fact…'

'In fact what?'

Dominic's next question was meant quite seriously.

'What's celibacy supposed to include – for you people – and what's it not?'

'Celibacy just means not getting married,' said Alex. 'But we're supposed to be chaste as well.' He smiled – a bit teasingly, Dominic thought. 'That's a whole lot harder. It's something we're supposed to be aiming at, but not everyone gets there all at once.'

'What about wanking then?'

'What's wanking?' asked Alex.

Dominic gaped at him in astonishment. Then he realised that, though his new friend's English was pretty faultless, he might not know all the colloquial words to do with sex. Rather than wade embarrassingly into a verbal explanation Dominic did a high-speed mime with hand and wrist.

'Oh no!' said Alex, laughing, but blushing furiously at the same time. 'How much did you see?'

'Only from there down.' Dominic drew a line with his finger across his own thigh, halfway between crotch and knee.

'Well that's a relief at least.' Then Alex reached forward with one of his hands and gently took hold of one of Dominic's. He looked into his eyes a little diffidently and said, 'Now you've made me embarrassed.'

Dominic returned Alex's gaze steadily and then there occurred that seismic moment when two people of the same sexual orientation look into each other's eyes and learn from them, *He's like me*, and, a second later, the message's perfect anagram, *He likes me*, too.

There was an unmistakeable outline now in Alex's jeans, straining against the fabric. With his free hand, which trembled, Dominic reached forward and undid studs to give the pent-up form release. He was not surprised now to find Alex's cock unencumbered by any underwear as it came popping smartly out, framed only by a small neat triangle of shiny black pubic hair, while his jeans slid down his legs. Alex was cute-cocked rather than well-hung: something Dominic found reassuring – he was not such a very big boy himself. He watched as a clear droplet began to form at the tip of Alex's foreskinned penis like a dewdrop on a budding rose.

Within a minute they were both stripped naked and all over each other on the floor, busy with hands, wet tongues, and wet and glistening cocks. Then, before they'd even negotiated who would do what to whom, they'd done it anyway, coming simultaneously in floods, pressed hard and pulsating against each other's bellies.

They lay still together for a while. Then Dominic got up to get a towel.

'I'll have to go in a minute,' Alex said, sounding suddenly flustered as he mopped himself down. 'College supper.'

'Couldn't you skip it just for once? I was rather thinking of checking out Trastevere, do a few clubs or bars. It would be nice if you came too.'

Dominic could see prudence struggling with desire in Alex's eyes, but only for a second. Desire quickly won. 'OK, I'll come. To hell with the consequences.' Then his face fell. 'I don't think I've got the right clothes.'

'Come as you are,' suggested Dominic to his still naked friend. 'You'll be a sensation. No, but seriously. Your jeans'll do just great. And I'll find you a nice shirt. We're about the same size.' He tweaked Alex's waning erection playfully, to point up the double entendre.

They explored the bars, they wandered the streets, they saw the city's lights reflected in the Tiber like stars, they drank and danced, they exchanged the stories of their lives. Alex told Dominic the tales he had heard about exorcists and demons and possessions. 'Even the very experienced exorcists have to be careful. The spirits are full of tricks.' He told one story about a priest who had successfully carried out the exorcism rite, as he thought, then found himself breaking into a sweat. Reaching in his pocket for his handkerchief, his fingers had encountered... *'not a handkerchief but a lump of human shit.'*

It was after one o'clock when Dominic and Alex returned, a little unsteady on their feet but very happy, to the *pensione*. The duty receptionist gave them a discreet nod and they made their way up the dimly lit stairs. 'We'll check your room out first,' said Alex in a businesslike tone. Dominic had almost forgotten there was a problem with it.

They didn't need to turn the light on when they opened the door. They stood in the doorway and gazed, appalled, at the scene before them. The bed, Dominic's bed, was illuminated from within like something in a religious painting. The table lamp was inside the bed, mounding the bedclothes and shining, glowing, through them. In the very place where Dominic should have been. Would soon be? Not on his life. For the light was not the only sight they saw. Dominic's clothes were strewn across the floor. 'Jesus Christ,' he murmured, almost without breath. The chest of drawers was a substantial pile of firewood, of jagged, broken planks that leaned at awkward angles against each other and against the wall. Involuntarily Dominic and Alex clutched at each other.

'You're not sleeping in here tonight,' Alex said firmly. 'You're coming to bed with me.' They kissed each other fiercely as soon as they left the room, and Dominic locked the door on whatever had taken control within.

John got the room number from reception and went up to find his friend. Although it was ten o'clock, Dominic had not been out yet, they told him at reception, or even been seen. Still, it was a Sunday morning.

John knocked and waited. He knocked again. Waited some more. Knocked harder the next time, and louder. After five minutes he gave up; people would be coming to complain. He went back to reception. A handsome young man was talking earnestly to the receptionist. He was tall and muscular, as was John himself, with a healthy tan and the strawberry blond hair and blue eyes of northern Italy. What a waste, thought John, noticing – you could hardly help noticing – that he was clad from shoulder to shoe in priestly black. Only then did he begin to register what the new arrival was saying.

'…didn't appear at supper … breakfast … morning Mass. … not answering his door…'

'He returned very late last night,' the receptionist said. He looked up and caught sight of John. 'With the young man that our friend here is looking for.'

A minute later, escorted by the duty manager, John and the blond young man in black were climbing the stairs together. They reached Alex's room first. After a quick courtesy knock the manager opened the door with a master key. They walked in. And froze. They were unable to utter a word, any of them, though their gasps of shock and distress were as audible as cries. John's fingers sought and clutched spontaneously at the other young man's hand.

The bedside light was on. Its improbably long, strong flex was hideously tangled around the necks of the two young bodies that lay – limbs caught by death in desperate flailing motion, their two heads drawn together by the wire – among the dishevelled and thrown-back sheets. Somehow their two heads were raised a little above the pillows and the light projected their two shadows – so black they were, it seemed to John that they made two real holes, like the pair of eye sockets in a human skull – against the bright ochre wall.

It was many hours later, as the two of them waited in an arid waiting-room to be seen by yet another police official, that John and the blond young man – who's name was Antonio, he said, and who wasn't a priest yet (if he ever would be) but only a student for the priesthood – found their fingers interlocking, almost involuntarily, for the second time that day. John and Antonio looked into each other's eyes, and through the pain and hurt there John saw something else. He thought, *He's like me. And he likes me, too.*

STRAIGHT MATE

We used to pass on the stairs, or coming and going from our twin front doors, which stood just inches apart. Paul and I. Rachel and Scott. Mostly we'd be in couple formation when we met. We knew one another's names but that was about it.

Then came *all that*. The break-up between Paul and me. I won't go into it. The day Paul left I got drunk at home by myself on red wine. At least Paul hadn't taken that. But I struggled next morning to get up for work. The second evening I went out. Walked down Warwick Avenue to Little Venice and the Warwick Castle pub. It was a cosy, old-fashioned pub which I liked, although for some reason Paul and I had seldom used it, preferring to use the Warrington near Maida Vale tube. But now as I entered the Warwick Castle on my own I saw Scott seated at the bar, alone. I didn't think anything of that. Perhaps he often came in here on his way home from work. Whatever work he did.

He caught sight of me and motioned me over with his head. I hopped up on the empty stool beside his. We were then both struck by something: we were dressed alike. Both in light blue jeans and denim jackets. Both in white trainers and T-shirts. We didn't comment on this. A twitch of smile said all that needed to be said.

Scott asked me how I was. Just in the routine kind of way, but I couldn't tell him I was fine, or good, when I was not. I told the truth. Paul had left.

'Oh God,' he said. 'I'm so, so sorry. But it's weird. Three days ago,' he hesitated a second. Perhaps he found it difficult to say the words that came next. 'Rachel left me.'

'Oh blimey!' I said. I agreed with him that it was a weird coincidence, then said how sorry I was to hear it. It always comes out a bit awkwardly when two people find themselves exchanging mutual sympathies at the same time. Scott called across the counter and ordered me a pint, and a refill for himself. When those had been demolished I got another round. And after that... Well, we spent the whole of that evening in the pub. Forgetting to eat, we got drunk.

We wouldn't necessarily have made such an evening of it. Had the coincidence of splitting up with our respective partners in the space of three days been all we had in common we probably wouldn't have. But we quickly found we liked each other, had more in common than just a taste for denim jackets and jeans. We realised that, without knowing it, we'd both been living next door, for the best part of a year, to someone who could have been, could yet be, a mate. Gay boy, straight boy. There was something very nice about that.

Scott was a historical advisor to the National Trust. It sounded a plum job. I worked in the Planning Department at Westminster City Council. Though as we compared notes I found that our jobs were not as different as all that. We learnt more and more about each other that night. And all of it we liked. We could see that mutual liking reflected in each other's eyes time and again as the evening progressed.

But there was something else. On my side at least. I liked the look of his thighs in his sky-coloured jeans, splayed on the bar stool, angled further and further towards me as the pints were sunk. I liked the look of the neat but prominent mound he displayed at the crotch. I liked his face, his build... I liked his height; he was the same height as I was, that is, a little less than average. I liked the look of his hands too, which were also the same size as mine, and that told me (I have always believed this, whether it's true or not) all I needed to know about the size of his cock. Well, not quite all. I'd have liked to see it. Would have liked to unzip him there and then, sitting on a bar stool among the regular clientèle of the Warwick Castle, and get it out, then put it in my mouth. I fancied him, in short.

We didn't arrange to meet again. We lived on opposite sides of the same wall, after all. So three days passed during which, although we heard each other's front door open and shut a couple of times, our paths didn't cross. Then he knocked on my door, startling me by being there when I opened it, and asked me if I fancied going for a pint. I might not have seen him for three days but he'd been anything but absent from my thoughts. By now there wasn't much I didn't fancy doing with him. I said yes.

We drank a bit more circumspectly that second time. After a couple of pints I suggested going on to eat. A bit diffidently, afraid he might not say yes, or misinterpret me. But he did say yes. We went to a Thai restaurant I'd used to use with Paul. It turned out that Scott had often gone there with Rachel too. We'd just never been there on the same night.

There's always a bit of a frisson when two regular customers of a restaurant, whom staff know as halves of couples, make an entrance à deux. Nothing is said, of course, but quite a lot is felt and thought. An atmosphere was thus created that we hadn't thought to expect. How do you describe an atmosphere? This one was suggestive of slightly raised eyebrows and intrigued and expectant intakes of breath. It was very palpable in the room, and it propelled us closer together somehow, drew us across the small table further into each other, as if we'd become fellow conspirators in something we didn't yet know about. As if we were having – or about to have – some sort of a thing together. We weren't, of course. We were simply two bachelors who lived in adjacent flats and had decided to go out together for something to eat.

Afterwards it felt a bit odd to be standing next to each other at the top of the stairs, unlocking our two front doors and wondering what words we'd use to say goodnight. Then Scott said it. Said what I, the gay one, wouldn't have dared to say myself. 'Do you want to come in for a nightcap? Or is it too late?'

It wasn't too late. Too wonderful was nearer the mark. I was in through his front door before my heart could beat twice.

The flat next door is a mirror image of one's own. Except it isn't. It's been lived in by people with different tastes from yours, with different ideas about where the furniture should go and what the décor should be like. Yet our two flats had one particular thing in common which struck me at once. There was a sparseness about them. Bookshelves stood half empty. Among the pictures and ornaments were gaps. Flats that had housed two lives apiece were now quite literally half-abandoned. In the case of each of them one of the two lives had fled.

'Where did Rachel go?' I asked. Up to now I hadn't felt able to do this.

'To her mum's in Enfield,' he said. 'For the moment at least. Though I'm pretty sure she's seeing someone else. And Paul?'

'Cambridge,' I said. 'And he's definitely seeing someone else. I do know that.'

We laughed, though on both sides there was a bit of awkwardness in it. He gestured towards a sofa, and I sat while he went to the kitchen and poured us a glass of red wine, after checking that was what I'd like.

He had two sofas in that living-room. He sat on the other one. In my flat there was just one sofa, and two arm-chairs. I found myself wondering how we'd end up sitting when – if – he came in to mine.

I don't remember what we talked about. It didn't seem to matter at the time, so it certainly doesn't now. The thing was, the way we talked. I'd spotted that our first evening together. We found the same things funny; we had the same quirky way of examining the world. We found each other funny, quirky, too. Exploring each other more and more deeply we went on liking what we found.

Two nightcaps later I knew the time had come for me to get up and leave. Don't push it, I thought. He's straight, you're gay; there's nothing more for you here with him tonight. I wondered, as he turned the key in his door to let me out, if we'd part with a hug. Although I wasn't going to initiate it... But he did. And it was nice.

We'd given each other our phone numbers and email, but didn't make use of them over the next few days. If we needed to get hold of each other we had only to knock on the door. Actually, in every room except our bedrooms we could have thumped on the wall. We were too self-conscious to start sending each other texts. What would they be about anyway? Nor did we take to forwarding each other silly internet jokes. So it was that another four days passed before we saw each other again. By the end of that time I found I was missing him. I wanted his company again, quite a lot. Then I ran into him by chance in the Portobello Road, a good mile away from where we lived. We stopped, talked, facing each other in the busy roadway full of shoppers, among the market stalls. I didn't want to let him go. The reflex of the lonely, that. But I realised suddenly, with a sensation like a punch in the chest, that he didn't want to let me go either. He kept on chattering about not very much, not wanting to stop, as if our conversation had become a thread that linked us and that he couldn't bear to break. This discovery, that he needed me as much as I needed him, and the adrenalin rush that it induced, gave me the courage to suggest we went for a coffee. He looked for a split-second at his watch. 'I'd rather have a beer,' he said.

We sat in the Duke of Wellington, drinking pint after silly pint. Sometimes I saw his knee in motion, bouncing as his foot drummed the floor. Then I discovered the same thing happening to mine. The questions began to come, on about the third pint. The ones we're all familiar with. How long had I known I was gay? Had I ever been straight? Wasn't everybody a bit of a mixture, after all, of both? Of course, I answered that last one with the growing confidence of the increasingly drunk. Sexual orientation wasn't a black and white thing. We were all at different places on a plectrum. Sorry, I said, I meant spectrum. We both laughed.

Where did that afternoon go to? It was evening suddenly and getting dark. We wended our homeward way along Golborne Road and Elgin Avenue; we called in, on the way, at The Skiddaw for another pint. Then, as we spilled out of it and floundered across the Chippenham Road he grabbed hold of me amidst the swirling traffic. Caught at my arm with both of his. 'Hey,' he said, with a laugh in his voice that had an edge to it. 'My first time with another bloke. Be gentle with me.' This gave me a real shock. But it had to be a joke. Did he even know what he'd just said? I laughed back at him, but found I couldn't speak. Instead I discovered I'd put my arm around his waist.

We knew we needed something to mop the beer up. The open door of an Indian takeaway beckoned directly in front of us as we tacked across the street. We had to wait, seated in a row with other people, while our order was cooked. With his hands Scott began to explore my arm and neck. Then he laid his

157

head experimentally on my shoulder. He poked his tongue into my ear at one point, then giggled after he drew it out. At first I felt nervous and uneasy about this, and looked around to see if, among the queuers for their supper, there was anyone I knew. But there wasn't. Nor did anyone look likely to remonstrate with us, or to give us a bashing when we got out into the street. Actually the people near us were trying not to look at us, pretending this wasn't going on or that they were somewhere else. So I relaxed and gave myself up to Scott's attentions. I began to return them. In for a penny, I thought. Hung for a sheep as a lamb I didn't know where this was heading. If it went ... well, that way, God knew what the repercussions were going to be for our new friendship. How we'd deal with each other tomorrow and the next day. Did I care at that moment? I didn't give a twopenny fuck.

But I had just enough of my wits about me to suggest, as we climbed our stairs, that we went into my flat to eat our takeaway rather than into his. If Scott was going to have a dreadful awakening tomorrow it would be marginally less dire for him to find he'd made a fool of himself in someone else's gay bed rather than in his own straight one, and he would at least be able to retreat to the bastion of his own unsullied flat.

While we ate, and drank a rather superfluous bottle of wine, we kept our clothes on. Just. We sat side by side on my sofa, listening to some music which he'd put on, turned up very loud. I've no memory of what it was. We fished one-handedly with forks into our tinfoil boxes of curry and rice, which we were balancing on our thighs and cocks. We used our free hands to grope each other a moment at a time, in between the other moments at which we had to employ them urgently to steady our precarious suppers and prevent them tipping into our laps.

When we'd finished eating I uncorked another bottle of wine and we got undressed. We were both thirty-one years old but now that we were doing this, removing first T-shirts, then shoes and socks, in front of each other's gaze we regressed to shy-bold seventeens. Part of the attraction lay in the fact that our bodies looked reassuringly familiar – the form that each of us saw more and more of as we removed our clothing looked similar to our own. We chuckled at the sight of identical CK underpants. Then those came off. And even now we were a pretty similar pair. Matching, rigid cocks, and nearly identical pairs of balls.

We each stared at the other's hard-on but for the moment didn't touch; our hands explored chests and buttocks first. He, whose eager tongue had delved in my ear in public now seemed to hesitate, to hang back, when it came to the matter of starting to kiss. So I started that ball rolling myself, and a few minutes later we went into the bedroom.

We were not a success in the sex department because of the ridiculous amount we'd had to drink. Paul and I didn't wear condoms as a rule – we'd been given the all clear after our tests some years earlier and had been faithful to each other since. But there were a couple of rubbers on the bedroom mantelpiece. They'd been handed to us in a club and

we'd kept them, sort of just in case. In case of a
situation like tonight's. We need not have bothered
with them, though. Neither of us was firm enough
to penetrate the other by this stage. And despite a
further hour of trying to bring each other off by
hand we didn't even manage to achieve that.

He came in my hand in the morning, when we
both woke up parched, though I, despite all the
willpower I could muster and a manful, energetic
effort on his part, still did not.

We spoke a bit but our conversation ticked over, it
seemed, as if in neutral, gears not engaged.
Eventually, still in neutral, he got up and said it was
time he left. When he was dressed I got out of bed
and we briefly hugged and kissed. Wrapped around
each other, one naked, one fully clothed. That's
always been a turn-on for me. For most other people
too, I think. Funny how we seldom think of doing it.

Then he went. I let him out of my front door,
stood naked in the doorway for a second or two
while he let himself into his. I don't know if he went
back to bed when he got in – the two hallways lie
between our bedrooms so I couldn't hear – but I
know I did.

I tried to phone him later but got no reply, nor did
he call me back. I spent the evening in painful
indecision about whether I should knock on his door
or not. I didn't in the end. I spent the next evening in
the same agonised state. The third day, I went and
knocked.

He looked shocked to see me, almost reeling back.
He half smiled for a second, but it was like a match

that half strikes and goes out. He looked awkward and ashamed of himself. I said, 'I wondered if you felt like coming out for a drink.' I knew, though, what the answer would be before I got the words out.

'I'd rather not.'

He shut the door slowly, so as not to hurt my feelings even further than he knew he already had. I stood on the landing for a second, just looking at our two closed doors. I felt myself shivering. Then I turned down the stairs and went out to the pub by myself.

As the days passed things returned little by little to the way they'd been before. I mean, before Rachel and Paul had left. We said hi if we passed on the stairs. We did so awkwardly at first, exchanging shifty, not quite eye-holding looks. But the days became weeks and we would begin to exchange a sentence or two about the weather or the traffic, and it was quite like old times. We never referred to what had happened between us that Saturday, of course.

Then yesterday evening, when I'd come home from work and was climbing the stairs, I met him coming down. A young woman was with him. He said hallo and smiled very nicely. So did she. She was pretty, I thought. Even prettier than Rachel. 'This is Holly,' he introduced us, 'Holly, Mike.'

I said hallo to her, then continued on up the stairs, while they continued down. I heard Scott say, when there were two flights between us. 'He's my neighbour. Gay. But quite nice.'

THE NAME OF THE WINE

I had hardly been in Cambridge two days before I was startled by the apparition of old Parry emerging suddenly from the doorway of a newsagent's. There was no mistaking him, though I daresay I had not seen him in twenty years. Here were the same spectacles, seeming almost too thick to see through, the same thinning hair – quite white now – the same ill-fitting clothes that had once been expensive, the same aristocratic disregard for their shabbiness and failure to match and the same apparent absence of a face as a focus for the whole ensemble. Everything looked somewhat older than I remembered, but then of course it was.

Parry had been nearly, but not quite, head of the History department at Bristol when I had arrived there all those years ago as a very junior lecturer. I remember those spectacles peering out from an armchair over the issue of Speculum in which my first paper on the Forest Laws had just been published. I had been feeling very pleased with myself. 'Nigel,' the spectacles had said, 'you are an unsystematic young man. Alarmingly unsystematic.' A few years later our paths had diverged. I had an idea that he had gone on eventually to a fellowship at All Souls'. We had not met since.

To my surprise Parry recognised me as quickly as I had him. He showed no sign of surprise himself. Looking back, it occurs to me that he might have had some prior knowledge of my appointment through his contacts at the university – for he himself would have been retired for a good many years by this time. 'Hallo Nigel,' he said benignly, 'What brings you to Cambridge?'

I told him about the Readership at Peterhouse. He treated this as news and I was duly congratulated. We stood and chatted for a few minutes. He now lived, he told me, a few miles outside Cambridge on the Royston road, at a place called Bearpark. By the time he had spelt this odd place-name, explained that it was a corruption of the French *Beau Repaire*, that it had originally been a sort of holiday home for some thirteenth-century Benedictine monks, and then indicated with the aid of both hands how one would find the place if arriving by car, he had little choice but to invite me to visit him. We fixed on Saturday lunchtime and I made a point of noting the date in my diary to show him how systematic I had become.

I drove out to Bearpark accordingly on what proved to be a fine, dewy October morning but when I reached the spot to which Parry's painstaking directions led me I was quite astonished. Instead of the country cottage I had been expecting, I found Parry's home to be the imposing gatehouse of an immense mansion which was partly visible further up the long drive. Both buildings were flamboyant eighteenth-century neo-Gothic: all ogee arches and fancy crenellations. Parry was sitting outside his pointy-arched front door in a garden chair, sipping a whisky. He had clearly thought it worth braving the lukewarm sunshine in order to relish the astonished look that must have appeared on my face as I caught my first glimpse of his rural retreat.

Inside, the house was a good deal less than immaculate but even more exotic than the exterior. It was full of exquisite furnishings and ornaments of different periods and styles, each one of which must have been priceless but which, taken together, created an impression of spectacular unease and disharmony. The principal room was too large for comfort and an enormous mirror over the mantelpiece effectively doubled its size and halved its cosiness. Nevertheless a cheerful log fire burned in the grate and when a large whisky was pressed into my hand the room took on a more friendly aspect altogether.

'And you live here all alone?' I said. Idiotically really, because Parry had been a lifelong bachelor when I'd first known him in his mid-fifties, and that was hardly likely to have changed now. Besides which, there was no sign of anybody's presence in the house except his own. He was looking his usual self. His sports coat might have come from Savile Row, though it looked as if he had been gardening in it. He frowned at my question as though I'd asked him something difficult. Then he said, 'Yes, I live alone,' pausing before adding, 'My lover shot himself last April.'

There was a dreadful silence. I had not the smallest idea what to say. I had been taken totally by surprise. Not so much surprised that Parry's proclivities lay in that direction but that Parry had proclivities at all. I had thought of him, when I thought of him at all, as sexless; I had seen nothing beyond the ill-assorted clothes and pebble-thick spectacles. Clearly I had been wrong. I now had to come to terms with the fact that the elderly scholar who sat opposite me, faceless behind spectacles, bow tie and lead crystal whisky tumbler was, despite an acquaintance that spanned more than twenty years, an almost complete stranger.

'I'm sorry,' I said. 'I really don't know what to say.' I paused again. 'I don't quite know how you expect me to react, that's all.'

'Don't react at all then,' Parry said blandly. 'And don't bother about how I react to anything *you* say. You strike me – always have done – as far too worried about what other people think of you. Yes, I know you. But as for me,' he took a sip of whisky, 'I couldn't care a fig. At least, not now.'

It was the *yes I know you* that I found disconcerting.

'I was surprised, if you really want to know, that you should want to talk about something like that with a … with someone you only know slightly. I was also surprised … I mean … I didn't know you were … 'so'.'

'So!' Parry almost boomed. 'What an extraordinary, old-fashioned turn of phrase. How clever of you to dig it up. A euphemism from the past. And much more descriptive to my mind than … gay. Hardly dignified. Especially as one approaches eighty. Thank you, Nigel, I'd forgotten that one. You've given it back to me. I shall remember it now. Now where was I?'

'Your lover,' I said. I felt I had turned red. 'I'll happily change the subject if you like. On the other hand …' I thought this was quite perceptive of me '… it may be that you'd like to talk about it, and in that case I'll just as happily listen.'

I had never been aware of Parry's eyes before. Now, suddenly, I was. They were narrowed like a hunting cat's as they peered at me through their shatter-proof windscreens. 'You must be nearly fifty, Nigel,' he said, 'yet you're still making pretty little speeches like an eighteen-year-old boy. You haven't changed a bit.' There was a hint of amusement in his voice that I disliked. I felt a small shiver run down my spine. 'But thank you for your indulgence,' he went on. 'Yes, I would like to talk about Alan. But just for a few minutes. Not all through lunch; that would be tedious. Bring your drink. We'll take a turn round the garden while I tell you about him.'

The sun was warmer and the dew had gone. We rambled round lawns and shrubberies and the following – I have tried as far as possible to recall his actual words – is the story Parry told me.

'I first met Alan more than forty years ago. Long before Bristol, long before I set eyes on you, Nigel. Do you know what Alan did for a living? He worked on a building site. Called himself a brickie. We met in a... On second thoughts I don't think I'll go into that. You've probably got enough experience to work it out for yourself.'

Which I had. It wasn't something I liked to think about though, and I was horrified at the idea that he had guessed it for himself.

'He was very, very handsome. And only nineteen. We had only known each other a short time before we fell in love. Fell, as if from a sea cliff into the waves below. Not something you'd ever plan to do – or be able to reverse after it had happened. There was no possible question, at that time, of our living together. I was a very junior lecturer at UCL. Setting up home with a nineteen-year-old bricklayer would have been professional suicide. I don't need to remind you that this was several years before homosexual acts were decriminalised. And it was just as impossible for Alan. His workmates would have ... well, you can imagine. So for years, and I do mean years, our social lives never touched. I never met Alan's friends and he never met mine. The times we spent together were hard-won. Something as simple as a drink or a visit to a cinema had to be planned like a military operation.

'But then I went to Bristol and Alan came with me. And now he did move in with me. It seemed extraordinarily daring at the time. (I'm still talking about more than thirty-five years ago.) But we weren't really very brave, looking back on it. I still never met his workmates, nor was I mentioned in their company. We never met each other's family. If one of us entertained at home the other had strict instructions to stay out of the way.'

I interrupted at this point. 'I came to your house, I don't know if you remember, with Doctor Sanders. It never occurred to either of us that you didn't live alone.'

'Quite so. And we never went anywhere together where we might be recognised. It made life together difficult, even dangerous but ... also ... exciting. You see, real romance sometimes thrives in the pragmatic squalor of deception. The need to keep a job down, the need to keep the dull old world turning. But there was a reward for all this, for all this inconvenience, for all these small deceptions. The reward? Call it magic. Call it what you will. It kept us bound together for a – for his – lifetime.'

The garden was extensive. Most of it actually belonged to the big house though Parry evidently had the run of it. As well as rolling sweeps of lawn and planted borders there were wild areas and there was even a lake picturesquely surrounded by trees. He named plants as we strolled, but I was getting interested now in the story of himself and Alan. 'What did he do in Bristol?' I asked. 'More building jobs?'

'No,' said Parry. 'You can't go on swanning around on scaffolding for ever. He took a job in a warehouse for a while but found indoor work didn't suit him and so he went to work for the Parks and Gardens department of the City Council. He never became at all middle-class in his occupations or attitudes. Moving in with me was as far as he was prepared to go in that direction. Even then his accent became more aggressively cockney as the years passed. But he did develop one or two tastes that were rather endearingly out of character... No, not out of character, just at odds with his background. Wagner, lobster thermidor, Shakespeare's sonnets, Chateau Yquem with the rhubarb crumble. You know the sort of thing.'

I supposed I did.

'Eventually we went to Oxford. I was never happier than when I was there. I knew I was never going to get a chair and somehow it was almost a relief. You can be quite second rate and still be happy in Oxford, as you'll find for yourself one of these days. Alan worked at a school for problem children. At first as a handyman gardener. Then he took over some of the woodwork classes. And I think that's when he really found himself. He had a natural gift with the little toughs, and the school authorities let him take on more and more responsibility. The kids loved him. We were at Oxford for nearly twenty years and they went in a flash. But because all good things come to an end, Oxford ended. I retired.'

'But why retire back up here when you were both so happy in Oxford?' I asked.

'Look around you,' Parry answered. 'It is all rather splendid isn't it? The big house belongs to a cousin of mine, while my flamboyant gatehouse was left to me in an uncle's will, many years ago. Alan and I used to spend holidays up here, and as time passed he grew as fond of it as I was. If he hadn't taken to the place I'd never have asked him to pull up stumps in Oxford.'

'But he gave up his job,' I protested. 'A job he loved. That must have been a terrible sacrifice.'

Parry looked grave behind his glasses. 'Unfortunately you are right. And equally unfortunately, neither of us realised it at the time. One of us would have to sacrifice something, and he, I'm sad to say, convinced himself that his sacrifice would be the smaller and more easily made, because he was captivated by the idea of living here,' he gestured widely with both arms, 'with these glorious gardens and in our small, higgledy-piggledy palace. As he said, Bearpark had the casting vote. Unfortunately it cast it wrong.'

'You mean he couldn't settle?' I asked.

'Oddly enough it wasn't that. He loved being here. You see, although it's a bit bleak and un-cosy in winter, that didn't matter when there were two of you. Alan took an almost childish pleasure in all this … opulence. Never mind that it was a faded, unkempt, ill-assorted kind of opulence. All those chandeliers, Persian rugs, inlaid writing desks and monogrammed sheets, they were the stuff his childhood dreams were made of. And although I don't doubt that he missed the challenge of his old job – he became a gardener again – it wasn't that that made things go wrong. Nor was it the fact that we were under each other's feet rather more now that I was retired. We were pretty used to each other by this time. No, the real problem was something else.'

We had turned the last corner of the garden and were heading back towards the house and – I hoped – some lunch. Our whisky glasses were empty.

'The thing was,' Parry resumed, 'that everybody up here seemed to know about our relationship and nobody could give a damn. And, ironically, tragically, this was the one thing that Alan was not prepared for. Here he was among all sorts of new people, gardeners on the estate, people in the village, old colleagues of mine at the university, and they all seemed perfectly ready to accept him for what he was – a pansy. He had always cherished the belief, I suppose, that if anyone ever found out they would refuse to believe it. He with his rugged, bearded face and broad shoulders and cockney accent, he couldn't be 'like that'. And I realised for the first time that something that the rest of the world was beginning to accept as quite natural was something that he could not accept at all. At the very moment in this country's history when you could at last arrive at a party and say quite simply, 'This is Alan', just at the time when we could begin to share our social lives, we found – what? That Alan, God rest his immortal soul, had never admitted to himself that he was a bloody poof. I tried to explain to him that the world was changing and old prejudices and stereotypes disappearing. Homosexuals like us – I mean of course, homosexuals like Alan and me,' he said this with an exaggerated carefulness that I did not much care for, 'were suddenly socially acceptable. But my arguments were to no avail. Alan sank slowly, oh so slowly that I didn't even see it at first, into a profound depression until, about eighteen months ago, I realised he had become unreachable. He was like someone living the other side of a glass wall. We could see each other but not, so to speak, hear, or talk, or touch. It was unbearable. Then last year, one spring day, he borrowed a shotgun from the head gardener and went decorously away to the edge of the lake…' he turned round and pointed towards it '… where, considerately far removed from the silk wall-paper, the brocades and the monogrammed sheets, he shot himself tastefully in the mouth.'

We had arrived at the front door. Parry paused on the threshold. 'I loved him as I have loved no-one else. But now I think that is enough about Alan.' He motioned me to go in ahead of him and when I did so I was astonished to be met by a demure, grey-faced woman who announced that lunch was ready in the dining-room.

'Mrs Craig is my daily woman,' Parry explained when she had withdrawn. 'It's a courtesy title only, though. She comes in once a week – and cooks occasionally if I have company.'

I had to admire Parry's composure. Within minutes of his finishing his tragic tale we were both spooning away at watercress soup and discussing, if I remember rightly, construction methods used in early pianoforte manufacture. Lunch was really excellent and, surprisingly, the conversation never morbid. We washed it down with a bottle of Gevry-Chambertin. But this, coupled with the tendency I share with most academics of wishing to show off in front of more senior colleagues, proved, as the meal drew towards its end, to be my undoing. 'Now was it Belloc or was it Chesterton?' I said, and quoted, 'I forget the name of the place, I forget the name of the girl, but the wine was Chambertin.'

'Belloc, almost certainly,' said Parry. 'Chesterton would have forgotten all three.' Then he looked straight at me across the table and for the first time ever his eyes were so clearly visible, so wide-open and so blue that I scarcely saw the spectacles. And he said, 'I forget the name of the place, I forget the name of the wine, but the boy was you.'

'Oh my God,' I thought, but I must have said it aloud; it must have slipped out, because Parry then said, in a flat voice, 'I appear to have been unsubtle.' And I was thinking, behind those spectacles he's been watching me all this time, watching and waiting, knowing just who and what I was, for all these years.

'Do you know something?' Parry said. 'I never really saw your face until the other day. My glasses have got thicker as the years pass and human faces have come to seem more of a blur and less coherent. Any system behind the arrangement of the features seems to be lacking. Then, as I saw you outside the newsagent's, your face sprang into focus for the first time. There was a system behind the features. No criticism intended.'

I said a chilly thank you. He was not to be put off. 'And now, Nigel, I am thinking I should like to make you a proposition. No, don't flinch. I don't mean that sort of a proposition. Where do you live?'

'In college,' I said.

'And do you like it?'

'I have two rooms. My own bathroom.'

'And are you comfortable?'

'Yes,' I said. 'It's splendid. Couldn't really be better. Nice view and a genuine medieval window to admire it through. Warm, cosy, and all meals provided.'

'And you hate it,' said Parry matter-of-factly. 'I know. I wish I had someone to share this place with, Nigel. Not a lover, I think, at my age, but a companion. And since we met last week I have found myself thinking, perhaps unwisely, that it might be you.' He peered at me again, leaning halfway across the table to do it. 'You find the idea abhorrent? Impractical? Liable to misinterpretation … or what?'

'I don't want to appear rude,' I began, but he cut me off.

'You see, Nigel, in some ways I think I know you better than you know yourself. And I am aware – as you are not, so that you will think me a monster of arrogance for saying this – that I could possibly be good for you.'

'How dare you,' I said, and stood up.

'Yes,' Parry said calmly, 'I did think that might be your reaction. There's blackberry pie on the sideboard. And cream. Do help yourself. Mrs Craig will have gone home.'

'I really couldn't eat any more,' I said – and heard the expression 'through clenched teeth' in my head.

'Nigel, do sit down. And if you like we can change the subject.'

I stayed standing. 'I don't want to change the subject, thank you very much. You've been talking to me as if you own me already. But nobody owns me and nobody's ever going to. You have in your mind some idea of me, some image of me, filtered through those God-awful spectacles, but that isn't me. It's you who you're seeing. It's you who has never loved or been loved in his life. I don't believe Alan ever existed. He was just a figment of your warped spectacles and…' I gestured around the opulent room, '…and your distorting mirrors. You invented Alan. Just as you're trying to invent me.'

'And there you rest your case,' said Parry quietly, sitting back in his chair. To my astonishment he took out a small cigar from a case in his pocket and lit it before he continued. 'It would suit you down to the ground if Alan never existed. But he did. In the churchyard, where we can take a walk after lunch if you like, you will find a stone with his name on it. The verger will tell you how he remembers Alan. Mrs Craig, when you next see her, will happily tell you his favourite menus. Or I can give you her phone number if you wish to conduct your own researches. On Monday morning you can even ask your own head of department, Professor... Professor... hell...'

'Professor Williams.'

'Thank you. Professor Williams met him. Alan cut down some trees for Professor Williams that were keeping the light off Professor Williams's garden and if you go there you will see the stumps! Three in a row. The ivy has hardly begun to grow over them.' Parry got to his feet, slowly. 'Oh yes, Alan was real. Very real. And so am I. You fail to discern me behind these spectacles of mine because you are incapable of perception, incapable of seeing, incapable of feeling anything much at all. How mistaken I've been. For a little while I'd been thinking that you had a face, Nigel, or were beginning to acquire one. But now I look at you more closely it seems to be fading away. Fading slowly away. These extraordinary glasses. I'm afraid, Nigel, you are once again ... just a blur. Now, shall we adjourn to the living-room for some coffee?'

Needless to say I didn't stay for coffee, but made my escape as quickly as I could, and I wish I could say that that was the end of the matter. But honesty compels me to admit that, over the next few days, I found myself thinking quite often, in my dreary college rooms, about Parry's unexpected proposition, and to my further surprise, considering it quite hard. The material considerations were a bit of an inducement after all, and

Parry had stressed that he was looking for a companion, not a lover. But a little whisper of newly acquired self-knowledge warned me that I would find even that hard to cope with. I had not exactly risen to the occasion when Parry had bared his soul to me. And he, not I, had been right as to which of us was the faceless one. It was mine that proved to be wanting. Behind the learned articles, the Readerships and Fellowships it was I, not Parry, who lived in a world untouched by the rays of love or friendship. I was probably not even up the challenge implied by his possibly justified belief that he could be good for me.

I decided to give myself one more chance. I wrote him a conciliatory letter in which I thanked him for lunch and invited him to dinner at college High Table.

But he never replied.

TIFFER

Long ago…

A tigress bounds sure-footedly along the narrow edge of the bath, her stripes blazing intermittently between jungle-green fronds and grasses, her eye a blazing roundel, black on yellow, her teeth fierce triangles, snarling at the sheeting rain. She is Rousseau's Tiger in a Tropical Storm, in a nearly full-size wallpaper print that covers most of the bathroom wall, making this room in Tiffer's parents' house strikingly unlike the bathrooms of any of Rory's other friends.

Rory himself is stretched out in the bath's warm shallows, alongside Tiffer. They've been sharing baths at intervals for the best part of a year, and still manage to fit in side by side – though with a little adjustment of the hips these days: they've been growing quickly since they both turned eight.

'Lighthouses,' Tiffer says, for that is what their two upstanding dicks remind him of, poking up out of the water among the reefs and headlands of their bellies, thighs and knees. No light beams from them however, so Tiffer does the next best thing, projecting his own water in a brief upward spring that then tumbles down again like rain upon his groin. A second later and Rory brings his own lighthouse sparkling into commission in just the same way.

Tiffer's elder sister looks up from the washbasin just alongside the bath. 'Stop that,' she says. She has come in here to brush her bedtime teeth – and perhaps also to cast her eye over the spectacle of her little brother naked in the water with his best friend. 'Stop it. It's dirty.'

'Can't stop till it finishes,' Tiffer answers, sweetly, reasonably, unchastened. And for a further half minute he and Rory continue to pretend they are lighthouses as if to prove the point. Rory thinks of other things they do together, and have been doing during the course of this last wonderful year and which Tiffer's sister has never seen them at. She might think them even dirtier if she knew. But to Rory, and to Tiffer, they don't seem dirty. Just good.

It's almost an effort now for Rory to remember how it all began. The wonderful improbability of it. The serendipity of it. Not that that word has entered Rory's vocabulary just yet. Tiffer – actual name Christopher Marks – joining Rory's school last September. Three months older than Rory and bigger, burlier and more boisterous. Better at football too. But it was football that became his undoing – and the happier sparking off of what has followed. Rory, standing at the edge of the playground where the ground rises just a few inches as asphalt gives way to turf – on a rough grassy patch where a lichen-clad, still leafy apple tree stands. Raised voices a little distance away, and Rory turns to see that Tiffer has tried to join a football game played by the nine-year-olds. Rory could have told him it wouldn't do. Tiffer is roundly told to get lost and then the ball is kicked gratuitously against his backside as he turns rebuffed away.

By chance he is now walking towards Rory. Who calls to him. 'Hey, Tiffer!' And Tiffer comes on towards him, relieved, unconsciously, that Rory's greeting has given him a destination, somewhere to make for when a moment ago he had only somewhere to retreat from, and this masks to some extent the ignominy of his dismissal. It's a matter of a few yards only. So now here is Tiffer standing facing Rory and, because of the tiny rise in the ground under the apple tree, Tiffer's eyeline is an inch or two below Rory's instead of the usual half inch above, and for the first time Tiffer finds himself looking up at

Rory. The high afternoon sun is more or less behind Tiffer but not so completely as to reduce him, in Rory's eyes, to a silhouette. 'They wouldn't let me play with them,' he says, his deep blue eyes meeting Rory's in a candid gaze. It's the first time he's taken much notice of Rory, let alone confided to him such an ego-bruising summary of events. And Rory sees that Tiffer's admission has cost him something. Tears have welled up in those blue eyes, have overflowed their lower lids and are now balancing among his long black eyelashes like dew on spiders' webs.

This in turn makes something well up inside Rory, though it isn't tears. He doesn't know what it is. If he's ever had intimations of this feeling before, they've never been as strong as this. All he knows is that it's the most important feeling that he's ever had. Wonderful, shocking, surprising, like sudden light and heat. And also – puzzlingly – it hurts. He feels as if his heart will burst. And the sensation is doubly powerful, doubly strong, because somehow, mysteriously, the knowledge is given to him that Tiffer is experiencing the same thing.

Some gesture seems to be needed. But none comes easily. If they were standing side by side Rory might risk placing an arm across Tiffer's shoulder. (Risky because normally only the older boy is supposed to do that, and it might in any case be roughly shaken off.) A hug is out of the question – they're both too old for that. Words then, perhaps. But what words? Older people have phrases in their heads like, 'I love you,' and, 'Be mine for ever', or simply, 'Darling.' None of these is available to Rory, aged not quite eight. Which is probably just as well. Instead he says, quite softly, 'Show me your willy,' and is moved rather than surprised when Tiffer unquestioningly obliges, hitching up a leg of his shorts to reveal his ivory-skinned little soldier to his new friend. And Rory, with only the briefest look around to check that no teacher is at close range, follows suit.

It hasn't been a very public sort of friendship. They don't spend all their break times together at school, nor always sit next to each other at lunch, nor have they asked to have adjacent desks. So not everyone is aware how close they have become. Most of the time they share together is out of school. They are forever visiting each other's houses. For both of them home is a working farm, with all that that entails in the way of open spaces to play in, and private outbuildings where they can enjoy their secret pleasures in the dim light. Because farms are necessarily spaced widely apart their long-suffering parents spend much time at weekends driving them to and fro. They sleep over at each other's places often, and always, always demand to sleep together in a double bed. Like the shared bath and the lighthouse game this has become a tradition – honoured now with some eleven months' observance.

Twenty minutes after bathing and the two boys are tucked up together in the spare room double bed. The routine is pretty fixed. Tiffer calls, 'Pyjamas down below knees.' His pyjamas are blue like his eyes; Rory's, though his eyes are also blue, are red and silver striped. Both pairs slide down. Rory switches on the torch which lies – placed there with some forethought as always – between their two torsos, pointing down. The top sheet, tented over raised knees, becomes a bright-lit cyclorama in front of which their two cocks take centre stage. They're stiff of course – which the boys are hardly aware of, since that's how they always are, at the age of eight, when they get them out or take notice of them for any purpose whatever. Now they're to be played with and explored. They are slightly different, because Rory, unlike Tiffer, has been circumcised. They don't take much account of this either. People are born differently after all. It's probably just like the fact that older generations were born with wildly different shapes and sizes of nose. Like the fact that Rory's hair is fair and curly while Tiffer's is straight and nearly black. Just one of those things.

WT is what they call their nocturnal game. Willy tickling. Which is exactly what it is. (Even years later, Rory will never be able to hear the initials, referred to in news bulletins, of the World Trade Organisation, without experiencing a tug of memory that takes him in imagination back into bed with Tiffer.) 'Lovely WT,' says Tiffer as he runs a finger for the umpteenth time along the underside ridge of Rory's small erection, and traces its continuation in the seam that rides up over the dome of his ball-sac until it disappears mysteriously into the tight vortex of his bum: a place that Tiffer has occasionally explored with a tentative finger, amid Rory's feigned protests and secret delight. Lovely WT. Funny, the use of the word lovely by an eight-year-old. Tiffer doesn't consciously make the connection between that word and the shorter one that it derives from. One might almost say, a pre-pubescent Freudian slip. Half an hour later both boys are fast asleep and in a position they would never consider adopting while awake: enfolded in each other's arms.

Not so long ago…

Marco is in bed in his college. But it is not his own bed, nor his own room. Bed and room both belong to a fellow first-year student, whose name is Rory and who is right now snuggled up against Marco's left flank, contentedly asleep.

Marco hardly dares to breathe. Not because he is afraid of waking Rory up but because he is afraid of waking up himself. Afraid of finding that the beautiful journey of the heart that has been his for the past six weeks and has cumulated in this night has only been a journey in a dream. Yes, it's been as good as that.

Marco met Rory, or rather simply saw him, at the auditions for a Dramsoc play. Both of them were cast – which was a bit of a coup, in their first term as they were. In a play set during the First World War, they were given the parts of brother officers. As rehearsals got under way Marco found it wasn't difficult to play his role with conviction. Understated affection, poignant tenderness, masked by the stoical bravado that war engenders were easy to convey, he discovered, when he was acting opposite Rory. Rory with his fresh pink cheeks, light brown curls and sky blue eyes. Rory who was as reserved and gentle off-stage as the character he played when on it. Rory who was diminutive and cute, yet blessed with impressively developed little muscles… Marco had just managed to winkle out from him the information that he was brought up on a farm.

It was all a new sensation for Marco. Half Italian as he was, he'd always taken it for granted that he was attracted to girls. Even if, at the age of eighteen, he hadn't yet bedded or fallen in love with any. But there had been plenty whom he'd liked, had been attracted to, and anyway, time was on his side. To say nothing of his looks: the raven hair, the lustrous dark eyes, and other attractive features of which it sometimes seemed that the fact of having at least one Italian parent was the only cast-iron guarantee.

Attractive. Attraction. Attracted to girls? The thought made Marco's lips twitch involuntarily towards a smile. He now realised that before meeting Rory he hadn't known what attracted meant. Did that make him gay? He didn't care. He was way past worrying about niceties of nomenclature. People might call him an Inuit, for all he cared, or a fork-lift truck. Sticks and stones… He knew only that he wanted Rory more than he'd wanted anything in his life. But life thus far lived had given him no guidance as to how he might set about getting him. And Rory himself – though not, admittedly, publicly flaunting a girlfriend – was giving no clues as to whether, let alone how, he might be got.

The last-night after-show party might have proved the moment of truth. Yet somehow it didn't. Marco and Rory met often in the course of it – as how could they not in the handful of adjacent student rooms where the party was being held. They stood near together. They talked, about the play, and about other, less consequential things. And all the time Rory smiled sweetly at Marco and Marco wanted to ravish him. In his frustration Marco, untypically, drank too much and was sick in the gutter during his solitary walk back to his own college room. What was the point, he asked himself foggily, in having the looks of a model, plus the size and strength of an oarsman, if those things couldn't deliver that on which you'd set your heart? Marco's big athletic build might come in handy in a fight but, in thinking about Rory, fighting was the last thing that came to mind.

Marco and Rory shared the same college but the college was a large one. They studied different subjects, ate at different ends of the dining hall with different sets of friends. They didn't even live in the same building. Marco lived above the main quadrangle, while Rory's room was in an annexe around the corner in a nearby street. They might not meet again properly until the next play in which they both got cast. Which might not happen. Even if it did, then what?

Twenty-four hours after the end of the post-production party Marco, having spent most of the day recovering from a very unpleasant hangover, finds himself unable to sleep. It is two in the morning. He gets up, puts on jeans (without underpants) trainers (without socks) and, after a moment's thought, a black denim jacket – his new one with the rivets – with nothing underneath that except his manly chest. It is a mild autumn night and he isn't going far – and he's only just eighteen.

Marco knows where Rory's room is, though he's never been there. Nor has he ever before stood in the street below his window in the middle of the night – nor below anyone else's – and looked up at it from the exquisite misery of unrequited love. This night is going to be a first.

The streets are not entirely empty. It is after all a student town. A few other young people are wandering home from parties or setting off on mysterious errands of their own, alone or occasionally in twos. The few youngsters Marco passes do not see anything amiss with Marco's sartorial style – bare-chested on a November night in the English Midlands.

Marco is quickly there. In the building where Rory sleeps all lights are out – save one. Rory, as Marco knows, has the room above the front door. And that's the light that's on. For a moment Marco's heart seems to stop – and so does his whole life. He wonders whether he will find the courage to climb the stairs and knock at Rory's door, a door which may open into who knows what new chapter of his life.

'Marco, I'm over here.'

Marco turns. Rory is standing watching him from the pavement across the street. As far as Marco can see by the light of the nearest – not all that near – street lamp he's wearing jeans and a sweater but nothing else, not even shoes. Yet, when he's crossed the road to Rory, Marco, standing in the gutter, finds his eyes looking an inch or so upwards to meet Rory's who, bare-footed though he is, is given a few extra inches by the accident of the kerb. The full extent of Rory's beauty, outward and inner, hits Marco like a punch just below his diaphragm. He takes the onslaught like a man, but can not stop the tears that mortifyingly spring to his eyes. For a moment they stand looking at each other in surprise, not knowing what to say. Neither is going to ask the other what he is doing in this street at such an hour, loitering and half-clad. Sharing a glass house, you do not ask: *please pass the stones.*

Rory at last speaks. He is the one who is nearer home ground. 'D'you want to come up? I've got some whisky.'

The whisky is nice but barely necessary. They sip at it, sitting side by side on Rory's slim bed. It seems a more natural place to settle – though neither of them thinks this consciously – than in any of the chairs. To Marco's surprise they don't talk much. It doesn't seem to matter. The little they do find to say is so unimportant that they won't remember it in the morning. After a while Rory leans backwards on the bed till he is resting his back against the wall. He seems totally at ease and relaxed, as Marco has never seen him before. At ease and relaxed himself he leans back, side by side with Rory. They turn and exchange a smile of the kind that is usually the preserve of people who know each other very well indeed. And Marco is quite sure of himself, and of Rory, when a minute later he places a firm but gentle hand on Rory's trim taut thigh.

And now, a couple of hours later, with Rory asleep beside him, Marco is looking back in wonder at the best thing that's happened in his life. He has sucked a cock for the first time, and had his sucked (what an unanticipated miracle of exquisite sensation!) in return. He has fucked Rory gently, mindful of the boy's smaller size in all areas and Rory, with no such constraints to consider, has eagerly and more easily plumbed Marco's hidden depths as well.

Where does all this come from? Marco asks himself, safe and strong now in his new intimacy with Rory, the adored one, who is fast asleep on his shoulder. How do we know this thing about ourselves – about each other? How came it that I was right about Rory, that he instinctively got it right about me? What is it that steers us, like ships that pass on the dark ocean, into each other's way? Rory stirs in his sleep and nuzzles against him. Contentedly he splutters a little sound. Like a sneeze or a snuffle. Or almost even a word. To Marco's ears it sounds like 'Tiffer'

Anthony McDonald

SUNDAYS

...In a town in the English Midlands, 1980-81

I

I hate Sundays. In the evening I usually go to the Duke of Clarence for a pint or two, then collect a takeaway on my way home to watch TV. This evening in late December the pub is nearly empty. Outside it's tipping down sleet. I'm getting up to go at the end of my second Guinness when a smallish, slightly-built young person arrives with a drink at the next table, at which he sits down, and sinks immediately into the folds of a black duffel-coat. We catch each other's eye. Half-smiles of recognition. I'm fairly sure he's the new ASM. Alone, his first weekend in a strange town on a dreary Sunday night. Do I go over to him? Talk to him? No. It probably isn't him at all. He'll think I'm trying to pick him up. He won't remember he's met me – that David introduced us, standing on the pavement outside the theatre. He may be the most boring young man in the world, and I'll be lumbered for the evening. By now I'm halfway to the door so I can't go back. My feet are making up my mind for me. But now I can feel his eyes on me. They are staring at me from behind – I just know this – boring holes into the back of my head. So it is him after all. He does know who I am. He is very aware of me. I could turn round and go back. Could I? Do I? No, I don't. It's too late. I can't.

The technical rehearsal of the pantomime was scheduled to take two days. I looked in at the end of the first afternoon to see how things were going and whether there was any chance David would be able to get home for tea. I went and sat in the dress circle. They were running the last few minutes of Act One. David was

185

imprisoned in his transformation costume, while the complicated business of attaching his sequinned train to three tiny hooks under cover of a dance routine and then flying it upward at the end of the act was tried time and time again. Someone scampered in and sat down just behind me. The new ASM. I turned and spoke to him over my shoulder. 'It's a bit of a shock seeing your boyfriend dressed like that.' Just in case he thought I found it the most natural thing in the world. 'I'm not sure I like it very much. Though of course someone has to play the Dame.' He didn't attempt an answer. I went on, 'It was you I saw...?'

'In the pub on Sunday night? Yes.'

'Sorry I ignored you. I'd gone before I'd quite realised who you were.' I was simplifying things.

'I wasn't quite sure till you'd gone, either.'

'I'm afraid I've forgotten your name,' I said.

'Graham. I've forgotten yours too.'

'Rory,' I said.

I had begged David to ask the stage manager if I could have a job backstage during the run of the panto. I started on January the third. On January the fourth the box office manager went sick and the general manager begged me to put in as many hours in that little aquarium as I could be spared from my work backstage. Nine months out of work, then two jobs in two days. Three, actually. David and I have a two-man show based on the life, letters and piano music of Mozart. David reads the letters, I play the solos. It's quite straightforward but I do have to put in a lot of practice before we do the show in public. We had arranged to do it as a late-night event on January the sixteenth. So my days were suddenly crammed. Nine till ten o'clock, practise the piano with freezing fingers in the orchestra pit; ten till twelve-thirty, brave the box office at its panto season busiest; twelve thirty, down a couple of beers with David in Shipman's; one thirty till nine thirty, work the scene changes and the sliding iceberg effects at matinee and evening show with only the briefest break in between; nine thirty, more beer, supper and bed – with David of course.

At the end of that week Graham changed his digs. He'd found somewhere closer to the theatre. As it happened it was even closer to where David and I lived. He told me about it over coffee in the green room, woebegone blue eyes gazing into mine. The new flat was damp and unheated, almost unfurnished, and as his mother hadn't yet sent his trunk down from Lancashire, and the trunk contained his bed linen, he was having to sleep curled up under cushions. He asked me if I could lend him a sleeping-bag.

'Graham does surprise me,' I told David, explaining why we were walking in to work with me carrying a sleeping-bag, 'He's been around a bit and looks able to take care of himself, yet in everything he says, even in the way he looks at you, he seems to be calling out, help me, I'm lost.'

'Well, watch it,' David said. 'He'll be moving in with us next.'

I was part of the stage right crew. Graham, stage left. Viewed from the side the stage has a different character from when seen from the front. It has the appearance of a river, a long narrow stream of bright light, kingfisher blue, flowing between tall shady banks of wing flats, sliders and machinery. Bright pantomime creatures dart in its currents, while we, a totally different, sombre-hued population lurk in the shadows on either side, out of sight of all except our opposite numbers. They, stage crew left, stand one or two to a crevice, awaiting the next scene change. Joining them briefly from time to time are actors waiting to make their entrances. Some are blowing kisses at us across the great divide, or mimicking the action in progress on the stage. They look so close that you feel you can reach out and touch them. An actor – David – can cross that stream in seven good strides. A crewman cannot cross it ever. Directly opposite me stands one particular dark blur with a pale face attached. He looks a bit more bored and hunched up than the rest. Graham. Almost close enough to touch but a hundred miles apart. What is he looking at? Another pale-faced blur, like a reflection in a dark mirror. He is looking at me.

My mother travelled up from Kent for the Mozart show. We fed her trout and sparkling wine, then delivered her into the audience at the start of the pantomime, while David gave his all as Mother Goose and I heaved sixteen-foot flats around, wearing gloves on this occasion so as not to damage my hands too much, my fingers running through Mozart figurations inside them. Half an hour after curtain-down the pit piano had been hauled up and placed centre-stage, and David and I were transformed by three-piece suits and performing to an audience of about sixty. We were considered a success. There was a party afterwards. 'Do you realise,' David said later, 'that at least three men kissed you goodnight in front of your mother?'

'That's as it should be,' I answered, confident at that heady moment that nothing in life could have consequences I wouldn't know how to handle. 'By the way, Graham's very pleased with the sleeping-bag. I said I hoped he'd be comfortable in it – and then that I wished I could be in it with him.'

'You didn't!'

'I did.'

'It's time there was a law against you,' David said.

*

Actually, Graham looks a bit like Tiffer. Tiffer (short for Christopher) is the boy whose photo I carry in my wallet. He's nine in the picture, sitting at the wheel of his father's tractor and looking as if the world were his oyster. Probably by now it is. We met at seven, fell in love at eight, and from then on we slept together as often as circumstances permitted, till we were thirteen. Maybe he's now six foot seven and married, with five children. Don't care to know. I do know, though, that Graham, who is twenty, reminds me of Tiffer at thirteen. He also has a small gap between his top front teeth, something that is considered attractive in a young man. I have a similar gap myself.

I was talking about Graham in the pub with David – and Clive, the director of the theatre. They couldn't see his appeal somehow. 'Those pallid limbs,' Clive said.

'Nobody looks their best in January,' I countered.

'Rory's mad for the boy,' David explained coolly.

'As a matter of fact,' I said, after a bracing swallow of White Shield, 'I've asked him to join me for a lunchtime drink at the Queen's Head if he's on his own tomorrow. Since I shall be on my own. Though I can foresee that leading to complications. I can't imagine him shopping for his weekend. I shall probably end up having to carve my pork chop in two. I suppose such a thing is possible?'

David raised his eyes towards heaven. A bit melodramatically, I thought.

But Graham didn't come to the Queen's Head. He'd had a better offer, from a girl in the pantomime chorus. 'I'm sorry I didn't make it yesterday,' he told me on Monday. 'I don't like not to keep appointments. Only I overslept.'

Well, that was one way of putting it, but it was nice of him to apologise. I told David this. He could have said, I told you so, but was kind enough not to.

Graham came and sat down beside me on a laundry basket full of props behind the backcloth. He told me all about the girl. 'I've screwed her of course,' he said. 'But where do I go from here?' I can't remember what advice I gave. Though I did think it was better for him to have a girlfriend than be hanging around a twenty-eight year-old poofter like me. Selfless? Self-protective, more like.

Whatever advice I did give him, it was it was clearly not good enough. It was a solitary Graham who wandered into Shipman's the next Saturday night. He looked disconsolate, yet eager for companionship. Wagging his tail, yet half expecting to be kicked. It's nearly closing time and after one drink we are all out in the street. David's car is nearby. He drives off, leaving Graham and me to walk together towards our two flats, his in Denmark Road, mine in Palmerston. I have eaten, Graham has not. We decide to get an Indian takeaway for Graham from a restaurant that serves drinks while you wait. It's a good idea, but I get an appetite as soon as we enter the spice-fragrant place and we end up with two takeaways rather than one. Never mind.

We're slightly nearer to my flat – David's and mine – and so that's where we go to eat. It's something I haven't done for a few years: take a younger boy home on a Saturday night. I'm very conscious of the way the flat looks, and of Graham's reaction to it. It's an oddly upside down place, with the bedroom on the ground floor by the front door, while the stairs rise beside it, emerging into the kitchen; the living room is entered from there.

Graham likes the flat. It's warmer and more comfortable than his. We polish off our curries, then at last Graham, whose curiosity has been nibbling at his natural diffidence for an hour or more, asks the question that sooner or later everyone must ask. 'Where has David gone?'

'He has a cottage near Oxford which he goes back to most weekends.'

'Why don't you go with him?'

'Because he shares the cottage with someone else.'

There was a moment's silence. Then Graham said, 'That's a bit rough, isn't it? On you, I mean.'

'Bit rough on everyone. But we've juggled around with the situation for three years now and it's on a sort of even keel. David shares his life with me, and his mortgage with someone else. Terry – the someone else – also has his own little lover, who David isn't supposed to know about.'

'So why does David keep going back?'

'Property, tradition, and a kind of loyalty. Probably in that order. Also, Terry's a sort of backstop. They'd been together fifteen years before David and I met. In David's eyes I'm still the flighty kid who may not go the distance.'

'And will you?'

I shrugged.

Graham decided he would have to go back to Denmark Road to get some cigarettes, but was determined to return and continue the conversation. It seemed silly for me to sit alone doing nothing till he returned, so we walked there together. He gave me a quick tour of his grotty flat, gave me back my sleeping-bag (his mother had sent his trunk at last: he had his duvet now) then we walked back again to mine. We made coffee and watched television till it went on the blink – it overheats after a solid hour of use and has to be shut down – and then we just talked till half-past two. Then I walked back with him as far as his front door. He needed to give me his key, he said, so I could get in and wake him in the morning. He was definitely going to have a drink with me next day, but was sure that if I didn't intervene, he'd oversleep. It was one of the crazier arrangements I'd made in my life. I pocketed Graham's door-key and thought, as I walked home, that with a bit of company for a change, I might end up not hating Sundays quite so much.

II

'Your little friend helped you wash up, I see.' David has eyes like a hawk.

'Has he put the teaspoons in the wrong drawer?'

'No. The bread-knife. You know,' he went on, examining the utensil carefully before restoring it to its proper place, 'you and Graham are very bad for each other.'

'He's just a bit lost and helpless at the moment,' I came back. 'In a strange town in the dead of winter, living in a cold miserable flat. Nowhere to go at weekends. He needs a bit of looking after. I happen to be around.'

'You also happen to be quite the wrong person for the job. You're far too much alike. Also,' he went on in his severest voice, 'you're kidding yourself. You wouldn't be doing this big social work act on the boy if he wasn't actually rather pretty.'

Well, at least David has come round to my way of thinking on that.

There was a party at the theatre the following Saturday. David and I had been invited, Graham had not. Walking back home afterwards, and after David had driven off, I saw Graham's light still on, and found I couldn't go on past. He was startled by my knock. He'd been smoking a joint and playing his guitar and for some reason thought I might be the police. He took me upstairs and made coffee. We were both a bit down – he because he hadn't been invited to the party, I because David had just left. But wallowing in each other's depression and forensically discussing the shortcomings of the theatre cheered us both up, and Graham brightly suggested we head out and buy a bottle of wine. I pointed out that it was well after midnight and that we might not have much luck. I suggested instead that we pay a visit to the Queen's Head ... that was, if he didn't have any *a priori* objection to being taken to gay clubs. He did not.

I couldn't help feeling pleased with myself as I walked into the Queen's Head with Graham in tow. He looked very presentable, I thought. The sort of person you could be seen alongside without wanting to place a paper bag over his head. Our arrival attracted those fixed blank stares from strangers that I'd learnt to take as a compliment, while the open-mouthed astonishment of those people I did know – including several who worked at the theatre – was even more eloquent.

I didn't suggest a dance. We sat together at a table in a corner, drank a lot, and talked about being gay – or not. 'How does someone know they're gay?' Graham asked. 'I mean, I know that I'm not, but...' I gave him the usual lecture, about trial and error in adolescence, then settling down, if you were straight, into doing what most other people did, and what society in any case expects. Adding that gay youngsters found a bit more self-scrutiny was called for as the process led them little by little along a less usual track. Perhaps mischievously, I added, 'David was a married man of twenty-two when he realised he was gay,' Graham, still twenty, opened his eyes unusually wide and said, 'Christ!'

We changed the subject. A pint or so later Graham came back to something I'd slid into the conversation earlier. 'You said I looked OK just now. Do you really think so?'

'How do you expect me to answer?' I said. 'But yes, all right. Because I'm a healthy young poofter I not unnaturally find you attractive. Will that do?'

'See what you mean,' he said thoughtfully.

We staggered back to Palmerston Road with an armful of bottles and lurched from topic to topic for a further three hours. Graham finally crashed out in my armchair at half past five. I woke him by scratching the top of his head and told him I was going to bed. He could either walk back to Denmark Road or re-acquaint himself with my sleeping-bag among cushions on my living-room floor.

When I awoke in the morning the sun was shining and I didn't have the hangover I deserved. Two cheering discoveries. Then came the realisation, thudding down like a mallet, that there was a young man asleep upstairs. It wasn't a guilty feeling, just an *Oh God, here we have a situation* feeling. I had behaved myself impeccably, Graham wasn't gay, and David was in any case spending the weekend with someone else. This was all very fine; the problem would lie in explaining it to David. Pretend it hadn't happened? Greet him brightly with, 'Guess who stayed over on Saturday night?' The whole thing, thanks to this heart-searching, was gaining an importance it didn't deserve. Fuck it. I got up and made coffee for us both.

We went for a walk by the river. Not beside the flood channel where there are weasels, and it's enchanted and just for David and me, but only along the main stretch. It was February the first and it felt deceptively like spring. Among the reeds we passed two young men who looked as though they'd just spent a night together for the first time. They wished us a familiar good morning with twinkly smiles, imagining, I suppose, the same about us.

Make the best of it, Rory. Yes, it would be better if David were here. It would be nicer if you weren't feeling the weight of an unreasonable guilt in the pit of your stomach. But here you are on a spring morning with ducks paddling, and this sweet and gentle creature by your side, trotting happily along and chatting non-stop about his dog, about the countryside in Yorkshire where he was brought up... And he likes you, which is the best thing of the lot. A morning like this was made to be enjoyed, so shut up, Rory, and do just that.

'That's because you're twenty and I'm twenty-eight,' I said at one point. I don't remember what we were differing over, only that we were leaping over the puddles under the bridge that carries the by-pass. Memory's like that.

'You keep harping on the difference in our ages,' Graham said, landing with a bit of a splash. 'I hardly notice it. What does it matter? You're just you and I'm just me.'

Rather flattering, that. But do I really go on about my age a lot? I don't feel older than he is. I can turn cartwheels as well as he can. Run as fast. (We've checked both those out.) I must be wishing too much that I was younger. I only feel twenty. Yet he keeps telling me that I keep telling him I'm twenty-eight. Dear God!

I did us roast lamb for lunch, then I went to the theatre to do some piano practice while he practised his guitar back at his flat. He came to join me later and I gave him a piano lesson... Well, he's been asking me for some time about that. Then we joined the rest of the backstage staff in the Mail Coach for a folk evening. He was going to play his guitar but his nerve failed him and he didn't. Instead we both got drunk.

I steered him home. He was full of despair by now. About his lack of success with women. About his guitar playing. About his lack of talent and general worthlessness. 'Very busy being sorry for ourself tonight, aren't we,' I said.

'You're laughing at me,' he said, though he was trying hard not to laugh himself.

'You need laughing at sometimes. And to laugh at yourself. But I'm only laughing because I'm fond of you. I hope you know that.'

'I wish there were a few more people like you around the place,' he said. 'You're worth more than most of the rest put together.'

Well done, Rory. Keep on turning out the feed lines and eventually, when everyone's incoherent with drink, you'll hear what you want.

We went back to his flat with a takeaway. When we'd eaten it Graham said, 'I'm going to be sick in a minute.'

'No, you're not.'

'Then I'm going to bed.'

I stood up. 'You're certainly not going to do that.'

He stood up. 'I'm going to be sick. I deserve it.' He started to cry.

'You're a bloody fool.' I ruffled his dark hair.

'Yes, I'm a bloody fool. My own fault. Christ, I feel awful. I think I'm going to throw up right now.' He lurched a bit. Tears spilled down his cheeks.

I lurched a bit. 'Stop wallowing in it. You're coming for a walk around the block. With me.' He sank back onto his chair.' Don't argue,' I said, though he was hardly doing that. I yanked him to his feet, marched him once round the block, then delivered him to his front door again. Depression, sulks and tears had gone. He told me next day that he wasn't sick after I'd left him, but went straight to bed and was asleep before the room had had time to spin round once.

*

'Why are all the windows open?' David asked.

'I wanted to give the place an airing,' I said. Graham smokes a lot, and any room he occupies for very long ends up smelling like an ash-tray. I'd opened the windows the previous night and forgotten to close them.

'Has that child been here again?'

'Yes. He came round on Saturday night.'

'Why?'

'We'd been to a pub and taken some bottles out with us.'

'The pubs were already closing when I left you. So it wasn't a pub you went to but a club. Right?'

'It was the Queen's Head, which is both a pub and a club. OK?'

'What time were you there till?'

'About two o'clock, I think.'

'Why does the radio alarm say five a.m?'

'I played Graham some tapes. I must have forgotten to reset it.'

'And what did you do on Sunday?'

'I cooked Graham lunch and I went to a folk evening in the Mail Coach.'

'You? A folk evening? At the Mail Coach?'

'Most of the stage management were there. Tom was singing...'

'And Graham was there.'

'Yes.'

'Did you arrive with him?'

'Yes.'

'Did you leave with him?'

'Yes.'

'And were seen to do so by the whole stage management?'

'I suppose so.'

'You suppose so. And what inference do you suppose they drew?'

'What they inferred or didn't infer is their business, not mine.'

'But it also happens to be my business, or had you forgotten that?' There was a pause and I could see David's chest heave. I knew what was coming. 'Did Graham stay here Saturday night?'

'Yes.'

'Why didn't you tell me before?'

Here we go, I thought. 'You didn't ask until now. I need hardly add that he slept on the floor upstairs, in my sleeping-bag.'

'God, you don't do things by halves! Do you think perhaps I should be feeling grateful there's still room for me in the bed?'

David seems to think I did it all on purpose, to hurt him. Why must life be so difficult? Why do non-existent problems have to rise up and become such stumbling blocks?

That week was all words. At least, the words are all that remain of it now. There were Graham's. 'David's stopped talking to me.' There were mine. 'I'm sorry.' David's. 'You can't play fairy godfather to that boy. Nor can any poofter. Your motives will always be suspect.' Later, 'I'm an older man, you're a younger one: I'm jealous, quite simply.' Why does David harp on about the difference in our ages? I hardly notice it. David's just David and I'm just me. Anyway, what's all the fuss about? I don't have designs on the boy, though I notice that every other gay man around the place seems to have. I'm not going to leave David and run off with him. Graham says, 'Can't he see that we're just good friends?' Just good friends... Dear, dear Graham, don't you yet know that you never, ever, use that expression if you want to be believed?

The pantomime closed on Saturday. Then the work really started. Seven weeks had passed since the set went up, and no-one remembered the order in which it had been put together. And whoever cross-threaded the screws or rendered them slot-less by careless use of a screwdriver or jammed the pin-hinges with paint is either not around or not admitting it. Striking the set took half the night, and half the skin off my hands. Graham and I took an infinite number of mangled screws out of an infinite number of pieces of wood, then got the job of carrying all the rostra down the road to the furniture store in the dark together, then manhandling all the flats upstairs into the paint shop. Graham managed to set off a fire-extinguisher with which, in his efforts to aim it away from the newly painted scenery for Guys and Dolls, he drenched me thoroughly. He made amends by cooking me an omelette at four in the morning.

Sunday we began the fit-up for Guys and Dolls. We continued on Monday, working without a break for lunch or supper, until two the following morning. By the time we were putting the finishing touches to the set before the dress rehearsal began in the evening everything was a blur. Rushing upstairs into the carpenters' workshop to return a hammer and screwdriver, I ran full-tilt into Terry. I didn't stop to chat. 'You look as though you've seen a ghost,' said Graham a minute later.

'I've just seen Terry,' I said.

'Terry?'

'Co-owner of David's cottage in Oxfordshire.'

'Oh hell. Did he see you?'

Apparently he had. He came back later and had a blazing row with David. He too had seen a ghost. He believed that David had finished with me a year earlier. To find that I was now not only sharing a flat with David but working in the same theatre had given him a dreadful shock.

David was a bit edgy at the end of the dress rehearsal, when we set off for home on foot. 'Wait for me,' said Graham. 'I'll walk with you.'

'I'm going,' said David, and went.

Graham rushed to get his coat, realising he'd added to the tension rather than lessening it, then the two of us set off after David, dogging his footsteps a hundred yards behind. I called to David to stop and wait for us but he wouldn't. I knew what he wanted to happen instead: what I had to do next. 'Look,' I told Graham, 'if I keep on walking with you a hundred yards behind David all the way to Denmark Road it's going to make all our domestic situations more difficult than they need to be. So, sorry, but goodnight, and see you tomorrow.' Then I sprinted away up the dark street to catch David up, leaving Graham to walk home alone. Haring along, I knew that I looked as ridiculous from behind as I did from in front.

III

There were three of us on each side of the stage for Guys and Dolls. Graham and I had been placed on the same stage left team now – it was hardly a secret that we liked to be together – and with us was a boy called Mick. We lived, the three of us, huddled up on a laundry basket behind the proscenium arch when we were not in use. We made a rather handsome trio. This had quite a bit to do with Mick whose own looks – which could make him a fortune if he ever cares to try – upped the average somewhat. He is a little Viking boy of nineteen, with wild blond hair, bright blue eyes and an impish smile. Sitting on our laundry basket together, clad in uniform black jeans and roll-necks, our little trio became a focus of attention for the acting company which, girls excepted, was at that time almost entirely gay. Across our corner ran a hefty beam on which the three of us used to practise pull-ups. Not to be outdone the actors joined in, between their cues. Including David. We got up to fifteen per show. Which made thirty a day when there was a matinee.

Graham and I were now practically living together whenever David was away, in the sense that when we were not together there was some reason for it and each knew exactly where the other was, what he was doing, and when we would next meet up to eat. As for when we were at work together we were scarcely ever further apart than the length of whatever piece of scenery we were handling … and that was when not huddling shoulder to shoulder on our laundry basket with Mick.

I flirted outrageously with Mick, who loved it, though he was as straight as a die, and it worried David not at all. I deliberately didn't flirt with Graham, and perversely that worried David all the more. He took the cessation of frivolity as a danger signal. There were conversations late at night.

'I don't care about you flirting with Mick. He isn't available. Graham is.'

'Graham's straight.'

'He'd go to bed with you like a shot in return for a square meal. You know that.' There was no way I could pretend to myself that I cared for both boys equally. But I'd no intention of taking Graham to bed. There was no physical need to. David and I are a horny pair and make love, one way or another, most days of the working week. Lust wasn't the biggest danger to be looked for in my relationship with Graham. If only because there was another one: the enjoyment of power – one of the few things that can draw lust's teeth.

It seemed suddenly that I had the power to get Graham his next job. People tend not to believe me when I tell them I was general manager of the Maltings Theatre in Berkshire when I was just twenty-five, so I don't go on about it much. But Graham has applied for a job there as DSM – that's deputy stage manager, one rank above that of assistant stage manager, ASM, which is his current post – and I wrote a letter supporting his application. They wrote promptly and interestedly back, and Graham began to take more of an interest in my brief past.

I vetted his letter of application for that job – unnecessarily, it turned out: he was a capable little letter writer. I'd done other things as well as that. Advised him, when he got elected Equity deputy by default (it's a job that no-one ever wants) how to avoid getting squashed between the twin mill-stones of union and management. I taught him how to cook cabbage so it doesn't go soggy, helped him compose a letter to the tax office about his arrears and showed him an exercise to get rid of his slouch. To say nothing of the piano lessons...

He enjoyed all this immensely. I need hardly add that the same went for me. I felt strong and useful and wise. With David it's always the other way round.

It was after hearing me play the piano at the Mozart evening that Graham began to work hard at the guitar, and took to playing it to me every time we were alone together. And it was after I'd told him I fancied myself as a bit of writer, and kept a diary, that he began to keep a diary of his own. I never read what he put in it, though I saw it: an exercise book full of a neat flowing handwriting that was startlingly at odds with his chaotic approach to most things in life. I don't know if imitation is the sincerest form of flattery – but it is the most flattering.

*

I took Graham to the club again the next Saturday night. To my astonishment he asked me to dance with him. So we danced. Companionably, not sensually. He looked nice, wearing his best green jacket over his open-necked white shirt … and his flares. He looked as out-of-date as I did (me in my old flares too, of course) but all the cuter because of that. After we sat down I asked him primly, 'Are you in the habit of dancing with men?'

'No. That was the first time. But I just like dancing. It makes no difference who with.' Hmm. He looked into my eyes a bit urgently. 'Was I all right, though? Do I dance OK?'

'Yes,' I said, 'you're fine,' and felt something pricking at my eyes and throat.

He slept on my living-room floor again, in that adventured sleeping-bag of mine that now looked like becoming his. In the morning there was four inches of snow outside.

Snow brings out different things in different people. David hates it. He curls up into a small squirrel-like ball and has to be stroked and comforted till it has gone away again. Me, it brings me to life. Brings out the explorer in me. I discovered, this sudden white morning, that it had the same effect on Graham. We drove out rather recklessly through a landscape like a white womb, for a drink in a snow-thatched village pub. 'It's not just that it's beautiful,' Graham said, as the car did a semi-circular pirouette near the canal bridge. 'For one day in the year everybody and everything is different.' We drove home even more recklessly. We fell asleep in our armchairs, at my place, after lunch.

There was a concert at the theatre in the evening, and Graham and I strolled down there to have a drink. I lent him my Polish Air Force great-coat for the snowy walk. He did it up so tightly under the chin I don't think a germ could have squeezed down his throat. I wore my long leather coat. 'We look like the Gestapo,' Graham observed as we scrunched through the churchyard, our usual short cut, though I had a suspicion that we didn't quite look dangerous or butch enough. I had to phone David from the theatre about next day's rehearsal times. (There was no phone in our flat, or in Graham's, and mobile ones hadn't been invented yet.) 'What did you have for lunch?' David asked.

I took this to be a question about Graham. 'Half a pork chop.'

'Very cosy,' David said, in what was not his cosiest voice.

When I put the phone down I was trying not to cry. Graham, at my elbow immediately, asked, 'What's the matter?'

'David. About you.'

'Why? We've done nothing wrong. He ought to know – surely – that you couldn't be much safer.' A suspicion crossed his mind. 'You don't exaggerate things, do you? To make him jealous on purpose? I hope you don't.'

'No, Graham, that I do not.'

We had fish and chips for tea, back at Graham's place. The next day would be a big one for him. Rehearsals for the next play of the season were starting, and Graham was going 'on the book'. The play was a two-hander – a budget breather following the epic spends of pantomime and musical. It was called Staircase, and its two cast members were … David and Clive. The director ... well, they hardly needed one. They would direct each other to save costs. This threw even more responsibility than usual onto the stage manager on the book. Graham would attend all rehearsals, prompting and taking notes. Later, during the run he would sit hidden in the prompt corner, headphones on and script in front of him, co-ordinating the proceedings, cueing actors, stage management, sound and lights. I gave Graham a little lecture on the importance of being punctual and on the ball, partly to avoid David's having any ammunition to use against him, me, us ... and partly because I'd recommended him so highly to the Maltings. 'You sound as though you don't believe in me any more,' he said in a pained tone of voice. 'Have you changed your mind about me?'

'No,' I said, a bit uncertainly. Working as closely with him as I now did, I had discovered in him a dismaying tendency to leave most decision-making, responsibility and hard work to others when he could. Often the others meant me.

'It's just that you *are* sometimes late and things like that, and you don't always do the best work you can,' I wriggled feebly.

'I will do my best,' he said. 'It's just that...'

'I know,' I said. I wanted to hug him. He looked so sad and vulnerable, sitting in his duffel-coat in his cold little flat as I got up to go. 'I really do know all about it.' I gave him a sly smile. 'It comes with being twenty-eight. But promise me three things.'

He looked doubtful. 'What are they?'

'One, make sure you do a bloody good job on Staircase. Two, make a good start by being early for rehearsal in the morning. Three, let me take a couple of slices of bread home for my breakfast. You ate all mine this morning.' We laughed. I filched the least green slices from his bread-bin and went home.

'Does he pay for all the food he eats when he's here?'

'For every meal I've cooked him he's cooked me one back. Ditto every takeaway. I'm not out of pocket.'

'Must be me, then.'

'Where's your old coat gone?'

'I lent it to Graham.'

David exhaled with a noise like air-brakes. 'You like to flaunt it, don't you. You really do. In front of me. In front of everyone. Parading him around dressed in your clothes! Can you honestly say there are no sexual overtones, undertones, or whatever, in your relationship?'

Leaving aside a certain difficulty I had with that word *honestly*, I said there were not.

Walking to work through the slush in the churchyard with David a few days later, I said incautiously, 'You should have seen this in the fresh snow on Sunday night. The black trees outlined in silver, and the light streaming through the windows from inside the church.'

There was a short pause, during which I wished I could have bitten my tongue. Then David said, without emphasis but a little wistfully, 'It must have looked very different with a romantic young man at your side.'

I had no answer to that. But David had stumbled on the right word. Romantic in the wider sense, of course. Leaving aside the question of love, such as between myself and David, maybe there's no other kind of relationship I can have with a man. Friendship, but with this inconvenient, sometimes absurd, element of the romantic thrown in.

It was Terry's birthday next day. Terry had invited David to dinner. I had asked David to find out if the invitation extended to me, and he said he'd ring up and find out, though we both had a pretty good idea what the answer would be. David returned home at tea-time. 'Bad news first,' he said. 'No, you're not invited to dinner, so I'll be going on my own. Now the good news. John's handed his notice in.'

The world spun round. John was the general manager. He'd been on the brink of resigning for over a year but the jobs he'd been after had fallen through. Meanwhile

I'd been after his job since I first saw the theatre two years ago and it was assumed by many that when John went I'd automatically slot into his place. But now the moment had come I saw a yawning gap of uncertainty between the two events. The many a slip included the question of my relationship with the theatre's leading actor, and having to explain what had gone wrong at the Maltings, why I'd been out of work for a year, and what I was doing crewing a show, trundling scenery and sweeping the stage floor every night. 'Good heavens,' I said.

'You'd just better get it,' said David.

'What's up?' Graham asked me when we were setting props before the show. 'I've never seen you in this mood before. You're all on edge. And you've been biting your nails, which you never do.'

'Tell you later,' I said. Then, 'Do you fancy going for a takeaway after the show?'

Graham thought about this for a moment. 'OK, then,' he said. 'But if David's going to have a proper meal sit-down meal with Terry, I don't see why we can't do the same.'

By the end of the show the theatre was buzzing with the news of John's impending departure. Twice I walked into the green room to find conversation stopping abruptly. No doubt the question of whether I would apply for his job was being discussed with equally interest.

We walked towards our usual Indian, and I told Graham I was definitely putting in for the general manager's job. Then he told me he'd been offered an interview at the Maltings. 'Hey, that's brilliant,' I said. 'Why didn't you tell me before?'

'I wanted you to tell me your big news first.' That's when I did hug him, publicly, out on the cold pavement.

Nothing really. Except that this was Northampton. And January. And 1981.

We were the only customers. Our moods had changed since the early evening. I was no longer in a whirl of conflicting thoughts and fears about John's leaving, nor depressed by David's spending the evening with Terry. I was feeling warm and relaxed and optimistic. Graham, who had been tense with anxiety about his interview at the Maltings, was now in extrovert mode, laughing and chattering. He had his jacket off, on the chair-back behind him, and wore just a loose white shirt with most of the buttons undone, showing off most of his hairless but very pretty ivory coloured chest. His eyes were shining, he was flashing his gap-toothed smile and, yes, flirting with me. Flirting with his favourite poofter without even knowing it.

And me? Well, I'm doing it too, of course. It comes to me as naturally as it does to him. More so, perhaps, as I'm officially gay, while he's officially not. And right now I'm noticing something else. I'm looking across a restaurant table at a young man with lovely cobalt blue eyes, a gap between his front teeth and a half undone shirt and thinking: you're beautiful, and all this time I've tried to pretend I haven't noticed that. We've both gone through the motions of picking each other up, though without actually doing anything, and without understanding or admitting to ourselves what's really been going on.

We finished the meal before the bottle of wine we'd bought to go with it was empty and the restaurant staff, anxious to lock up, were more than happy to send us away with what was left of it. We went back to Graham's. We talked about loneliness. We talked about God. We talked about our respective flats. 'Really, yours is just as cold as mine,' Graham said, 'but it never feels it. It's cosy and home-like – and it has better furniture of course.'

'It's also better organised,' I said, 'and two people have made a home there together, which makes a difference, instead of just using it to doss in, the way you do here. There's things like salt and pepper, and pictures with real frames, and wine glasses, and food in the fridge.'

'And Earl Grey tea and cups with saucers...'

'Yeah, but there's another thing,' I said. 'When you come to Palmerston Road you're always with me. You associate my flat with companionship. You never go back there alone and cold, late at night, as you have to here. But I do. When I'm on my own there, without David, without you, then it feels as bleak and cheerless a place as this ever does.'

We looked across at each other from the two moulting armchairs in silence for a minute, we slurped some red wine. Then Graham picked up his guitar and played to me. Nothing new in that. Yet he played especially well that night. Simply because the atmosphere was special, different from anything that had been before. He played in the way that I play best – playing to an audience of one, because they are there, but not exactly for them; not bothering to think about them, just perfectly relaxed, totally at home in their company. Graham is no accomplished technician, but he isn't trying to play difficult things or trying to impress. He's simply playing music with delicacy, sensitivity and complete assurance. Not *to* me, but because of me. It's a very introverted performance. A breath of wind from the outside world would blow it to pieces and us with it. Yet his playing means everything to me at this moment, which is all that's necessary. It's not intended for anybody else.

I've come to like the way he looks when he's playing: thick dark hair, white skin and long dark eyelashes. The dark blue eyes are firmly set on his guitar.

I've come to like so many things about him, like the way he pronounces the letter O, its careful over-refinement a comical erratic amid his homely Bradford speech. I even like the way he sits, his knees wide apart and his absurd desert boots that he calls Cornish pasties crossed over each other as if for mutual comfort...

He finished playing and looked suddenly up at me, his eyes very wide. They glistened strangely. Mine were wet. 'Thank you,' I said. 'That was beautiful. I never need to hear you play better than that.'

We talked more. We had coffee. There came into my mind a quotation from somebody or other that defined a romantic evening as one that begins with a conversation about God and ends in bed. And that particular end to the evening seemed at that moment entirely possible, and much to be desired. The cold flat seemed suddenly as cosy and home-like as mine appeared to Graham and for a few agonising moments I basked in the glow of comfort and promise it radiated. Then, 'I think I'd better go home,' I said, with no trace of enthusiasm in my voice. I stood up. He stood up. We walked down the stairs together. We said goodnight, and thank you, to each other on the pavement. We hugged each other awkwardly for a few seconds. I turned abruptly and ran off fast up the road.

IV

David didn't seem surprised that I'd gone out for a meal with Graham and he made no fuss about it. He was hardly in a position to. But from this point on I began to notice that something was changing. I was finding it difficult to talk about Graham. Before, I had had to stop myself from prattling incessantly about him, which had got on David's nerves. Now there was almost too much to say and my thoughts were becoming too confused to be expressed coherently in ordinary conversation. Things that Graham said, things that other people said about Graham, went scurrying through my head, chased by ghosts, pursued by echoes, from my own past. They swirled by, merged with each other till they grew thick and opaque and volatile as fog, and in the middle of them all there was I and I was getting lost.

'There's something sinister about him,' said one person and I thought, not as sinister as you, mate. 'Something very vulnerable about him,' said someone kinder. 'A hopeless case,' came from someone else.' A lost soul,' and, 'He's a slut.'

I found myself having to say to people, 'I don't actually sleep with him.'

'Really?' they all replied. 'We assumed you did.' The powerful engines of theatre gossip.

'I don't want money,' Graham said. 'I don't want responsibilities. I just want to live in the country and play my guitar.' Substitute piano for guitar and David could have told him he'd heard the same pathetic plea from someone else. I was able to pass on David's response.

'Unfortunately this is the real world we're in, and there's the little matter of earning a living.'

'To hell with earning a living,' Graham said. 'You should just chuck it all up and play the piano and write.' In his defence I should say that he was both drunk and stoned when he said this.

So was I, but I had experience on my side. 'I have actually tried that, Graham, and now look at me – earning thirty pounds a week, and relying on David's generosity to maintain my standard of living. It's all very well for you not to worry about money when you're doing very nicely, thank you, on seventy pounds a week plus overtime.'

Temperamentally Graham would make a very good kept man. He'd never have a conscience about it. But he'd never stay with anything or anyone. Fickle boy. Changeable as a March day. But that's the thing about being twenty – and part of the attraction. Hope he gets the job at the Maltings. I shan't have to worry about him. And he won't be surrounded by gay men there, as he is here, unless the place has changed radically since my time there. Yes, he must get the job. He's putting a strain on the most precious thing in my life, my relationship with David. No, that's not true; he isn't; I am. And I'm not just worried that he's getting unhealthily dependent on me. I'm also becoming dependent on him.

'David, hold me.'
'What's the matter, little one?'
'Nothing.'
'Tell me, though I know anyway.'
'Just hold me.'

Graham's interview was scheduled for Thursday at eleven. In London. 'Your friend in Putney,' he said. 'The one you went to see because her parents were ill.'

'Yes,' I said. That had been before Christmas. But I'd been expecting Graham to bring it up now.

'Will you be going to see her again?'
'Probably. Next time I'm in London.'
'Do you want to go down on Thursday?'
'No, Graham, I do not. We both have to be back for the matinee. You'll only just have time to get back from Leicester Square as it is. No way can I get over to Putney. And I'm not coming just to hold your hand.'
'I don't want my hand holding. Just a lift.'
'Same thing. Same answer. No.'

'I'd pay all the petrol.'

'You certainly would. But still no. Just get on the train, look at the tube map, go there and come back again.'

'Oh easy,' he said, exasperated with me. 'That's if you don't have my nervous system to cope with. I'll have to have a drink before I go in. I get all screwed up.'

'You'll be fine. If you must have a drink, get yourself a packet of Polo or something. People who walk into eleven o'clock interviews reeking of booze may as well not bother.'

I relayed this conversation to David. He rocked on the balls of his feet for a second then looked me in the eye with his unique twinkly stare. 'I'd been waiting for you to tell me you had to go to London on Thursday. I was going to hit the roof.'

'Well I'm not going, so you won't have to. I've helped him get his interview, looked up train times with him, told him what questions to ask, and I think that's enough.'

'Did you tell him not to slouch?'

'Of course. I even told him not to slouch when he was phoning them to confirm.'

Later that day David said, 'I have to admit that Graham's doing a good job on Staircase. He's good about prompting. Very sensitive.'

Graham returned from London just before the curtain went up for the matinee. He looked very spruce. 'How did you get on, Sweetheart?' I asked. *Sweetheart* came into my head on the spur of the moment. I'd never called him it before. It was a spare weapon in my armoury of endearments and as I'd never used it on David there seemed no reason why it shouldn't do for Graham now.

'Oh, I don't know. All right perhaps. Tell you about it in a minute. Have a Polo.'

*

That evening there was a late-night show. This meant the bar staying open late and everyone getting pleasantly tight. The atmosphere seemed rather lovely. David and Graham and I sat chatting together, just the three of us. Graham suggested we both went back and had coffee with him Then he remembered he had no milk. Then... But what happened next? The order of events becomes confused. I remember suggesting that Graham came back for coffee with David and me and that at roughly the same time David slammed out of the bar, saying he was going home. I remember thinking drunkenly, I can handle this.

'Come on,' I said to Graham. 'We're going after him.' It took a while to get ourselves together. Graham was by now buying beer to take out – we were too drunk to notice this was superfluous – and finding coats and letting ourselves out of the theatre's front door, on the latch, in the dark foyer proved more difficult than we'd expected. I was confident that lurching back home with Graham and an armful of bottles was the best way of putting things right between the three of us once and for all. Graham was less sanguine. 'Are you sure this is a good idea?'

'Course I am.'

He shot me a look as we wove along the street. In it was the sadness of one who has just heard the jingle of silver. 'Are you sure you're not just using me to make a point with?'

'Quite, quite sure,' I said, looking back at him dressed in my grey greatcoat. I fully believed I was telling the truth.

We continued in silence through the churchyard, then,

'Do you think I *am* gay?'

Dear God, Graham, you do choose your moments! 'I honestly don't know,' I said. 'You shouldn't ask questions like that at moments like this … with drunken poofters who fancy you. It complicates life no end. Perhaps you're bisexual. You may well be. Like I said, that's how I thought of myself when I was...' I stopped myself. *When I was twenty, rather than twenty-eight.*

He let the matter rest.

'Come in,' I said, when I finally managed to turn the key in the lock. 'I'll see if David's awake.'

'There's no lights on.'

'Just run upstairs. I'll be with you in a minute.' I went into the bedroom and turned on the light.

'Get out of here,' came David's unequivocal greeting from beneath the duvet. 'Who's just gone upstairs?'

'Graham.'

'Get rid of him.'

I climbed the stairs and met Graham standing in the kitchen, looking thoroughly uncomfortable. I wasn't feeling too good myself. 'I'm sorry, my love. I think you'd better go.' I said. 'I'm afraid I've rather fucked this up.'

'Yes,' said Graham, more assertive than his usual self. 'You have rather.'

'I'm really sorry, Graham. Look, don't forget your beer.' I gestured to where it slouched, semi-upright, on the draining-board.

'You keep half of it. It was meant for all of us. You may need it.'

He shouted a friendly goodnight to David through the closed bedroom door as he left. As an attempt to withdraw with dignity it was not a total success but I gave him full marks for the philosophy behind it.

I undressed in silence and climbed into bed. A moment later I was sitting bolt upright. 'I think I'm going to be sick,' I said miserably.

'Oh, for God's sake!' David said. But he sat up beside me nevertheless and held me till the room stopped spinning round, with a tenderness he couldn't hide.

'What did David say about last night?' Graham asked me in the morning.

'Nothing at all. I nearly threw up but didn't. We both went straight to sleep. Breakfast was a bit silent. David fucked me as I sat in the armchair before doing the washing-up and everything's been fine since.'

Some hours later: 'He's said hallo to me, at least. So he can't be too upset.'

The strike of Guys and Dolls lasted till three in the morning. It was quite a pleasure to rip apart the colossal set that had caused us so much trouble to put up. When it was over the production manager drove Graham and me home. 'Your place or his?' he asked, smiling in the particular way I've noticed people do when dealing with the two of us.

'Mine,' I said. When we got there Graham cooked me an omelette and we consumed the beer that hadn't been required on Thursday night. In the morning I went over to Denmark Road. Graham had decided it was his turn to cook Sunday lunch, if I could provide some sausages and cooking salt. Following a few pints in the local it proved a pleasant meal. We sat and drank coffee. 'Remember when we first met?' I asked.

'In that dreadful pub.'

'And out of shyness neither of us spoke. We abandoned each other to our miserable evenings alone. I went back and watched telly.' I remembered it all too well.

'And I stayed and got pissed, and thought what a place I'd come to!'

'I was afraid you'd think I was trying to pick you up...'

'Yes, but we didn't know we were going to be such good friends. We might both have been someone different. Then we'd have been stuck for the rest of the evening.'

He has a disconcerting way of standing things on their heads sometimes.

'I remember the look on your face as I left,' I said. 'It made me want to turn back but it was too late.'

'I remember the look on yours,' Graham said. 'It said everything I was feeling. Fed up and lonely and hating Sunday.'

I said, 'Sundays have got better since.'

V

Staircase opened. The first night went beautifully but the party afterwards was a little tense. Terry was there, upset because I'd applied for the general manager's job and complaining to David that I was becoming irremovable. I stayed close to Graham. Later the cast were invited for stew and wine at someone's flat. David wouldn't go unless I was invited, and I wouldn't go unless Graham was. So we all went. It wasn't great...

I was out of work again. My time was my own and I could write and play the piano to my heart's content. At the end of the show I'd join David and Clive in their dressing-room and we'd wander over to Shipman's for a few beers before closing time, picking up Graham from the green room on the way. David was very nice to Graham these days. Sometimes the three of us would drive home together in David's car. But sometimes the strain of it all showed.

'If he's not actually gay he's pretty borderline and you know it. Probably better than anyone else. And if he is straight, well, that's never stopped you falling in love with anyone before; you've a whole history of it. You actually live with him when I'm not here. Showing him off in public, dressed in your clothes... That's your idea of being faithful to me...?'

'What do you expect me to do at weekends? If you go off every Saturday leaving a hole in your lover's life someone was bound to fall into it sooner or later.'

'Be pulled in, more like.'

'You spend your weekends with a man who was your lover for years. That's public knowledge too. How do you think I feel about that?'

'Significant that you balance Graham against Terry. He must mean a lot to you.'

'So? Terry does to you. Listen, Darling. When I want to be unfaithful to you I'll do it properly. Not mess around at weekends with a mixed-up boy who isn't even gay.'

'Thank you for that,' said David. 'But you're right. You don't need to be unfaithful to me now. Your track record's dodgy enough already. Just play around, needle me now and then, just enough to remind me of the threat you hold over my head. It's a little mean of you.'

'What threat?' I really didn't know what he was going to say.

He sighed. 'That you're a young boy and could spread your wings at any moment. That's the threat you keep underlining so unsubtly. In your conscious mind everything you say may be true. You may tell me the truth – I believe you do – but it's never the whole truth.'

'I try to tell the truth as far as I can see it. No-one can do more.'

'A pretty speech.' He didn't say this harshly. Sadly was more the mark. 'You've been worried lately. I know that. I've said things that have made you examine your motives a bit more deeply. You've not always been easy with what you've discovered about yourself. You've realised you don't need to jump into bed with Graham for him to be a threat to us. His youth and helplessness are as big a danger to you as yours are to me.'

Something clicked into place. I hadn't thought of this before. 'You're not worried about Graham, are you. It isn't him at all. It's the prospect of a lifetime of future Grahams stretching in front of you. That's what really bothers you.'

Next day we learned that Graham had been offered the job at the Maltings. He would be leaving in two weeks.

*

Graham had to make a trip to London, something to do with collecting props, with a girl his own age who had joined the stage management team that week. She'd be his replacement when he left. I, who had spent the day unloading a lorry for some extra cash, went to the Queen's Head alone. He'd said he'd join me there, but though my eyes leapt to the door every time it opened, I doubted him. I sat in what I though of as 'our' corner, drinking pints of Guinness on my own, remembering the first Sunday we'd met. He won't come, I thought. He won't come. If he does, maybe I'll take him to bed at last. Though why? To spite David? I don't want to do that. To make a point? What point? Don't know. See what happens. Not that he's going to come.

He did come – with the girl in tow. We had more drinks. 'You've had a bad day, haven't you,' he said.

'Yeah.'

I thought, no, Rory, you won't take him to bed. Not tonight, not ever. He's too real to be used as a weapon, a real boy, not something to make a point with. Now that he was here, flesh and blood in front of me, the idea became laughable.

At closing time he walked the girl home. 'Can I come back to your place?' he asked as we all left the pub.

'Of course you can. The bell's on the blink. I'll leave the door on the latch.'

219

'I'll only be a minute.'

He was nearly twenty. I began to think of locking up and going to bed. Then I heard his footsteps on the stairs. 'I'd just about given you up,' I said.

He looked pained. 'If Graham says he's coming he always will. You should know that.' Then he grinned and said, 'I may be late occasionally but I'd never not come. I got lost on the way back actually. Walked miles and found myself back at Denmark Road. Anyway, I'm here now.'

'I'm glad.'

We sat down. I had a half-empty bottle of wine – oh all right, a half-full bottle – and we got into it. 'Our last Sunday,' he said.

'I'm glad you came back from London.'

'So am I.'

We drained the wine bottle. I wanted to say something understated and not banal. I failed. 'It's been a good time.'

'Oh don't say that!'

I was startled by his sudden vehemence. 'Why?!'

'Because good times and all good things have horrible endings. If you say we've had a good time together something will go horribly wrong, I know it.' This put a damper on things for a minute. I got up, went into the kitchen and made coffee while Graham embarked on a sort of soliloquy from behind me. 'I could be much more successful, if I wanted to be, with men than women. Ironical, really. People say I lead them on – you know, the gay crowd – but I try not to. I just have the choice of being sociable and friendly with them or saying, 'I'm straight,' and sitting at home alone, freezing. There isn't anything else.' Well, there is. There are plenty of straight people working at the theatre but somehow Graham never clicked with them.

My mind went back to a conversation we'd had the day before, huddled in our overcoats around the Calor-gas stove in Graham's flat, eating malt-loaf. He'd said at one point, 'Maybe each of us is like what the other would have been like if I'd been gay or you'd been straight, if you see what I mean. We are alike, of course.' He chewed a fragment of malt-loaf thoughtfully. ''Cept I don't talk quite so posh.'

I said to him now that I wasn't quite sure about some of that. It seemed to me that the character traits we did have in common were the ones that I – and most other people – associated with the gay disposition. That's what we called it back then.

He shrugged. 'Maybe I am gay, then. Maybe it's really men I should be into. But I'd like to let that wait a few years. At the moment I'm still into girls. Though I'm not really into sex at all at the moment.' We've all heard that one. It translates as, I haven't been getting it lately.

'You're an extraordinary boy,' I said. The words came out in the tome of voice that is usually reserved for *I love you*.

'Am I'

'Oh yes.'

'Have you any music we could listen to?'

'Not a lot. There's a tape of me playing Beethoven...'

'That's fine.'

'I wish I had a piano here. I'd much rather play to you live. Return the compliment you paid me with your guitar that time.'

'Did you ever tell David about that?' he asked, unexpectedly, wickedly.

'No.' And a whole jungle of thoughts echoed to that answer. The boy's a mind reader. With that question he's very cleverly staked a claim to me. Something shared that time that was just for us. While my answer is in itself an admission of a kind of unfaithfulness to David. Does Graham know all this? Of course he does.

It was the first piano sonata. F minor. Graham began to doze before the end. His head lolled out of the chair towards my lap. I scratched the top of it. 'Listen to the finale. I played it rather well.'

He didn't move. 'I'm not asleep,' he said distinctly. 'I'm listening.' Still he didn't move a muscle. And I didn't stop scratching, then stroking his head. Stroking his soft dark hair till the music stopped. He enjoyed being stroked, quite passively, like a warm cat.

Why, I asked myself a day later, did it not occur to me to experiment with his zip? You mean it didn't? Yes. I mean no. I mean, cross my heart and hope to die but it never went through my head. I know that sounds unlikely. Unlike me. But it didn't cross my mind... Um... I think. OK, maybe it did. I know even less about what was going on in Graham's head, in intimate contact with it though I was. I think perhaps he would have accepted it just as he accepted my stroking his hair. But acceptance has never been enough. I'm too vain for that. I've let other people take me to bed with them without particularly wanting to go, but I've never inflicted my company in that way on anyone else. If I'm making the running they've got to want it too. So my hand never made that inviting twenty-five inch journey from head to crotch. Perhaps I was simply tired. Certainly, neither of us was excited. (Yes, I did look.) It just didn't happen and that's all there is to it. Perhaps we have guardian angels after all and the obvious, the almost inevitable, simply escaped us. Everything was right between us then. One more move and everything would have been wrong.

I turned the tape off. 'That was beautiful,' Graham said. 'Thank you. Can I borrow your sleeping-bag and stay the night?'

'Of course.' How could he not? Why, David had asked once, when he only lives a hundred yards down the road does he have to stay the night? Think about it, Rory! A few days later an actor friend of mine, Ian, joining the company, and meeting Graham for the first time, was to ask the same question. Well, I had thought about it. Why does a young man choose to sleep on my hard floor rather than in his own bed? And why do I feel honoured by that preference? Because it's cold outside and the wind blows hard when you're alone. There's warmth and comfort and company together, even if you're in separate rooms. The good-fellowship you've built up over an evening is not dispelled by an opening door, a curt goodnight and a journey to an ice-cold flat; the warmth is still there to be shared again at breakfast time. And there's danger too, of a sort; complicity, conspiracy, and a faint whiff of scandal. But most of all, it's just being with someone else. Neither of us is much good on our own. The wind does blow so.

I sat down on the floor at Graham's feet, my elbows on his knees, looking up into his eyes the way David sits and looks up into mine. 'Do you realise,' I said, 'that if I lived here alone instead of with the man I love, you would have moved in with me three months ago?'

'I suppose I would.'

'You'd have been very welcome. Probably we would have slept together. Almost certainly it would have been a disaster.'

'So it's better the way things are?'

'Definitely. Now I'm going to get you that sleeping-bag.' I stood up, 'I'm afraid I'll have to get you up early in the morning. David'll be here at eleven o'clock. I'm not going to pretend you haven't stayed the night but I'd prefer it if he didn't actually trip over you on his way in.'

'Quite.' We said goodnight.

*

I made coffee and toast in the morning. In the middle of breakfast the yard door banged. Graham and I looked at each. We froze. 'Is that David?' Graham asked in a husk of a voice, although it was only nine. His face was ashen. We looked hard at each other – it was like seeing deep into the other's soul. We saw fear there, and then we saw the reflection of our own, so that fear grew between us, like the light of a candle between two mirrors, to infinity.

'I don't know,' I said. The words were a faint rasping sound. 'I don't think so.' I knew I couldn't handle the situation if David burst in on us now and I knew Graham could see that in me. But that wasn't the worst of it. Fear was only one of two candles that stood multiplying to infinity between us. The other was guilt. I'd always assumed that if there had been anything to feel guilty about then it lay on my conscience alone. Yet now it was obvious that this wasn't the case. Graham was feeling just the same as I was and it showed. He was sitting in his usual place, having breakfast with me, same as every weekend. Yet his usual place is really David's place, his chair is David's chair, his view of me across the table David's view. Graham is suddenly aware of all this. And so am I. A biting wind is blowing and it will tear us apart if David comes in now. Neither of us can deal with this on our own and our unfledged little relationship isn't ready to hold together in the face of big trouble. We have to row back.

'I think you'd better finish your coffee and go,' I said. 'We're both getting too jumpy to enjoy a leisurely breakfast.' That was an understatement. I thought I was going to be sick. So, I could see, did Graham. Neither of us managed another mouthful.

'I'm scared of bumping into David on the way out,' Graham said. He sounded it.

'I'll come with you. If we're going to bump into him unexpectedly at least we'll do it together. You won't have to meet him alone.'

I escorted him out through the yard and into the street. It was the least I could do. 'I've got to get some milk from the shop, anyway,' I said. We didn't run into David. We said, see you later, on the pavement and parted. And two more whey-faced, craven children you could not have found.

VI

When one show closes another one opens and yet another goes into rehearsal. Now rehearsals were about to begin for an Agatha Christie, and new actors joined the company. Ian was an old friend of mine from Maltings days. Tall, sturdy and blond, almost exactly my own age, he was regrettably straight. Over a lunchtime pint that day we caught up on the last few months. He'd split up with his girlfriend, which was sad, but straightforward enough. I told Ian about myself, and Graham, and David, and Terry. 'Graham seems a nice chap,' he said. They'd met during the coffee break. 'My God, though. You lot do go in for complicated lives.'

I didn't see Graham again till the evening. David was rehearsing and I had arranged to go down and meet him for a drink when he finished. I set out a little early though, and, seeing Graham's light was on, went up to his flat, letting myself in with his spare key, which I now kept. He was trying over some Beatles songs on his guitar. He was too young to know some of them, I discovered. I sang them for him. Not very well. We gave up after a while and walked down to the pub.

'Have you told David I stayed last night?' We'd got as far as the churchyard.

'No. Once I'd tidied the place up and he came back I found I couldn't. He usually asks, and I usually tell him, and there's a bit of an explosion, but this time, no. He waited for me to volunteer the information and I waited for him to ask the question but neither of us did. So it didn't come up. I've felt wretched all day.'

'Will you tell him?'

'If he asks. If it becomes that important, yes.'

Graham changed the subject. 'Two days to go.'

'I shall miss you.'

'I'll miss you too. Our Sundays have been good.'

'Right,' I said.

'And no dreadful endings?'

'No,' I said. We came out of the churchyard.

'Lucky we met up,' Graham said.

'We've been company for each other.'

'When no-one else seemed to want us,' he said.

'Yup,' I said.

After the pub the three of us walked home together. David, Graham and I. First time we've actually done that. I went leaping over the litter-bins en route. David actually proposed a visit to the Queen's Head but I warned him that both Graham and I were nearly penniless and he changed his mind. So he and I went back to Palmerston Road, leaving Graham at the fish and chip shop on the way.

Wow! I'd been short-listed for the general manager's job. The interview was in a fortnight. There was a party that night at someone's house. No connection with the job interview: it was someone's birthday...

Graham was rather quiet, considering it was his last night, or perhaps because of that, and left the party early. Before that, though, he sat and talked with Ian, across the room from where I was sitting at David's feet. David leaned close to my ear and said, 'What are you thinking?'

I didn't reply.

'I'll tell you,' he said gently. 'You're thinking about Graham and Ian. You could have either of those young men for a lover. Only you've got me instead. Do you mind that?'

'No,' I said. But something I said later, or something in the way I said something, or something in my face – I never knew exactly what – must have upset him, and not long after Graham went, David went too, without telling me he was going. Ian and I hunted the house and garden for him without much expectation of finding him. I cried drunkenly and Ian held me in his arms until I stopped. Then I was given a serious talking-to by Tanya, the design assistant. She lives next door to us in Palmerston Road. She too took me in her arms. She told me I was an appalling flirt. 'You've got something very special with David,' she said. 'Don't risk losing it. It's not worth it. Especially for little sluts like Graham.'

'He's not a little slut.'

'Oh?'

'I know you've seen him round at the flat a bit...'

'A bit?!'

'All right, frequently.'

'Whenever David's away. It does notice. It's upset David a lot. You know that.'

'Well, he leaves tomorrow.'

'Good thing too. But don't go getting another one.' She talked as if I'd lost a pet dog or cat. 'Please? I know it's a kind of retaliation for David going away at weekends. But just don't. Promise?' It was funny to think I might be her boss in another month.

I laughed. 'All right. I won't.'

I'd quite enjoyed being cuddled and lectured at the same time, but I now disentangled myself and rearranged my arms around Ian again, who cuddled me without much in the way of a lecture until I felt ready to go home. 'Good luck,' Ian called from the door as I lurched out into the night, as uncertain about my state of mind as I was about how to manage my feet.

VII

'Yes, I love you,' was what David said in the morning as he got up to go and rehearse. I stayed in bed to nurse my hangover.

I was woken by what sounded like the doorbell. Then came the voice of the old lady who lived the other side of the yard fence shouting that someone was ringing the bell from the street. I pulled jeans and a sweater over my startled hard-on nakedness and went barefoot across the yard. There, when I opened the street door, was Graham. 'Were you in bed?' he asked.

'I was fast asleep. Come in.' As we crossed the yard Graham announced to the world, and especially to the old lady still hovering on the other side of the fence, that his zip was bust and had I any pliers.

'You're outrageous,' I told him. 'And you look obscene standing there fiddling with it like that. Go upstairs and see if the pliers are in the right-hand drawer. If they're not, they're in David's car, to which I don't have a key. Put the kettle on while you're up there and I'll find some socks and underpants.'

'No pliers,' he shouted down a minute later, 'but I've managed to do it with a fork.'

'Good,' I said. 'The neighbours will be delighted.' I hope he washed the fork afterwards.

He had come round not only to tell me his fly was undone but also to ask me if I could take him and his trunk to the Roadline depot in the afternoon. I agreed a bit reluctantly. My car was not in good shape and the depot was on a labyrinthine industrial estate several miles from the centre of town.

And by the time the afternoon came, we'd enjoyed enough of a boozy farewell lunch, involving two pubs, to restore our blood-alcohol levels to roughly where they had been the previous night. There was plenty wrong with the car too. One wheel-bearing was squealing like pigs from hell, the exhaust pipe was hanging by a thread, the petrol gauge was reading less than zero, and the MOT had expired the previous week. I was seized by the conviction that something terrible would happen: that the dreadful ending Graham had gloomily assigned to all good things was scheduled for this afternoon.

We loaded the car. In the process I ripped half a thumbnail off. We nearly crashed into the district nurse during the first hundred yards and she gave us a sound telling-off at the first set of traffic lights. It took us an agonising two miles to find a petrol station, willing the car not to come to a stop. Graham insisted on buying three quids-worth of petrol. He told me to save some for a trip to the Maltings.

'It would have to be the most beautiful day of the spring so far, wouldn't it,' he said. 'The day I'm leaving.' I had to agree. The end of March, and the sun dazzled from a cobalt sky. There was no wind. We had petrol now, but I was more than ever convinced that something bad would happen. The lapsed MOT... The shrieks of the wheel-bearings were causing pedestrians to look at us. 'It'll start growling before it eventually falls off,' said Graham. He'd worked in a garage once.

'I'm worried about being stopped by the police,' I said.

He said, 'My guitar case is full of dope.'

'I thought it might be.' Having it confirmed hadn't cheered me up. I realised we were both shaking uncontrollably. But it wasn't because of the car or the police. Nothing as simple as that.

Found the depot with difficulty. Delivered up the trunk to be weighed, labelled and dispatched. 'What does M stand for?' I asked, staring at his initials, GMA, on the lid.

'Martin,' he said.

Back in the car. Off towards the station. 'Don't you want to do your seat-belt up?' I asked. My teeth were chattering now and I couldn't stop them.

'Doesn't matter.' His teeth were chattering too. I could hear them. We were getting a bit intense. 'If I go through the windscreen, so be it. I'm not that keen on living. I mean I'll give life a chance but if it decides to finish me off now I'll be perfectly content. Life's pretty bad really.'

'I know that, my love,' I said. I might have got angry with him but I didn't. 'Just don't be defeatist,' I said. 'Life has good things in it. Seize those. Make them fill the whole of it. Otherwise you're right, and it becomes unsupportable. Learn to grab your opportunities. You must do if you're going to stand any chance of surviving in the world or being happy.'

'Not everybody has those opportunities.'

'I think they do.'

'You will come and see me at the Maltings? Promise?'

'Of course.'

We were bombing down the straight. The station less than a mile ahead. Somehow we'd both stopped shivering. Our teeth were quiet. 'What do you keep smiling about?' Graham asked, scrutinising the side of my face.

'This morning. You on my doorstep with your broken zip. And I think, anyone who marches up to his friend's flat, finds himself alone with a half-dressed poofter and announces in that little boy lost voice that his fly is gaping has to be the second biggest flirt in the world.'

'And the biggest?'

'Sitting beside you, I suppose.'

'Am I really a flirt...?'

'It's the way you're made. You've flirted with me for three months, either without knowing or without admitting it; it hardly matters which. OK. Me too.' I was admitting it at last. 'I've been flirting with you for three months and pretending I wasn't.'

He ignored this. 'Well, if you say I'm a flirt, then I suppose I am.' In an apologetic tone.

'Don't pretend you're sorry about it. You're not. Anyway, I've enjoyed every minute.'

Graham half turned towards me. Across the gear-lever. He was wearing a red carnation in the button-hole of his green jacket. 'Does it look silly?'

'No. It looks good.'

'What'll my mother think?'

'She'll think you've spent four months with a load of poofs.'

'She'll be dead right.' He thought for a moment. 'It's been a weird experience.' Then, 'Do you think I've made a difference to you? Changed you at all?'

'Of course you have. Just as I've changed you. We could hardly have got to know each other the way we have done without doing that.'

We reached the station. Incredibly, nothing had gone wrong. We parked up. 'I really will miss you,' Graham said as we walked in the sunshine across the car-park.

'And I will you, of course.' There was nearly an hour till his train. 'I won't abandon you just yet. Let's get a coffee.'

A table between us, and a mound of luggage. When exactly was my interview for general manager? Ten days to go. For the hundredth time he wished me luck. And what would I do with my Sundays after he'd gone? he asked. I wasn't sure. Turned out I couldn't remember what I did with them before I met Graham. I'd no memory of Sundays before that. 'I'll have Ian for company,' I said.

'You don't do yourself justice,' he said. There was anger in his voice. I'd never heard it there before. 'Always falling for straight men...'

'I do do myself justice,' I returned with equal vehemence. 'My life's complicated enough by gay men falling for me without my falling for gay men too.' Graham let it go. I think he only half accepted my point.

'You lot are so ... immediate,' he said a little later. 'I think I'd rather be the sort of friends we are. Not leaping into bed at a moment's notice.'

'Hmm,' I said. 'I suppose I agree ... in our particular case.' But I knew by now that I wasn't telling the truth.

'Still, we got them all talking,' he said wickedly, the naughtiest grin of his life appearing on his face. He was more precious to me at that moment than he'd ever been.

'True... Flirt!' But the moment had come. 'I'm going to love you and leave you now. It's only ten minutes to your train. David's finishing rehearsals in half an hour. I said I'd have the shopping done. If I tell him there's nothing for supper because I was so long saying goodbye...'

He smiled. 'Quite.'

I stood. 'Oh dear. It's no fun saying goodbye, is it.' I felt my eyes fill up.

'No goodbyes between us. Ever. You're coming down to the Maltings.'

'As soon as my car's better.'

'So no goodbyes,' he said.

'No. Good luck then. Take care. See you very soon.'

'See you soon.' His smile had become fragile.

I left the tea-room and was in the booking hall. Through the plate-glass window we caught sight of each other: two woebegone faces. The sight made us both laugh suddenly. We waved extravagantly then, still laughing, I walked out into the sunshine. I had the feeling I'd been walking on eggshells all day ... or three months longer than that ... and that they hadn't broken yet.

PS

They didn't appoint me at once. My interview was followed by an ominous pause. Then Clive got a job in America and the board, in panic, called on David and me to run the theatre together, director and manager, two workaday oxen yoked together and harnessed to the same cart.

Graham went a splendid copper colour in the summer, gained muscle and self-confidence. He wrote music for guitar, performed and taped it, and it was used as overture music for one of the Maltings' plays. I visited him as often as I could.

We did a sequel to the Mozart show. David, Ian and I, and a woman friend. This one was about Schubert's songs. I went into the foyer before it started, greeting the audience as they arrived. I too had gained self-confidence and a bit of weight. Then Graham walked in, unannounced. I can't describe what happened to my heart. We hugged.

He came on stage and helped set up. Then before the doors were opened he made me play for him. 'Make you relax,' he said. He was wearing the same green jacket, blue denims and white shirt he'd worn when he'd played so beautifully for me that time – his wardrobe remained limited. As he went back through the pass door he said, 'It's your talent that matters, not the others'.' That was mean of him but I decided to overlook it in view of what he said next. 'Just play for me. And for the music.' So I did.

There was champagne afterwards. After that a meal in the Indian restaurant in Sheep Street. David caused a stir by eating the chrysanths from the vase on the table while we waited for the main course. Then Graham came home with David and me. The first and only time the three of us slept under the same roof. The famous sleeping-bag was pressed into service one more time.

At breakfast – I poached three eggs for us – there was a moment's awkwardness as we worked out where we'd all sit, David's chair and Graham's having been the same one in the past. As on the last occasion Graham and I had breakfasted together we couldn't quite finish the meal. Maybe that was because of hangover. Maybe not.

Graham and I said, hugged, goodbye on the theatre doorstep later that morning. He drove off, waving, in the car he'd hired.

I'd gone to wake him earlier. He looked beautiful, familiarly asleep in his familiar place, in my familiar bag. Soft and vulnerable again. I woke him the way he was used to my doing it, softly scratching his head. 'Not a very nice morning, my love,' I told him as he focused his eyes on me. 'It's pouring with rain.'

Perhaps he was remembering, still half dreaming, a morning half a year ago when we'd woken to a fall of snow. 'At least it's better than nothing,' he said.

****

Anthony McDonald is the author of more than twenty novels. He studied modern history at Durham University, then worked briefly as a musical instrument maker and as a farmhand before moving into the theatre, where he has worked in every capacity except director and electrician. He has also spent several years teaching English in Paris and London. He now lives in rural East Sussex, England.

Novels by Anthony McDonald

IVOR'S GHOSTS
ADAM
BLUE SKY ADAM
GETTING ORLANDO
ORANGE BITTER, ORANGE SWEET
ALONG THE STARS
WOODCOCK FLIGHT
RALPH: DIARY OF A GAY TEEN
THE DOG IN THE CHAPEL
TOM AND CHRISTOPHER AND THEIR KIND
DOG ROSES
SILVER CITY

Gay Romance Series:

Gay Romance: A Novel
Gay Romance on Garda
Gay Romance in Majorca
The Paris Novel
Gay Romance at Oxford
Gay Romance at Cambridge
The Van Gogh Window
Gay Romance in Tartan
Tibidabo
Spring Sonata
Touching Fifty
Romance on the Orient Express

All titles are available as Kindle ebooks and also as paperbacks from Amazon.

www.anthonymcdonald.co.uk

Manufactured by Amazon.ca
Bolton, ON